Bearskin

Heather Strickler

Wyrd Bard Tales

Contents

Chapter 1
TURNED LOOSE

Rough polished wood cut into Gregor's hands as he gripped the center pole of the munition's tent. The lingering tang of gunpowder hung bitterly in the air and permeated the fabric and stained the honest wood.

He leaned his massive shoulder into the sturdy beam and heaved, slipping it free of its earthen hole. His feet slid in the musty damp as he walked the beam down with dreary finality. Fighting his way free from the heavy canvas and stepping into the weary sunlight of the camp.

This was what defeat looked like: the rattle of the carts picking up supplies, the murmur of men moving back and forth, finishing their tasks with as few words as possible. The drovers avoided his eyes... and each other's.

Gregor wiped the sweat from his amber eyes with the back of his sleeve, only to replace it with rainwater. The doleful drip of the trees carried even here.

He glanced over towards the paymaster's table and grimaced. That was a trek he was less than eager to make. For it would mean leaving, and where had he left to go? Nevahs no longer was held by Bayr. It had been taken by Almarc and his own lord had lost half his lands in this futile war.

A line of cannon, gleaming bronze even in this fitful, strangled sunlight, mighty... and useless now. Packed on their caissons ready to be hauled to wherever whatever lord kept them. Cannon were expensive so he suspected they would return to the capitol and the king's armory.

Was the man even his King anymore? He supposed he'd find out soon enough. He cast a weary glance up at the sky but found no hope there.

"Gregor! Heinrich, here!" One of the sergeants called, and Gregor straightened his back and stepped over to the Sergeant who barely topped his shoulder.

"*Debron*, Little Man." A deep voice from the other side of one of the wagons called and Heinrich joined them with a swing in his step. The big blond man from the northern provinces was the only one in camp who could get away with calling Gregor Little. For he was as much taller than Gregor as Gregor was than the sergeant, and Gregor found himself smiling up at him.

"*Marshet*, my friend," Gregor returned the Rithi greeting. The Rithi and his own Delmin tribes had been off again on again allies and enemies for all their histories. These days it was more a matter of curiosity than anything else, usually. "I think they have need of our muscles given the lack of horses about."

The Sergeant snorted. "You're not far from wrong. The horses for the cannon have been delayed, but we need to get them to the rock flat before they mire in deep. Do you think you two can handle that?"

"Pull or push, Little Man?" Heinrich asked with a smile.

"You're closer to horse sized than I am, you'll fit better between the arms. I'll push. Try not to be more stubborn than my old ox was." Gregor's mood always seemed lighter with Heinrich around.

He was the only man in camp who hadn't seemed to fret himself to a froth over the loss. Then again, he was from Isendorf which was far enough north that he had a home to return to. He could also forget. A luxury Gregor did not have.

"Just try to keep up!" Heinrich said with a laugh and stepped in between the bars of the limber.

Gregor stepped behind the caisson and lowered his shoulder to the bar. It was lower than even he liked, and Heinrich would have had trouble. Then again, Heinrich might have just picked up the whole assembly if he'd let him push.

Setting the thoughts aside Gregor called, "Ready!"

"On three," Heinrich called back and counted slowly.

Together they threw their weight forward. The whole assembly lurched, already mired deeply. Gregor worked a hand under the bar his shoulder leaned against and heaved up, letting it slide a little onto his shoulder. The wheels began to rock, and slowly, ever so slowly, the wagon pulled free of the muddy suction. At last, they had the first cannon on the rocky bit of ground next to the powder wagon.

Without a word Gregor turned back to the second, then the third. Seven times they heaved the massive bronze contraptions and their heavy wagons out of the mud and when Gregor straightened his back for the last time it was sweat, not the slacking rain that soaked him.

Heinrich came around, wiping his hands on his pants and flexing his fingers. He favored his friend with a speculative look and Gregor cocked his head up at the big blond. Normally he wasn't so reluctant to speak.

"You should have let me take more of the weight." Heinrich said gently then lowered his voice. "There is nothing to prove between you and I. Or there should not be after these years."

Gregor shook his head. "Nothing to prove my friend. But the work needed doing. I did it."

"You need not always do so alone," Heinrich reminded him and dug around in his belt pouch, drawing something out. "What are your plans?"

"Like everyone else... I will go home. I need to see if there is anything left." Gregor shrugged and looked away and a big hand touched his shoulder with feather gentleness.

"We cannot be the dead, nor can we replace them, but if you choose to look to the future rather than the past..." Heinrich pulled gently on his shoulder and offered the object he'd pulled from his pouch. A small, carved wooden bead rested in the giant's hand and Gregor looked up at him, genuinely surprised.

"I didn't know you knew about Delmin beads..." Rather than seek the words that were failing him he took the bead.

"You are not the only Delmin I have known, and I found the custom to be quite useful. Take it. If you should ever find yourself in Isendorf, everyone there knows that I carry these. Take it to my Marta, and she'll help you if I am not there when you arrive. You'll find your welcome warm as a friend of mine." Heinrich squeezed his shoulder and stepped back.

"Thank you... I..." Gregor trailed off and reached into his own pocket, drawing a bead out, one carved with a stylized bear reaching for a star. "I have no such welcome to offer you, but if ever I or any of mine... however many or few that may be... can help we will. May it please the Whispering Word that we meet again."

"Meet or not, I am pleased to have known you, Gregor von Nevahs. It is not often I meet a man with your honor, even if your memory means you know more than I find comfortable!" Heinrich tapped the side of his nose and Gregor laughed wearily.

"My gift... and curse. It may keep me fed. We shall see, but you should go. Your work is done, and your Marta will not be pleased at the delay." Gregor stepped back, and Heinrich nodded.

"I mean it. There will be work for you in Isendorf, honest work if not rich in glory." He stepped over to one side where Gregor now saw a pack and a fine crossbow. He raised a hand in fair well and Heinrich bobbed his head.

"You go see the paymaster. I have already had my last pay. Virtue guide your steps," and Heinrich stepped onto the road that led into the wood whistling. Gregor shook his head, ignoring the sarcastic mutterings and rolling eyes about him.

Believing in the Virtues and Vices had been increasingly unpopular in Bayr. After all they could not be weighed and measured, but Gregor knew better. There was Power in the world measured or not, and while the Whispering Word protected his people, man chose his own fate. And Power collected around his choices. Whether it would be Virtue or Vice that acted about him he wasn't sure he wished to discover. He shook himself and looked to the sergeant who waved him towards the paymaster.

Gregor squared his shoulders and retrieved his own meager pack and staff and stepped towards a future. What it held he could not say.

Gregor stepped over to the line with his meager belongings. The home-spun bag rubbed his hand roughly after the tight woven canvas's smoothness. The men in the line looked at their feet and scuffed the mud. No one spoke except the Clerk and whichever man he was speaking to.

Gregor's mind drifted as he shuffled forward through the clinging mud with the rest of the men. At least the rain had stopped at last. He tried not to think of fire and started reciting accounts in his head to block the images of the enchanted arrows that had consumed his home a year ago.

Two more men paid. Three more to go. He listened to the names and the amounts and tried to calculate how long such funds would last.

He gave it up in the end. There was no telling. Prices were strange now that the army was sending the levees home.

The mercenaries had collected their pay and marched out two days ago. No one was foolish enough to short them. At least not in this war. The story of Eislathen was enough to stop that foolishness cold.

Gregor shivered, which had nothing to do with the damp. He had been taught to read because of his Gift of Memory, and one of the books that he had read had been a history. Eislathen's was brutal. Iron mistress to four kingdoms and run by a mercenary company who had conquered it when they had been turned away without their due pay. It was no town to be trifled with.

And what about me? He wondered. He was not the same man he had been before the war had come. Who he was now he did not know. If his memory was correct...

Hah! as if his memory could be wrong with his Gift.

One more ahead of him. He turned his thoughts to his plans, rather than the past. Perhaps he actually should follow Heinrich to Isendorf.

There was usually work for clerks in such places. He wasn't afraid of hard work, so his size would be an advantage unless they were all built like Heinrich there.

He toyed with the idea of turning mercenary himself. It could be honest work if you could find the right company, and his path would pass Eislathen.

He certainly couldn't go back to being a farmer. Whoever would be given his lands would want their own vassals to farm it. Perhaps his own Lord would have work for him. Perhaps.

"Next," The Clerk called, and Gregor stepped up.

"Gregor von Nevahs."

"Nevahs does not look to Baron Hochritt," The Clerk said brusquely, then paused as Gregor simply stared at him in shock. A brief flicker of compassion crossed his face, only to be smoothed away. "Free Clerk Gregor, however, is owed ten Marks for help rendered in both the pay office and to the Quartermaster. I pray he finds good welcome wherever he can."

Free clerk. So, his Lord was ignoring the vassals in the lands he had lost. Or at least the common, easily replaced ones.

He unclenched his fist and gave the clerk a bow. He fished in his own belt pouch and drew a small, simply carved bead from it, offering it in exchange for the coin. "My thanks for the fair dealing. Please, render my thanks to the Quartermaster if you see him as well."

The Clerk lowered his eyes briefly then looked past Gregor who simply nodded and stepped aside to let the next man step up.

Ten marks. A month's wage for a skilled trade. Perhaps it would be enough. Perhaps. The next town would tell.

He had some of the bread from breakfast and most of the cheese from lunch. That should see him there. What should chance after that he wasn't sure.

He set his feet to the road Heinrich had so recently taken. It was likely the only time their paths would follow one another. The clouds thickened choking out the faint sunlight and it began once more to rain.

Chapter 2

WARNINGS

S unset touched the clouds with ominous fire and Gregor kept his eyes on the road and back to the sun. He needed no omens, nor did he wish any. The dirt path he had followed for so many days now joined another road, smooth, paved and arrogantly straight, bending the woods to its will rather than trying to evade it.

His eyes lifted once more as the first hoot of an owl reached his ears. The scent of the pines. The rustle of the leaves. Familiar yet foreign, all of it.

His feet touched the crossroads, but his eyes watched the sky. Fire dimmed to a gray smoky haze that carried the scent of ash.

He paused, leaning on the staff he had cut for himself, and inspected the carved sign which stood at the northwest corner of the road pointing each direction. North: Isendorf. West: Rhiesbrucke. East: Kupmauer. South... Nevahs.

Home. He turned north and fingered the bead Heinrich had given him. Then shifted the almost empty sack on his back.

There was no point in stopping. He had no tent. The marks he had had had bought him barely two weeks' worth of supplies and that didn't allow for such luxuries as tents.

Free Clerk. He was beholden to none. There would be no bar to him taking work in Isendorf if he went there. Or anywhere else for that matter.

His Lord had decided to cut his losses. And Gregor was a loss. Nevahs was a loss. He had enough mouths to feed on half the land.

He turned south. The road there was paved. Nevahs had been modestly important, once. A simple village where travelers between Bayr and Almarc could rest and resupply. A church, some inns, the bakery and the blacksmith--could everything really have burned? He couldn't see the whole town from where the battle had been. Surely something had survived. Surely.

"Turn aside, Gregor von Nevahs." A voice rang from the woods. A woman's voice.

He wheeled northward, staff ready. He faced the speaker in time to see a tall woman step out of the trees. She was dressed in olive green from her head to her toes, and her hair where it peeked out from the hood was blood red. Her eyes burned like coals. He might have thought her one of the Elven folk or the Sidhe, but her ears, though pointed, stuck out through the sides of her hood and put him more in mind of a fox or a cat. But he did not need that nor the four foot long flute she carried to know her. Fate's Minstrel would never be mistaken for anyone else.

He lowered his staff and met her eyes as best he could. Powers about in the night? That boded well for no one. She nodded slowly taking in his stance and repeated her warning. "Turn aside, Gregor von Nevahs. Your Doom waits you if you do not, and it may drag more under than yourself."

"I would risk no one but myself, m'Lady." Gregor favored her with a cautious bow. Rudeness to powers ended poorly, especially this power. Virtue and Vice followed her, and she drew on them at her whim. He knew himself enough to know she would have much to work with if he chanced to anger her.

"Yet those you care for and who share your care may also share your danger, not of your own will but of theirs," the lady cautioned.

He looked south then turned briefly north. "My fate is my own, Lady. Unless you have brought the doom with you?"

She shook her head at the tone and a small, sad smile tugged at her lips. "No. I am here but to warn. I touch neither virtue nor vice today. If you will not heed the warning, will you have advice?"

Gregor inclined his head to her. "When Powers speak it is wise to listen."

"Your folly need not bring your doom though it will be a difficult path. Cling to your virtues and nurture them. They are more subtle than Vices, but their reach is greater, not less for that." She bowed slightly herself, though it seemed more gesture of courtesy than subservience. Then she turned away.

"My Lady..." He hesitated and she turned back, curiosity burning in her coal bright eyes.

"Ask what you will. I make no promise beyond the hearing."

"I have heard of the beauty of your fife." Gregor rushed to get the words out before he could consider his temerity. "Would you play for me, please?"

She smiled and it took her face from strange and unsettling to beautiful. Then she raised her flute to her lips and began to play and all that faded from thought.

The world dropped away, his staff slid from his fingers, and not even the beauty of the stars, now beginning to come out, held any power for him. The low tones carried him places he never could quite remember and spun about his soul in bright laughter and tears so strong as to shatter any mortal. Yet as the song ended, he found himself still at the crossroads whole of soul and mind: with no memory of that song, only the memory of having heard it.

An echo of the tune flittered by in a nightingale's song, and he blinked realizing that echo had come from within him... and would every time he heard. She had left him whole when she could have captured him mind and soul and this time his bow was very deep. "Thank you for your indulgence m'Lady."

His voice was dry though he managed to keep his tone even as he realized what he had asked. She laughed. Startled he looked up and that laugh transformed her as the smile had only more. No longer was she a towering figure of doom. Instead she held out a hand to him in welcome, now something bright though no less powerful. He reached out to take it, once more wondering at his temerity and he found his hand closing on a smooth stone.

"That will be of use to you should you step into your folly. May you fair well whichever road you choose, Gregor von Nevahs. Have hope.

The future holds bright paths as well as dark, but you must find them yourself." She once more turned away, resting her simple wooden flute on her shoulder. Then paused and looked back over her shoulder. "And thank you."

"For what, m'Lady?" Gregor asked, startled.

"For requesting the song for the sake of the song, not simply for its power." She stepped into the woods and was gone.

Gregor looked at the stone in his hand. It seemed smooth, featureless and black. Then as he held it sparks seemed to play deep within it, yet whenever he tried to follow them consciously they faded away. He closed his hand on it and put it in his belt pouch, tucking the pouch inside his clothes. He had a long way yet to go.

He cast one more glance back towards the road, but in so many ways the choice was no choice at all. He had to confront his past before he could face his future.

Picking up his walking stick, he turned his face southward, and discovered he was no longer weary nor hungry nor thirsty. He glanced towards the woods where Fate's Minstrel had vanished and sent a silent prayer of thanks for her to the Whispering Word. Her song still wrapped around his heart.

Chapter 3
A Devil's Bargain

Cold stone met his fingers in the dappled warmth of the sunshine. Warmth that did him no good against the gnawing in his stomach and the hole in his heart. Old ash and older dust met his nose. Two simple stones, scored with the Whispering Word's starburst. But there would have been no one else here. Two graves: Anna and little Mirek.

His memory told the truth. As if it could be otherwise with his Gift, but he had hoped. Hoped he had not seen what he thought he saw. The stump of the house he had built with his own hands loomed in his peripheral vision. The charred bones still stood, but the fire had picked them clean leaving him with nothing.

His eyes fell to the markers, too real for his liking. Who had buried them? No one from Bayr. They had retreated from this battle. He would not have thought Almarc would have taken the time while on the march. He would remember the saffron and scarlet arms of the lead units. Their commander had been fiendishly clever with his blade. He had the scars to prove that.

He had also been fiendishly clever with his tactics. That was not the only battlefield they had met on. Whoever else he might be, the man was skilled in the ways of war. Too skilled. He tried to squash the simmering rage that sat right below the hunger. Focus on why he came.

The grass had grown over the little mounds of the graves. Soon the rich earth would reclaim them and only the stones would remain. He heaved a great sigh and bowed his head in prayer. Whispering Word keep them both... keep them all. The screen of dipping trees concealed the wreckage of what had once been a prosperous town. Surely not everyone was dead?

Well, he wasn't but none of the other levees were here. Had any of the other boys he had grown with found other ways to go?

He had searched the town, but there had been no sign of life. Nothing at all here, only rats and mice and cobwebs. No one had returned. Which meant any other levees had gotten the same answer he had and had followed what paths they could. Or if they had come back they had not stayed.

Could he stay? There was nothing here to stay for. He looked over to the cellar door, still firm, scorched but firm. The army had hungered and all that was left was a few rotted vegetables that they had not found and looted.

"Ho there!" A deep voice cracked sharply across the field.

Gregor's hand dropped to his staff, as he whirled, coming to his feet. A quartet of men in bright saffron yellow and scarlet tabards were walking steadily towards him. It was not quite a march step, but the lead man's square features were set.

Gregor tensed. He recognized those colors and the scarlet horse rampant: The same commander who had burned Nevahs. Was he actually in control of these lands now? Maybe if he'd been a little quicker with his spear... no. He ground his mental heel on that thought. He'd wish ill on no one, not even a former enemy. Not with the Minstrel's warning hanging over him.

"Who are you and what master do you serve?" The quartet came to a halt out of easy sword range, but within crossbow shot. And Gregor counted two of those, though neither lifted.

"My name is Gregor. I have come here to pay respects to my dead as a free man. No more." He kept his staff upright. The way the lead man was eyeing it he knew full well how dangerous a well plied staff could be. The others seemed more casual. He deliberately took in each of their faces. They would be less likely to remember him, though there were few Delmin in these parts. Fewer now with Nevahs burned.

The leader considered for a moment and nodded slowly. Was that a trace of sympathy in those hard, brown eyes? "As traveler's courtesy, there has been brigandage here since the end of the war, and Freiherr Rudigar von Neuen is currently tasked with patrolling these lands. There is a town about two day's travel south and an established traveler's camp between. You'll find little hospitality at the first. But we have maintained the clearing and the pit."

Gregor started and couldn't hide his surprise. "It is rare to find a Lord doing his road duty in these times. My gratitude. Also, if you know who buried the dead of Nevahs. If you could relay my thanks as well? I had not expected such a courtesy."

There the leader's face softened. "Honor where honor is due. It would have been wrong to let them rot or simply pile them in a pit as if they were thieves, and m'Lord Freiherr insisted we bury them properly when the battle was done."

"Then give him my thanks. From the living kin." He met the man's eyes but made no sudden move. They had been enemies but very recently. Still, he meant it. At least his family had not been left to the wolves and the vultures.

"I will. Now..." But a shout from the wood line drew his attention away. Another cluster of guards in the same livery had just emerged and were signaling. "No camping in the town. Stick to the campsites and be cautious. An immense bear has been seen in these parts. Larger than any we have heard of before."

He turned away and his men preceded him. After a few steps he turned back, "You wear no man's colors. The nearest town is the Free City of Steinburg. You'll need their permission to enter. Good luck they've been choosy of late."

Gregor bowed his head and turned back to the graves. Two days to the next town. With his stomach already empty and his pack long since dry. And no guarantee of work there either. Was this the doom the Lady had spoken of?

"**W**hat brings you to this wood?" A voice came from behind him. A man old by all appearances, wearing a green great coat, and leaning on a tall staff.

"Lost hope," Gregor gestured to the charred remains of his home. "I had hoped my eyes had lied to me."

The stranger nodded. "They have gone to their eternal fates. What will you do now?"

"That is a very good question." Gregor was very aware of how empty his sack and pouch were. "Who might you be, sir? and why are you so interested in a stranger?"

"Oh, I am interested in many things, some of which would doubtless surprise you," the old man smiled. "My name is not important. What might yours be since you're asking?"

Gregor laughed, "That's rich. You won't give yours then expect me to give mine? No, I think not. Old man. Let that name sleep with the dead. I shall be moving on before sun down. We shall see what comes of it."

"These lands are policed by Rudigar von Neuen. He is not a merciful man, though neither is he a needlessly cruel one," The stranger said. Gregor flinched. So the men had not lied. That would make things more difficult. Von Neuen did not have a reputation for flexibility any more than for mercy.

"Then I should move on sooner rather than later, so he does not take exception to me as more than a simple traveler," Gregor said grimly. Hopefully the camp would be as the patrol had said. It would give warmth if not fill his belly.

"You have not the supplies to last you until you could earn more. What might you say to a wager?" The old man cocked his head to one side and the cracked voice rippled with a hint of wheedling richness.

Gregor's eyes narrowed. Something tickled his Gift of Memory. The green great coat. The voice. The way the conversation was going. "Scratch."

"You have guessed it indeed," The old man laughed and drew himself up straight, no longer old, but tall and strong looking. "But you have let yourself become distracted!"

A roar of rage loosed behind him, and Gregor saw a great bear rearing up on its hind legs. It must have stood fully twelve feet tall! A massive paw swiped out at him, and he rolled away.

The bear flopped down onto all four legs and charged him before he could fully come to his feet. He kicked upward, keeping its teeth away from his throat, but it hooked a paw under him and stood once more.

He grabbed the paw and hoisted a leg over the brute's shoulder. It tore at him, but he managed to take the worst of it on his pack and twisted about until he sat astride the beast's shoulders.

He snatched his belt knife free as its paws came around and clawed at his back. One missed, the other glanced down tearing through his leather coat, but without the angle to do more, this time.

He plunged his knife into the brute's eye and into its brain.

The bear convulsed and fell forward. Gregor rolled off of its back and came to his feet, panting.

Slow applause came from behind him. "Impressive. Very impressive. I see you are a man of courage as well as of strength. Would you hear my bargain?"

Gregor eyed Old Scratch, the peasant name for the Devil himself, and nodded slowly. "I'll hear it, but it may be your eye the knife goes in next."

"If you could manage it, you would be the first." Scratch shrugged without concern. "My bargain is simply this: For seven years you will wear only what I cloth you in. You will neither wash nor trim your hair or nails. Neither will you pray to the Whispering Word. Calling on his Power would be cheating, and I'd be a fool to let you. In return you shall have wealth for the asking all those seven years as you wander. Should you see through to the end, you will have a fortune that will last you all your days. Should you fail or should you break any of my conditions, your soul is mine."

That was the usual penalty for losing such bargains and Gregor thought about it carefully. It was nearly two day's walk to the nearest town, and that would take him deeper into the lands conquered by Almarc. Yet there would be no work the other direction either.

He had the Gift of Memory and could read and write and do clerk's work but the army had turned their clerks loose and he had learned the hard and painful way that there was no work for him in the smaller towns.

The Free City of Steinburg was the next town. It was large enough, but the Free Cities were prickly about granting work other than labor to outsiders.

The nearest city that might need a clerk, and would be open enough to take him, was fully two weeks away, and he could never walk with no food for so long.

He slowly nodded. "I will take your bargain, and we'll see who gets whose soul..."

"Then, since you gave no name, Master Bearskin is your name now," Old Scratch slid out of his green great coat. "Wear this."

When Gregor had put it on, he found the scratches on his back had stopped hurting. He turned to see where Scratch had gone and found him kneeling by the bear's shoulder. He took the skin off as if it had been a great robe and smiled. "Wear this over all, and all shall know you as Bearskin. Return here seven years hence at sunrise. If you can."

And just like that Scratch was gone and Gregor found himself in the Bearskin with another long road before him. From afar the haunting sound of a flute drifted to him. Doom indeed. But the sound had not left him and the stone she had given warmed against his skin even through the pouch.

Chapter 4
MASTER BEARSKIN

The breeze ruffled the trees and the sun stood high. The warm, familiar scent of freshly manured fields drifted towards the road and mingled with the fresh, homey spice of the pines.

Gregor shifted the heavy bearskin on his back, growing used to its weight in the last two day's travel. The cobbles of the road poked his boots at awkward angles, and he stepped around clusters of nettles growing up through the grass.

He averted his eyes from the long, low hill lined with grave markers. Another city. Another battlefield, yet the walls of this city seemed largely intact.

He shook himself, and the Bearskin did not shift. It was uncanny but he wasn't sure he could take it off without deliberate effort. Even so, he intended to have a clasp made for it... just in case. He would leave nothing to chance with Old Scratch.

Voices, raised voices, reached his ears. He paused and his hand tightened on his staff. His pace quickened, though he didn't quite dare break into a jog. It was technically none of his business after all. Interfering in local trouble likely would not get him welcomed. Could he make it to the next city?

The scent of the fields faded as he came around the final bend and the skirting edge of the trees ended leaving two bow shots distance clear between the screen of greenery and the walls themselves.

A woman in the black habit of a religious order faced off with a richly dressed man on a warhorse. A blond-headed boy of about ten clung to her and around a dozen children clustered a short distance off.

Bearskin lengthened his stride, head up. He would grovel to no one, however well off. A knobbly old oak stood right near the gate, and movement caught his eye, but he thought little about it for the moment.

The man on the horse spoke sharply, "I say he was seen in the area, Sister. I would have him answer himself."

"M'Lord, he has been with the other children all morning under my own eye. I do not see how it could have been so. You, yourself have seen that he has nothing but a few pebbles and acorns in his pouch," The sister drew herself up to her full height and dared meet the lord's eyes.

Gregor stepped directly up to them. "If a stranger may ask, what trouble is there here?"

The man glanced at him and slowly took in the bearskin and Gregor's height. His shoulder came to the horse's easily.

Amber eyes met gray. The man inclined his head slightly, polite enough for what was obviously a lord when addressing a commoner. "This is not your concern stranger. Property is missing and the boy is a suspect. I suggest you be about your business."

Gregor nodded and again movement caught his eyes. He lunged sideways. The lord's hand went to his sword, but Gregor's path brought him away from the horseman and to that loan oak. "What have we here?"

The lord's eyes narrowed as he saw the thin, rat-like man with darting brown eyes. "That is a good question, stranger, though I would ask you treat my people more gently, even such as this one."

Gregor hauled the man before the lord. "He is undamaged, m'Lord. I will release him should he not be involved, but he was lurking and hiding behind yonder oak rather than passing on his business, as you bade me. I cannot help but wonder why."

"It is a fair question," The lord looked back at the sister. "I have not completed my business with you, but this may have bearing on it. Please remain here with the boy."

The Sister nodded and Gregor noted she winced a little at the address. Something more to her charge than he thought? Or perhaps the boy was a reasonable suspect.

He knew little enough of this town beyond what von Neuen's men had said. The war had not carried his unit this far south. It was unlikely anyone here would know him, either. "There was a hollow in the oak. It might bear investigating."

The lord nodded, but never took his eyes off the man. "So, Bertol, why were you lurking here eavesdropping on your master's business?"

"Nor I weren't, m'Lord," The rat-like man wrung his hands and hung his head eyes darting about and looking everywhere but at the lord. "I were just going 'bout my business like any other honest man. Standin' by the gates is no crime, m'Lord."

The lord snorted. "No, it is not a crime, but we are investigating one so how about you turn out your pockets while I investigate this hollow our brash guest was speaking about."

The lord dismounted and tossed Gregor his reins. The horse stamped a little at the smell of bear on him, but otherwise simply stood there, training evident. It also, conveniently meant Gregor couldn't bolt without first dropping them and alerting the horse's master. Clever. Not that it increased his likelihood of welcome.

The lord checked the hollow before sticking his hand in it. So more wood wise than Gregor would have given him credit for. In spite of the horse he seemed more the moneyed nobility than the warrior, but it seemed that appearances could be deceiving. The lord cautiously stuck his hand in the hollow and drew out a shimmering brooch, rich with the colors of gems and a pouch that clinked.

"I see. I see indeed," Said the lord looking from the sister to Gregor to Bertol. "Now this is a pretty puzzle. What might you know of this Bertol?"

"Not a thing m'Lord." Bertol scuffed his feet in the dirt and glanced at the wood.

"Ware the woods, m'Lord!" Gregor shoved Bertol into the lord and rolled to the side as a crossbow bolt passed through the place Bertol had been standing only seconds before. Gregor followed the course of the bolt back and knelt in the dirt. The lord followed, sword drawn.

"Gone, sadly. Some sense, though I would give much to know who wishes you dead, my little rat," The lord glared back towards Bertol who, to his credit, hadn't bolted. Though that might just mean he was more afraid of his lord than of whoever had shot at him.

"There was only one here," Gregor carefully examined the prints. And glanced up the tree to a small scrap of verdant green. "A clue... this isn't a forester's dye..."

The lord inspected the scrap and nodded, "Indeed, though there is not much this can tell us unless someone has the Gift of past reading."

Gregor shook his head. "My Gift is Memory which is of little use in this."

"Enough gift. You have proven that those with that Gift see things that others miss as well as remembering them well. What might I call you?" The lord simply shifted his gaze upward as Gregor stood and his shoulder stood over the lord's head.

"I am called Bearskin," He tapped the fur robe he wore with a rueful smile. "And I would credit more my time in the Army with my perceptions. It is not the first time I have been attacked out of ambush and I have traveled some ways alone."

The lord nodded. "You are not the only one. Though more honorable than some."

"That seems always the case. There are those of honor and those without, and those without seem more numerous, or at least louder and more obvious," Gregor shrugged.

"I think this does answer the question quite neatly of who stole these items. Come, let us deal with this," He strode over to the Sister and to Bertol.

"This is not the first time you have been caught in theft, Bertol. You will report yourself to the town Watch. Perhaps several nights cleaning the chamber pots for them will turn your mind to more honest means of employment. Though you are running out of chances. Your associates meant your death." The lord cocked his head at the man.

"I don't know who they were m'Lord. A man came to the tavern, and I was to leave the things in that knot hole and they'd leave m' money there when they got it," Bertol shuddered. "I'd not cross you m'Lord, but they're hard men. That much I do know. Mortal hard and...."

"And you let the fear in front of you overwhelm whatever good sense you have," The lord said with a sigh. "I'll take you to the Captain of the Watch myself."

Then the lord turned to the sister and bowed more deeply than Bearskin had yet seen him, "I owe you and the boy an apology. Perhaps some good will come of this. I'll not be so swift to jump to conclusions next time. Though, lad, keep your hands out of belt pouches if you want that to hold."

The boy nodded seeming to relax, but the lord was not, quite done. He turned to Gregor. "You have the freedom of this town so long as you remain honorable, Master Bearskin."

Then the lord turned away marching his prisoner off to his sentence. A more merciful sentence than Bearskin had expected.

He picked up his staff from where he had dropped it to go after the crossbowman and when he stood, he found the sister in front of him. Now that he was closer, he could see the twinned stars of the Sisters of St. Katheryn: an order that tended dominantly to orphans.

"I owe you a thanks as well Master Bearskin." She used the title that was common for a free man looking to no lord in particular, but owing his allegiance only where he chose.

"No thanks to me, I was glad to help. I have a stubborn streak. One that has caused me trouble, but it can serve Virtue as well as Vice. I am glad it was so this time," Bearskin smiled, and a thought occurred to him. He dug into the pockets of his robe and sure enough his hand closed on something cold. When he pulled it out it was a handful of silver coins. "Perhaps these will help your Mission? I know the war must have left you with more charges than you can handle."

"Too true sometimes, Master." The sister took the money after only a moment's hesitation, eyes widening at the weight and number of coins. "Is there nothing I can do for you? For twice you have aided where you need not."

"No, your thanks is enough. If you must do something. Pray for me. I have a long seven years ahead of me. Pray that I may come through safe to the other side," Bearskin smiled once more than turned away but not before he saw the sister's mouth tighten in speculation.

"Pray for you we will. I and the other sisters with me Master Bearskin," She signed the sign of the Whispering Word after him and then returned to her charges and their berry baskets.

T he town swirled about him. Eddies of people in plain homespun clothes, with finer flashes of color here and there. The scent of stables and of refuse, assaulted his nose and he drifted onward towards the center of the town, away from the fringes.

There were no other Delmin here and the crowd parted before him, none wishing to get too close to the immense stranger in the bearskin robe. His eyes caught several signs, the tanner. One inn, though only the poorest of inns would be this near the tanneries and more ramshackle buildings on the edge of town.

He followed the main eddies of the crowd heading into the town itself, perhaps there would be a market. Perhaps he could get supplies.

Even the scents from those poor inns caused his stomach to rumble. It had been two days since his bargain, and, as von Neuen's men had warned, there had been no towns between Nevahs and this one. He had managed to find some edible plants along his path, but it had been a poor meal for a man his size.

He stepped on his hunger and scanned the signs as he walked. Soon he was passing through sturdier houses, as the main street spiraled inward. The road jogged suddenly left and he nodded to himself, noting the abrupt change in architecture.

Older buildings here, but that jog created a bottleneck that choked traffic down to a crawl and would have done the same to any advancing army. He wasn't sure whether to resent the reminder or approve of the innovation. Instead he simply made note of it and set his own feelings aside.

The language was familiar at least, and they labeled their stores with words not just images, for which he was grateful. The Free Cities were a strange mixture, and this one seemed better organized than most.

A silver spiderweb on one sign caught his eye and the words: Smith, with the symbols for gold, silver, and copper framed it. He worked his way across the street, ignoring reproachful mutterings, having heard such directed at fellow locals who disrupted the flow of traffic to get where they were going.

He stepped into the smithy and found it several degrees warmer in here than out in the street, though strangely quieter. There was no sound of hammering though he could see a man working at an anvil through a door in the back.

Most of the view was blocked by a counter. The walls behind it were lined sturdy wooden shelves, simple and unadorned but polished to a high gloss with many boxes and caskets on them--also row upon row of books. Most in Astlordan--the language shared by Bayr, Almarc and a few of the surrounding countries though each had their own variant-- but some in a script he didn't recognize. It looked almost runic, now which-

"Can I help you sir? Master Silverweb is currently busy, but I can make an appointment for you." A boy who sounded like he should be fourteen or so, but only stood about four feet high with absurdly broad shoulders, stepped around the counter.

"Ah, yes, please. If you could tell him that Master Bearskin would like to speak with him when it is convenient and ask if there is some time today, he might be available for some business. I have need of a signet ring of a mercantile rather than noble sort." Gregor had little desire to offend any of the local nobility, even in the Free Cities. Perhaps especially in the Free Cities.

The nobles here tended to regard themselves as several grades above the station their holdings would normally allow, simply because they had so few nobles over them. He'd heard enough of those arguments while doing clerk's work with his old unit. It was amazing how invisible a ledger and pen made you even at six foot six.

"I shall tell him and see what the appointment schedule holds. Please wait here," The boy gestured to a long bench, also simply made of good wood shined to a high gloss.

He settled into it, surprised how comfortable the seat was for all it had no cushion. Whoever had made it could have taught the old carpenter in Nevahs several tricks apparently.

He returned his attention to the books and his fingers twitched. He itched for something to do. Now that he was not traveling, he felt more adrift than he ever had.

He closed his eyes, only to snap them open before he thought a prayer for guidance. This would be more difficult than he thought. At least he could make some preparations. He was fully expecting Old Scratch to cheat, but they'd see how that worked for the old liar.

Cling to your virtues, the Minstrel had said.

Well he had money abounding and had always been honest so perhaps he could make something useful of that. What he didn't know, but this place would be a start.

He firmed his resolve and once more set his eyes on the spines of the books. Those strangely written spines. He'd seen some Narskull runes before and these looked different. They certainly weren't Delmin runes. Nor any of the Elvish scripts he'd seen in some of the church accounts. But what they were he couldn't place. Who else used runes?

"Master Bearskin, my boy says you want a ring?" The man who stepped out of the forge wiping his hands was only about six inches taller than the boy but broad and strong as his anvil. So, dwarven runes. They must have been Dwarven runes.

"Yes, Master Silverweb. I would like a ring, fit to me, no make it a little loose. I'll likely be thickening back up after my time in the war," He watched the smith warily, but the dwarf only nodded.

"That will be no trouble. Once I make it, it will always fit your hand and never anyone else's unless you grant it to them as your Heir, will that be satisfactory?" Master Silverweb cocked his head and laid the cloth he had been using on his hands on the counter. Then he pulled a book down from the shelf.

"Quite satisfactory," Gregor agreed, looking curiously at the book.

Master Silverweb smiled and tapped it, "A record of all the nobility in Almarc and Bayr, enchanted so it's always up to date. What symbols had you in mind Master Bearskin?"

"Ah... I was thinking a bear either holding a star or with a star super-imposed on its chest," Gregor hadn't thought too much about it, but that was of special significance to the Delmin, though he doubted anyone from these lands would have such a thing. Most of his kinsmen were further away to the east, only a few of the tribes had drifted into Bayr and Almarc a century or so ago.

The Dwarf flipped through the book several times, making notes on a piece of paper in that strange runic language, "There are a few Lords with Bears, and one with stars. Some of the Clergy have stars, but no one combines the two. So, which would you prefer?"

Gregor thought for a long moment. "Make the star where the Bear's heart should be if that is workable?"

The dwarf sketched out something quickly on the same page he was making notes, then flipped it about, "Like this?"

Gregor looked at it and nodded, "That will do excellently and hope-fully is different enough in style not to cause me difficulty."

"Bah, this? No, no one will think twice about this. Half the merchant houses have their own rings and heraldry. The only ones who get in trouble for it ape the styles of the nobility and I don't think you'll have that problem," He cast a significant look at the bearskin. "Delmin, I take it?"

Gregor nodded, surprised, "You know us then?"

"I know." He switched into the Delmin language, that even the tribes abroad used when at home. The ache came back, but he ignored it. Anna was gone, and he'd not expected to hear his own language again. "My people in the Copper Mountains have done business with the Delmin from time to time. Though our territories only barely touch."

Bearskin nodded and responded in the same tongue. "It's good to hear my own people's speech from time to time. There aren't many of us here, and fewer than there were before the war."

"Sadly so, but I can have this for you in oh... a week if you have the money now for the fees. Half now, half when you receive the ring. That way I can purchase any supplies I might be short," There was a defensive note in the man's voice. But it was a sensible arrangement to Gregor's ears, though he knew some places only expected payment, in full, on delivery.

"Fair, what price?" Gregor asked, and the dwarf quoted him one. He considered then simply reached his hand through the bearskin to the pocket of the great coat and pulled out coins.

Silver coins from a hundred nations, many worn and ancient came to his hand. He laid them on the counter and then reached for more without bargaining. He didn't know what a reasonable price was. He had been a farmer not a merchant, whatever he was going to become now.

Pulling out a scale and weights, Master Silverweb quickly weighed the silver and Bearskin saw him muttering over it and felt a power in the room flex ever so slightly: a spell of purity most likely.

Well, he couldn't blame the man. After all Bearskin did not look like the kind of person to have that much silver casually in his pockets. But the smith nodded in apparent satisfaction and pushed about two-thirds of the coins back towards him. "This will cover the fee. Honestly if you wanted, the rest would cover the whole thing with some to spare."

Which gave Gregor an idea. "Do you sometimes keep such things for others?"

"I have on occasion," The smith said slowly. "I'm no money lender but I am one of the more reputable goldsmiths in town and maintain several boxes and accounts, though usually they are for customers who order regularly. Some ah... arrangements could be made unless you've gotten yourself in trouble with the Goldsmith's guild?"

Gregor shook his head, "To the best of my knowledge they would not even know I existed unless I was in the room recording accounts when they spoke with the army."

The smith snorted, "Them? They'd run first, but that's all to the good. I maintain connections through them and can set it up so you have an account you can draw on wherever the Guild has a presence."

"That would be most useful. Though I think I will finalize this when I have the ring. I have seven years of difficulty before me, and I may have need of proof," Gregor's tone was rueful, and the smith didn't ask. Some things it was wiser not to know about.

"Then let us make the contract. You can sign, and seal it when you have the ring. We'll draw up a separate contract for the ring that only would need a signature. You said you were a clerk? At least you'll be able to read what I write!" The man chuckled.

Gregor nodded, "It has its advantages. Though what they may be I am not completely sure."

"Hah! It means you can read a contract and the people who may try and cheat you have to actually be clever about it rather than simply waving a paper that could say anything and asking for a mark. It's getting more common since Riola started exporting paper." He shook his head, as he quickly drew up the contract and handed it to Gregor who read it, saw nothing objectionable and signed it 'Gregor Bearskin.' Bearskin he would be known as, and he would use his folly to forge a better fate.

The dwarf nodded, "I'll keep this provisionally and whatever's left over will go to your account with the guild."

"Excellent. Have you any recommendations on an inn?" Gregor asked.

"I think you'd do best at the Broken Anvil, mostly for mercenaries, but you'll fit better than the merchant guilds. You're big enough no one's likely to mess with you or look twice if you should acquire a weapon. There's no law here against that. Raising troops when not noble, yes, but arming yourself? Too many dwarves and mercenaries for that to ever pass!" He jotted down a few other notes, and Bearskin took that as a dismissal and ducked out the door which was far too low for him.

It was time to find his rest while he still could.

Chapter 5
Forged in Fire

Fire. Smoke. Gregor's eyes stung. The curling fumes assaulted his nose. He tensed as the wind brought a wave of heat with it. The acrid air reached to choke him.

His eyes fell on the village at the bottom of the hill. He drew a sharp breath, shifting his grasp on his quarterstaff as he took in the curling flames, the wooden walls, and the armored men with lit arrows surrounding it. A small cluster of defenders stood outside the wall and reacted as soldiers. They were the only ones.

A low growl came from his throat. It wouldn't happen again. He wouldn't let it.

It didn't matter that these were likely common, or uncommon, brigands. Or it did. It meant the law wasn't likely to have any objection to what he planned to do.

The road was rough under his feet. It had progressively worsened as he had wound his way through the battle torn provinces. For now, he only focused enough on it to prevent himself from twisting his ankle and his feet could manage that on their own.

His mind took in those raiders below him. He had only a staff, but none of them wore more than leather jerkins. Useful against the edges of weapons, but his weapon had no edge to deflect.

The farthest out archer glanced over his shoulder and raised a frantic shout as Gregor brought his staff around and smashed in his head. The shout attracted the other raiders' attention. They swarmed forward.

The bearskin caught several arrows, for once protecting him. An irony he wasn't prepared to concentrate on.

Ducking under a sword blow, he yanked a spear free from its owner. He flipped it around with a feral smile. None of them were near him in height or strength and he was stronger even than his size suggested.

His first spear thrust impaled one of the braver raiders, but one of his more clever opponents grabbed the haft before he could wrench it free. Four more were circling around behind him and he had to duck again, which cost him his hold on the spear. Another came in from behind and drove a knife at his back. It bit. Gregor roared in as much rage as pain.

A roar that began a human battle cry and ended in the terrible growling call of a great bear. Twelve feet tall and more Gregor swatted the bandits from him. Thick, furred hide deflecting all they could currently throw: the ones that still stood. He swatted them from his path, lumbering forward to chase those that ran from him, rage clouding his mind...

Until there were no more enemies to chase. Gregor found himself collapsing--rage ebbing from him-- human once more.

He blinked slowly and looked at his hands. The nails were slightly more pointed. But that seemed to be the only change that had remained.

What had that been? His wrath? He knew his vices and that wasn't the greatest of them though he struggled with it.

The wanderer's stone burned warmly against his skin. He touched the pouch that held it briefly drawing comfort from it and took stock of his injuries. Nothing serious. As had happened with the bear wounds he could feel them tingling as if they were healing already.

"Master ah... Bearskin..." A tentative voice sounded behind him, and Gregor picked himself up carefully. More tired than many a full day battle had left him in the past. Was it the change or something else? He didn't know.

"Yes, lad?" For the person before him was a boy or young man. Only about fourteen, but they'd had boys that young fetching and carrying on the front and many had fought bravely.

"Are... are you alright? They've got the fire stopped now that the arrows have stopped. They asked for someone to look on you... And..." The boy stammered but held his ground and Bearskin smiled.

"It's alright lad. I'm in one piece yet," Gregor reached a hand out and patted the boy's shoulder. "Though if your town would be willing, I was traveling this way planning to stay here the night. Though I'd not put more burden on you."

"I was sent to ask if you'd come." The boy ducked his head, a little embarrassed. "Most folk didn't want to."

"I'll not hold that against them. I'm a sight at the best of times, and this is not the best," Gregor stood. "Lead on."

The boy trotted ahead of him seeming to grow in confidence as Gregor had spoken. Gregor glanced at the walls and had to resist the urge to shake his head. It would take much to repair that and he hoped the walls had been the worst of it.

They weren't.

Several families gathered about charred out wreckages of thatch-roofed houses and Gregor winced. The slate roofed buildings further into town had fared better, but here thatch was murder when the fire arrows flew. A soot covered man in what had once been splendid clothing stepped up to him, speaking first to the boy.

"Thank you, Hans, please go see if you can help with the wounded," Then the man turned to Gregor. He was big for people of this region, and had once been a strong man, but age had thinned him. "And you, m'Lord. We owe you a debt we cannot repay."

Gregor shook his head. "Several days from here is another village. That one lies in ashes due to the war. How could I not help?"

The man nodded slowly. "I fear we have little room for you, but something can be found. It's the least we can do. It's another day to the next sizable village."

Gregor grimaced and ran his hands through his hair. "I appreciate the generosity. I'd not make your lot harder. I've slept in the woods before."

The man shook his head firmly. "We will find a place, though it may be on the floor I fear."

Gregor smiled. "That would be one of the better accommodations I've found of late. Though, m'Lord Mayor?"

At Gregor's question the man nodded, and Gregor continued. "Have you the resources to make all this good?"

"Yes, though it will be a near thing. We can rebuild the town, but not the houses. Places will be found for the families, but many have lost everything, and the town can either rebuild or help them. The Church will help as it can, but it is not as rich here as in the cities," The mayor reached out a hand then dropped it thinking better of the familiarity.

Another equally soot covered man in priestly raiment stepped up. "The church will do what the church can. Sister Raina is tending the wounded. Her Gifts will ensure we lose no one we do not have to. Sadly, I have no such powers myself."

Gregor nodded then considered. "I think I can help with some of this. While I am odd enough to look at there is one thing I have a surfeit of."

And he reached into his pocket, the pocket of the great coat, and pulled out a handful of coins, which he gave to the mayor, and a second which he gave to the priest. "Please, use these to make your town whole. In honor of the dead who did not have such a chance."

Both men blinked at him in then seemed to recover themselves. "My Lord..."

The mayor began this time using the title sincerely. Gregor held up a hand and shook his head. "If you must call me anything. I think the boy had the right of it. Master Bearskin is enough for me. Suffice to say I honor my own dead as best I can this way."

The priest's eyes narrowed, and Gregor felt Power touch him, though not a sort he was familiar with. It felt... almost like the Minstrel had felt though far, far weaker. A true priest indeed! But the priest's blue eyes regarded him steadily then he nodded slowly. "I see. I think I do see Master Bearskin. If there is anything we may do for you?"

"Pray for me." Gregor said simply. "I have a long seven years before my time of danger is done. Pray that I live."

"Perhaps you would do better not to fight whole brigand troops on your own, then, Master Bearskin," The Mayor smiled, taking some of the sting out of his words.

"Perhaps not, but I have never said I had any great claim on wisdom. Courage I will claim sometimes, though perhaps that also is foolishness." Gregor shook his head. "Now if there is anywhere I may help or may go to be out of the way and get a meal..."

"Of course." The mayor motioned Gregor to follow. "Come and we shall get you settled. I have duties to see to."

"I am rather strong, so if you need help with lifting, I have done that work before." Gregor mentioned, and they walked down the street making plans.

Rudigar von Neuen leaned back from his map table and glared at the parchment spread before him in the command tent. Its yellowed edges did not change, nor did the lines and demarcations within it. He pushed himself forward to feel along the smooth surface of the paper, paper not vellum.

He was a tall man for one of the Geroth, lean and dangerous dark of hair and blue of eye, but those eyes narrowed. Golden light streamed through the open entrance of the tent, pushing back the green tinged light that filtered fitfully through the canvas.

At least he'd managed to leave the gaudy pavilion his father had insisted he bring behind this time. Rank be damned, he was an obvious target without adding to it with useless finery. Besides his men were more comfortable in his simpler tent.

It was distinctive enough for his purposes. As was his uniform. Not that his father would ever agree. Well, the good Duke needn't to see and wouldn't sully himself stumping about with the troops. More the fool he.

"Any more word from Markault, Beren?" Von Neuen did not look at his valet, but he didn't need to to guess the man's expression.

"No, my Lord. the Bandits we have been tracking have been extreme-ly difficult to pinpoint. It is as if they know where we are and what we are doing at all times." Beren was a broad shouldered man, short, almost as if he had dwarfish blood in him.

Rudigar suspected he did but had never asked. It was none of his concern. He certainly appreciated the man's strength, skill, and quick mind wherever they had come from. That also was not his concern, merely the results.

Rudigar traced several lines from the marked points on the map and shook his head. "There are too many possibilities, and we have too few men left to investigate them all at once."

Too few men, that was a laugh. The levees and mercenaries had been released from their service and he suspected no few of them were now the bandits he was chasing. Even so there had to be an answer. If only he was clever enough to see it. "If they follow the pattern they should strike Markault next. Nevahs would have been a possibility, but mark it as burned out. It has potential for the base, if they have the stomach for hiding in the burned out ruins of a stone church."

"Surely not even these bandits would be that foolhardy. Whatever they may think of the Whispering Word, churches have Power to them, even small churches," Beren frowned and folded his hands behind him.

Rudigar pretended not to notice. He was not nearly so devout as his valet, but the man did have a point. He'd met too many venial priests to think the Church itself moved according to the will of any Power, but a faithful Church or one blessed by a faithful Priest held an enormous amount of Power, which made them unchancy places to hide for those of evil intent, even petty and stupid evil.

"Bandits are known for neither intelligence nor wisdom, so it is something to consider, Beren. It will harm nothing to check," Rudigar, privately, thought that the bandits would not take such chances. They tended to be a superstitious lot. "And see if the Town hall is still standing, they would have no qualms about using that building."

"A fair point, m'Lord, but we have no patrols to send at the moment they are all out except for your personal force here," Beren pointed out diffidently.

"Let me know when the first group of scouts-" His head came up as the shout registered and he caught the glance from his Valet. His own senses were extremely keen and he knew Beren suspected him of magic, but that wasn't where his magics lay, small though they were.

A man dashed into the tent, soot covered and fell to one knee. Truth be told, he almost fell over, and von Neuen caught him and eased him up into a chair. "Speak your piece when you've caught your breath man."

The messenger gulped in air and leaned forward, fighting the urge to stand back up, thoughts plain on his face. He was the bastard son of a peasant after all! His commander was nephew of the King.

Rudigar kept a hand on his shoulder and kept him in place. The message was more important than any misplaced pomp and circumstance. He didn't think he'd have to worry about undue familiarity from this one in more formal surroundings.

The messenger managed to catch enough of his breath to begin. "Markault was besieged m'Lord. There were far more of the bandits than we expected... They had fire arrows."

"Did anything survive? What of the townsmen?" That last drew a surprised look from the scout. Rudigar ignored it focusing on the information. It was pragmatism that motivated him not compassion. Especially if the King granted him these lands, which by all precedent he should after all he had been instrumental in their conquest, he would prefer to replace as few of the peasantry as possible.

"Most live. though a third part of the village burned. Anything with a thatch roof is gone." The man shook his head.

"Your squad did well, Halfrich," Rudigar thanked his easy way with names as he dredged up the scout's. The man's startled, and pleased, look was just what he was going for.

Surprisingly the man shook his head. "It wasn't us, sir. We did what we could, but we were pinned between the fire and the bandits when this big man. Delmin or Rithi for his size, came out of the woods. He was wearing a bearskin and... I think the smoke was in my eyes but for just a minute I thought there was a real bear there. But any way he laid into the bandits with a stick and his fist and they broke apart and scattered."

"Well, that's good news. Your squad may not have saved the town, but you still did well. I take it your commander is still at Markault?" Rudigar turning back to his maps and making a few notes on his paper.

The man nodded, sucking in another large gulp of air, though this one less desperate. He seemed to be more fully catching his breath. "He's assessing the damage. You are the King's only representative in the area so..."

The man trailed off knowing it was a touchy subject for his commander, but Rudigar simply nodded. "It was well thought of. I will send a messenger to the King myself and we shall see what aid can be had for this town. Hopefully they did not lose too much of their harvest. What of this man who startled the bandits?"

"I didn't see much but he was talking with the mayor when I left. They were calling him Master Bearskin and he seemed to be well off. Or at least I saw silver. He looked half like a bandit or wild beast himself though so, maybe it was my eyes playing tricks again," The man shrugged and lowered his eyes.

Rudigar nodded thoughtfully and cast a glance at Beren who frowned. Rudigar gave him a small shake of the head and turned back to the messenger. "Go, get cleaned up and get yourself some food at the mess tent. I will handle the other messages from here. Tomorrow you will likely be returning to Markault, hopefully with happier news."

The man stood and bowed deeply then left at Rudigar's dismissing gesture. Rudigar cocked his head at Beren who shrugged. "Your assessment?"

"Something new has been added. It may be useful to us or not. I find it interesting that a Delmin should be wandering about in a bearskin." Beren squared his shoulders, feet shoulder width apart, his usual stance when he wasn't fully sure of the reception of his ideas or was thinking or both.

"How so? My father's lands have few enough Delmin. Aren't most of them in the southern and central provinces rather than the north?" Rudigar's brow furrowed but he set the thought aside. There wasn't anything he could truly grasp with his small Gift, so there was little enough point in pushing.

Beren shifted slightly then settled, a sure sign that he thought Rudigar would not like what he was going to say. "Most of the Delmin live in the east on the other side of the Dead Wood. They revere the bear typically. The Bear constellation features very heavily into most of their rights and festivals and such. We've met more of them in the Mountains. They're not to be trifled with. They give the Rithi a run for their money in size and are often stronger than they look."

Rudigar started at that. "If they're that large and stronger than they ought to be that would explain much about the scout's report."

"Yes, m'Lord."

Once more Rudigar looked down at the map and then made a note on his page, one that said simply, 'find Master Bearskin.'

Chapter 6

WANDERING

Another day, another little town. Gregor wiped the sweat from his eyes and looked down at his increasingly grimy hands. He dared not wash them. He would not let such a trivial thing trip him up.

The last inn had asked he come in through the back and he had obliged. He suspected that he would soon have trouble finding any place that would take him no matter how much money he had. Even some of the churchman looked at him askance, though those were usually the over fed and pompous ones.

He leaned on his staff and closed his eyes, wishing... though he wasn't sure what he was wishing for. Fall had closed in on him and the breeze was chilly and crisp with rain. Four months already he had walked this path. His supplies were running low again. Perhaps this time he would buy a pack, or at least something he could sling over his shoulder. Better than going to town after town an outcast.

At least the bandits seemed to have decided to move on. He'd spoiled more than one of their raids, and that was worth something. One of the nobles, possibly von Neuen, was sending out patrols and they seemed to be actively trying to stop the brigandage, which was at least more than he had expected. What did he expect out of this? And what truly would come of any of this? Could there be anything good?

"Do you really wish to ask that, Gregor called Bearskin?" A familiar voice came from behind him, and he spun about. Fate's Minstrel held up a hand and smiled a gentle smile at him.

"No, do not be afraid. I bring no doom. Nor bargain. Merely answers. At least some. I cannot give you all of them, it is not the way these things work." Her tone took on a stern note and she waited until he nodded.

Before she could speak again, he made bold to ask, "If you have not come to warn, what is your purpose. You say you bring answers. But to which questions? I have so many. This is my own folly, as you said. Yet you helped me. That stone you gave me... Who are you m'Lady?"

She nodded and looked over his shoulder to the town below them. "I am she who warns. It was I who warned the Sidhe that their course would bring their own ruin when they were tempted with the destruction of humans. It was I who led Silverslip in the organization of those who became the Elves. It is given to me to ensure mortal, and power alike knows the Enemy and makes their own choice. It is given to me to ensure that what Laws need to be known are known."

She looked back at him. "It is this latter purpose that brings me here this night. Though I had not expected to be sent to you again so very soon."

"Sent, by whom?" Bearskin asked then flushed at his own temerity.

She threw back her head and laughed. "Oh, so straight forward! Not in ten thousand years of my dealing with mortals, Powers, and the walkers between has someone simply dared ask me whom I serve. I serve the Whispering Word and only he. Ask what you will, I will answer, and it will not count to calling on him for aid. The old liar cannot forbid this. He has not the power."

"Are you more powerful than he?" Gregor marveled, but she shook her head.

"No, it is simply that I have the Laws of the Whispering Word on my side, and he stands opposed to them. I have enough power that was given to me in the beginning of all things, that with it and the Laws he dares not openly oppose me. Remember that should he try to convince you our conversations constitute a breach of your bargain." But her face grew serious. "My time is brief, ask what you will of me, what I can I will answer."

"Will any good come of this?" Gregor shook his head. "No, can any good come of this. I've heard of no story that ends so."

"There are those who have seen through such folly. And I will tell you this, Gregor called Bearskin. The Laws regarding humans are very specific and come from the Whispering Word himself during that great war.

"No power has any hold on you that you do not give it. As you gave yourself into the power of the Enemy. As your actions and intentions build power about you that may be used. Each of you holds your own fate in your own hands. Use that power wisely, it is not granted so greatly to any other people. Even the Elves have only an echo of that power and only because they helped Humans," Fate's minstrel held up a hand. "Do not ask what makes you so very special. That is a question I cannot answer. But remember. No power has any hold on you that you do not grant them. Human wizardry blurs these lines, but even there they can only make use of what you give them to work with."

Gregor nodded slowly. That at least fit with some of the things that he had seen during the war. It was easy enough for a mage to simply use power to slay someone, even as the cannon could shoot clean through a man, but the horror stories of enchanters enthralling thousands did not seem to come easily true.

Even so, there were many ways powers could approach and the Veils concealed too much and for once he was very glad he did not have the Sight or anything resembling it. But what should he ask such a power? "Have you any advice then m'Lady? My fate is, as you say, in my own hands. I would not share it with any, yet something prevents me from simply retreating into the mountains and living alone. I seem to be able to do much good with the devil's promise, yet... do these people share my fate if I fail because I have helped them?"

The Wanderer once more shook her head and came to stand beside him on the hill. "No. Only those who willingly bind their fate to yours shall share it. It is their choice and little you can do will prevent it. So, I give you this advice. You will have four years of wandering before you come to your peril. In the last three years you will have a great chance for redemption. Do not cast aside aid, but neither let fear stay your hand from what is right. Your Virtues will see you through."

Gregor nodded slowly and inspected her carefully. The sharp profile. The strange ears and the unassuming green clothing. And there was a sadness in those gleaming coal bright eyes. Almost as if... And yet how could it be otherwise? She had seen so many fall to the dooms she had warned of. "My Lady, you have my thanks. I will take your advice to heart. I will not forget it. I cannot forget it. Though if you are what I believe you to be, you know that already."

She looked away from the town then up at the sky and the setting sun and her expression grew sad. "Now I am needed elsewhere. And who knows, Gregor Bearskin. Perhaps you shall be the salvation of some who would have otherwise fallen rather than their doom as you fear. Go in peace and..."

She paused and once more held out her hand. He took it and she pressed what felt like a carved bead into his hand. "You will know when to use this. Do not use this before the time is right. If there is any doubt do not use it."

His hand closed on the object, and she turned away walking down the road and simply faded away in the light of the setting sun. Gregor held up the thing she had given to him in the same light and found it was, indeed, carved bead, but the sigils and symbols it bore were strange and ever twisting and seemed to shine of their own light. How he was to use it he didn't know, but he slid the bead into his pouch alongside her stone and once more turned towards the town. He would take whatever fate was to come to him.

Cold water ran down Gregor's face the rain came down in sheets, penetrating even the thick canopy of pine and ash. He didn't bother to move. There wasn't another town for miles and the forest held some shelter. The bearskin gave him more, but it wouldn't protect the exposed portions of himself.

He tucked his hands into his arm pits as he huddled and tried to keep warm and as dry as possible. The scent of the earth and pine might have been pleasant some other time, but its dampness only underscored his current trouble.

He hated wet summers. Crops stunted from too much rain and not enough sun or drowned entirely. Struggling to keep the thatch from leaking. Anna running about, to and fro trying to keep the house as warm as possible and plug what drips she could. Anna...

He closed his eyes against the memories. Against fire arrows. Thatch ablaze. The Church bell ringing the alarm and the army arriving too late to set up their cannon before fire sunk its teeth into the city. It had rained that day too and ash mingled with the scent of wet earth for nothing but a torrent of rain could quickly quench mage fire.

He pushed himself to his feet and began to prowl at the edge of the pool he had found. The water seemed good enough and he hadn't had trouble drinking anything since taking up this foolishness, but that meant little enough. Between the Minstrel's gifts and the Devil's Coat he wasn't sure what could affect him. Though he had expected the coat to hinder rather than help him. What had the Lady said of that?

What had she said?

That everything must obey its own Laws. And all things were subject to the Laws of the Whispering Word.

He looked down at his rain streaked hands. Three times now he had turned into a bear in a moment of battle. He had heard of such things. There were those among the Delmin who were said to carry such a curse.

Was it himself? Or was this part of the Doom he had brought upon himself with his Bargain? The Skin changing him rather than something within him?

But it must follow Laws. While he could not call on the Whispering Word, nor did he expect yet another visit from the Minstrel, perhaps, perhaps there was something he could do. He closed his eyes and leaned against the rough bark of a pine, letting the sound of the rain and the scent of the wood play about him. How had it felt when he turned into a bear?

How had it felt?

Rage, but not just rage. Rage was mindless.

Something close to purpose.

Maybe desperation. His eyes snapped open as he singled in on the part of the memory with a clue. The change always happened when he refused to run, when he decided to act. Perhaps he could draw on that poised moment of determined decision.

He pushed away from the tree and centered himself in the clearing, once more closing his eyes. The sound of the rain faded from his ears to a gentle thrumming in the background as he turned his attention inward. Seeking that moment... the feeling of the decision.

Something stirred within him, and he recoiled from its snarling fury. Even as water ran down his neck and shed off the Bearskin in great sheets, a force assailed his mind such that he physically reeled away from it. What had he touched? He wasn't sure.

He settled himself once more and reached once more within. This time that force threw him to the ground. What was it? Was it him? If so, he wasn't entirely certain that he wanted to know where such a snarling angry piece of himself came from. Especially since it didn't seem to like the rest of him very much.

This time he settled, legs crossed, and called to mind one of the concentration exercises the old priest had taught him in happier days when his gifts had given him access to secrets and as much knowledge as he could cram into his head. He set aside the sensation of rain. He set aside the soft scent of the grass and the rich scent of the earth. The tang of the pines. The song of a lark. Each was acknowledged and set aside from his thoughts. Rather than turning towards the Whispering Word he turned his attention inward, seeking that thing.

That moment of decision.

That moment of rage.

His eyes flew open. No, not the rage. The rage might be some of the source of the power, but it wasn't the anger, the Wrath, that did it. It was... he wasn't sure what to call it. But it was not his temper's flash point that transformed him. It was the moment he realized he could not turn away or stand aside.

He rose to his feet, and closed his eyes, and reached for that determination and the echoing snarl that it always had brought to his mind. He felt Power flooding through him like a lightning strike and paws rested on the ground as he roared out his challenge, but there was nothing here to challenge. He felt the need to change back, but this time held to his determination. He must learn to control this.

Yet he couldn't hold on to it without the force of his wrath behind it. The bear's form fell from him, and he found himself face down on the ground panting from the effort of concentration.

Shoving himself back into a sitting position, he considered. Playing the last moments in bear form through his mind. The Bear left him when he was calm, no when the threat was past. When the moment of elemental stubbornness was gone.

Once more he touched his memories, this time of each time he had ceased to be a bear. He would not be controlled by a curse. He had not taken this as a curse on himself. Unless it had come with the bearskin? Yet that was not part of his Bargain.

Old Scratch was cunning and clever. It might be he had known the bargain would have this effect on him. And yet... He could not chase that thought down. His mind was trying to go in too many directions to too many memories.

First focus on the practical, then track down the philosophical. Perhaps the Minstrel's stone had something to do with it? At least his ability to return.

He recalled to mind the tales of the warriors from the far north who were said to change into a bear when in battle or in the heat of passion. The Delmin had similar legends except the Bear was a friend to the Delmin. Their totem, their guide.

There were those who followed the Bear as if it were a Power itself rather than a manifestation of some other power. For his part he had always thought the Bear was how the Whispering Word had spoken to the Delmin, but if that was so...

But he could not tell for certain. Though the legends of Delmin Bear shifters always included an eventual ability to control. Could he reach that ability? Was it in himself or something Old Scratch had laid on him? Could he control it either way?

Well, it was certainly time to try. He could hunt, especially as a bear, and if he needed there were towns behind he could return to if he needed food. He could take the time to practice and it seemed wise to do so.

The legends said the Bear came in the time of greatest need for the Delmin. He was the only Delmin about so was it his need that had called it. Perhaps starting there.

He once more drew upon memory and history and sought the emotion, the moment of change. He felt himself growing larger and heavier and tried to slow the change to examine it as it happened only to find himself snapped out of it and falling over on his side feeling uncommonly like a rabbit that has been shaken in a dog's mouth.

Had is focus slipped? It seemed likely. So perhaps the place to start was the concentration exercises Father Rufin had taught him when he was first learning how to control his Gift. First seek control. Then seek the ability.

It was going to be a long, long day.

Chapter 7

TRIALS AND TROUBLES

T wilight gathered about the streets and the raucous calls of the carters grew fewer. Isela hurried down the road alone, clutching the smooth fabric of her embroidery bag to her. The acrid bite of garbage heated by the summer sun wafted out of alley ways and made her very much aware of the heavy skirts and well-made shawl she wore.

She bit her lip and prayed as loud voices, raucous and uncouth, carried to her out of one of the taverns. She flicked a nervous glance at the lone lamp lighter plying his trade.

At least the money was hidden under her clothes as best she could manage. Sweet Maker of Man and Mercy, let the next Caravan go through or we are undone.

Her escort could have at least seen her home before he took his services elsewhere, somewhere other than a slowly fading merchant house, but that mattered less than the consequences. She was all too aware that a merchant's daughter, however troubled the times, had no business alone in this part of town!

But what else was there for her to do? Her escort had simply bid her fair well after she left the tailor and her choice was go ahead or back.

The uneven cobbles caught her feet and she stumbled in the dimming light. Her Gift stirred uneasily the world trying to go hazy around her rather than shadowy and she squashed it. This was no time for the Sight.

She had enough trouble in the here and now. Unless something was set to cross a Veil to get her, her present sight was useless, the past would not help and the future was unlikely to, either. A flash of insight caused her to duck away from a particular dark alley.

A rough laugh followed her, and three large men blocked her way. The lamplighter had suddenly discovered somewhere else he had to be for he was no longer in evidence.

Isela carefully started backing away. She had her sharp little shears and the blade she used to cut thread, but those would be small deterrent to determined trouble. Her soft grey eyes flickered from one man to the next down the line and they grinned at her.

They all loomed large and broad shouldered, though there was little other type about them. One blond, and two different shades of brown. Who were they?

The two on the ends shifted to cut her off from any of the other alleys or doors she might be tempted to bolt towards and the man in the middle with hard black eyes watched her speculatively. "So, looks like we found the right target boys, do you think she has it on her?"

"Only one way to find out," The blond one on her right answered with a slow cruel smile.

Both he and the one on his left lunged at her, but as Isela ducked backwards, she discovered the one on her left had lunged behind her. She found herself wrapped in strong arms with a hand firmly pressed over her mouth muffling her shouts.

She kicked back with all her might. Alas, she was a small woman and while he yelped, he maintained his hold. The one with black eyes assessed her calmly. "Careful boys. We don't want to do the wrong kinds of damage. We've got a message to send. Especially if she doesn't have it on her."

He reached up and fingered a trailing lock of gold that drifted down her face. And Isela twisted and struggled, but to no avail, save the one behind her grunting and saying to his leader. "Let's get her tied then. I'd've thought she'd've fainted rather than fought with her blood."

"Spirit comes in all forms. Come, the guards shouldn't be on this side of town for some time yet," And he pulled a length of rope out and a growl of rage sounded from behind them.

The leader turned and started to draw his short sword as a massive bear lowered from its twelve foot height down to all fours and charged. The blond was already backing away, but the leader ducked towards the alley slashing at the bear's face. His only reward was to be swatted into the brick of a brewery and he slid to the ground without a sound.

The one holding Isela hauled her along with him but another quick blow from the bear's paw sent them both sprawling. Isela scrambled away from the creature across the dusty, dry streets, trying to find her feet but stumbling in the dark.

The brigand wasn't so lucky. The bear was on him in a moment and that was the end of it with his head against the hard cobble of the pavement. The remaining bandit fled with the bear in hot pursuit. He ducked down a narrow ally and the bear slammed into the wall shaking the building as it tried to force itself after the lone escaping ambusher. But the alley was narrow, and the bear was large.

Isela took a deep breath and tried to collect herself. Her Sight had quieted, for which she was grateful. She could not bring herself to fear the bear. Her embroidery bag was still there, and she didn't seem to have broken anything.

She briefly let herself touch the place where the price of her commissions was hidden. It also was safe. They could pay the staff for at least a month and the new commissions in her bag did not seem to have been damaged.

"Are you whole, Mistress?" A voice sounded gently near her, using the term for a woman of unspecified rank. She looked up and saw a large man, larger than any she had seen before wrapped in what seemed to be a bear hide offering a dirty, untrimmed hand towards her. She took it after a moment's hesitation.

Had she simply imagined the bear? And yet he wavered, misty before her sight like something Veiled and energies played about him. This was no time for the Sight, so she held her tongue as he helped her to her feet.

"I seem to be in one piece, bruised and dirtied but better than could be expected. Thanks to you it would seem," She dropped to a deep curtsy. "Might I have a name to call you?"

"I am called Bearskin," He said simply. "I would escort you home if you do not think your family would find it amiss. I will not go inside. I'd not shame your house so."

He offered her an arm and she took it but shook her head firmly. "The shame would be in turning you away after such courageous actions."

"Then let us go before the constabulary come this way and ask awkward questions. I fear appearances mean I am not the most respectable or trustworthy to those in official positions," His tone was rueful, and he motioned for her to lead.

She considered for a moment then nodded. As her hand rested on his arm again powers swirled about him. Something sinister warred with something noble, all over laying the impression of a bear.

What could it mean? They quickly passed into more brightly lit streets and Master Bearskin, she had little trouble extending him the title, seemed willing to look anywhere but at her.

"My father will be grateful, Master Bearskin. Our House is in a poor enough state, but I am certain there is some way we can return the favor you have given us." She turned them down another street where the air was fresher and the faint scent of flowers wafted in from walled gardens. The cobbles here were even and well-fitting and the going was much gentler.

She waved aside the guards of two of their neighbors who stared resolutely ahead of them as they approached her own house. There Old Nathan, the old man at arms who had served her mother so faithfully, stood watch and shifted hand gripping his spear more tightly.

But she raised a hand and he subsided. Master Bearskin stopped. "I think I, at least should go no further. I do not think your tormentors will follow you here. And... take this. It has been a long time since someone has simply taken me as I am, no matter how grateful they were to me."

He pressed something into her hands and stepped away, bowing to the guard, and saying simply. "One of those who would have robbed her got away, please make certain she is not alone."

The old man with sharp blue eyes, and a broad frame that had once been strong bowed deeply. "Thank you for returning her to us. If you should need, call. You have my oath on aid."

Bearskin shook his head. "It was the least I could do. If you must give some reward, pray for me. I have yet three more years of danger ahead of me."

Then, he walked back in the direction they had come. Even as Isela tried to call him back, Old Nathan put a hand on her shoulder and shook his head. "There's a man who doesn't want to cause more trouble than needed. He's trouble enough of his own young miss. He'll not take from us."

"How do you know?" Isela asked looking up at him. "If he had troubles, you would think he would want allies."

"I know the breed," Was all the old guard would say. Well he was rarely wrong about the character of men, or women for that matter. Then Isela looked down to see what Master Bearskin had pushed into her hands and her eyes went wide. Three coins, but all solid gold, ancient enough that the symbols were worn off, and so large she hadn't recognized them as coins.

She held them up and Old Nathan and he nodded once more. "Let's get you inside, Miss. The Mistress, your sister, is in a fine temper."

"What's Karin done now?" Isela sighed as she followed the old guard up to her home.

Elf lights came up as Sophia swept into the room. The skirt of her fine linen dress swirled above the rich thickness of the carpet and the high gloss shine of the wood, now collecting dust at the corners. The elegant curve of the interior stairs rose up to the hall and glowed with the echo of more elf lights beyond.

Sophia's blue eyes narrowed, and she tapped a long finger, resisting the urge to run her fingers through her golden hair. There was too much to do here. She paused to wipe away errant dust from a priceless vase, now containing brilliant red roses, irritated. They'd lost another maid this morning. Fortunately the cook was more stubborn or she'd have to assume those duties herself. The woman would stay as long as she could reasonably do so.

Sophia closed her eyes and took mental tally, the cook and the butler were paid for this month, but next month was a question. The pantry was stocked. Thank the Whispering Word her father had spent the money on an enchanted pantry in more prosperous years. She ran a finger along the smooth wood of the dresser, replaying the echoes of her childhood in this room and her mother's laughter. All that was done now. She shook herself and turned resolutely back to the well paneled walls and above all the stairs.

Laughter floated down it and her sister breezed in, blood red hair tied up in the careless fashion that was so popular in court, wearing a dress of emerald green. The corseting accented her slender waist. The color set off her brilliant green eyes, but the skirts filled the entire staircase, making her look wide in the hip as a boat. It was a fashion that looked much better on a taller woman. Sophia planted her hands firmly on her hips.

"Just where do you think you're going, Karin?" She didn't bother to hide her displeasure.

Karin skidded to a halt in front of her and snapped a fan that Sophia hadn't seen open. She smiled coyly. "I have an engagement, sister dear, and since your beau seems intent on ruining us, someone has to make up the difference!"

Sophia shook her head. "I wouldn't say that without evidence if I were you. I've seen no indication of any such thing and accusing the son of a Duke and a Freiherr in his own right of that sort of thing is likely to undo anything your assignation will achieve. Whom are you taking with you?"

"Oh, I think old Nathan will more than serve," Karin brushed imagined dust from her skirt.

Sophia shook her head, "At least you're taking someone. Your wild reputation isn't helping Father's circumstances. You should exercise more control."

"What? And wind up an old maid like you, sister dear? The good Freiherr's been courting you for months and no sign of any more serious commitment," Karin stepped around Sophia and Sophia caught her shoulder.

"I mean it. Watch yourself, Karin. If someone is out to ruin us and this is not just a streak of poor fate, give them no more fuel for their fire than they already have. And watch your temper. That Vice will bring you to ruin if you don't take care," Sophia warned raising a finger on her free hand.

Karin pulled away, "I am not the one accepting the court of someone so high above my station. Why not seek someone amongst the other merchant houses? You tend to your Vices, I'll tend to mine. Pride will catch you as surely as Wrath."

Old Nathan stepped in followed by Isela, who pressed herself against the wall when she saw Karin's expansive dress. Karin beckoned to him, and he followed, after a quick glance at Sophia and a squeeze of Isela's shoulder.

Sophia glared after them, closed her eyes and took a deep breath to calm herself. She still had the household accounts to go over, and that was no task for someone beclouded by her own anger.

"Sophia..." Isela started hesitantly, and Sophia turned to the quieter of her sisters. They were a study in contrasts physically as well as temperamentally. Karin's face was as boldly boned as her coloration. Isela was all soft gentle curves, slim and quiet rather than striking. Her chestnut hair, had the same soft curls, but around a sweet heart shaped face, and the big grey eyes always made her seem younger than she was.

Sophia shook herself. This wasn't a time to coddle her youngest sister's innocence, unfortunately.

"What news, Isela? I hope it's good, we lost another maid while you were out." She couldn't keep the impatience out of her voice, and Isela's head dropped.

Sophia bit her tongue but the girl was far too sensitive for Sophia's liking. This world was very rough on the gentle. Pity their mother hadn't lived to teach her the ways to navigate it. Sophia had managed, but had not managed to pass enough on.

"I have the commission funds. It should be enough for a month and three more commissions and, sister," Isela hesitated.

Sophia tapped an impatient foot. "Out with it girl, I'm not going to eat you for telling me something I don't like. I take it your escort also decided to take his services elsewhere?"

Isela nodded. "Shortly after we left the Tailor's shop. And I was set upon by three men not long their after."

That grabbed Sophia's attention and she reached out gently to touch Isela's face, "Not hurt I hope?"

Isela shook her head. "Not more than bruises. A man in a bearskin robe chased them away and saw me home. He gave his name as Master Bearskin."

"I'm glad some benevolent Power or Angel was watching over you, but this will make things difficult. I need to do the accounts tonight so anything you can tell me about the commissions would be appreciated," Sophia gentled her tone and pulled her sister into a hug. "I am not making light of your saving. But we've only two more caravans this year to see us all through the winter."

Isela nodded, "I understand Sophia, there's more. He gave this. The man in the Bearskin robe..."

And Isela held out in her hand the three large golden coins. "He said it was a thanks for... taking him as he was."

Sophia's eyes widened as she took the coins. "I shall have to take these to father. He will know their value. I should have liked to meet your benefactor."

"He seemed embarrassed to be seen with us." Isela shook her head. "No. He seemed embarrassed that we should be seen with him."

"I see," Sophia looked down at the gold in her hand and closed her fingers about it. "Should you see him again, give him my thanks and Father's thanks as well."

"He asked we pray for him," Isela shifted uncomfortably. "He has a long road, sister, and his fate twines with ours. Something is coming, something powerful as a whirlwind. Please, please don't do anything rash. I... I'd give Karin the same warning or a stronger one, but I don't think she'd listen."

Sophia nodded slowly. She had only small magics in her soul, enough to run the household, but no greater. Isela's Gift of Sight made her profoundly uneasy, but while her visions could be maddeningly vague, they hadn't been wrong yet. "I'll be cautious, little mouse. And I'll do what I can for our wild one. And for you. We may not see eye to eye, but I'll see you as well cared for as I can."

Isela reached for her older sister and hugged her close and Sophia returned the hug, singing softly a song that their mother had taught them. She was not the musician Karin was, but her pitch was true. The household books would wait.

Chapter 8
CONFLICTS OF INTEREST

The wine was not up to his usual standards, even in the field. Rudigar set the glass down on the table in some disgust. He glanced at the letter in front of him. If he were honest with himself the letter more than the wine was the source of his displeasure. The wine could not help being what it was that letter on the other hand...

He ran a finger over the fine paper finish and touched the golden inks feeling a crackle of power and a shimmer of connections. Connections he could not see. Sadly, he never had been able to. Not enough magic in his soul, and for once he cursed his father's distrust of Powers.

They existed and it was folly to presume they were only hostile, as foolish as trying to ignore their impact. He pushed his plain chair back from the solid, though otherwise unprepossessing table.

The room was not truly large enough to pace, especially with all the 'fine' accouterments that the proprietor had crammed in here. All solid, well made, and quite serviceable, but he would not have called them 'fine'. Not even by merchant standards.

The lamp was high quality enough, wick and oil as well, that the room hadn't filled with smoke, for which he was grateful. Small blessings he supposed. Merchants. And that was the rub. His father had forbidden he see the merchant's daughter and further his courtship of her. More the fool he.

The woman was proud enough, more proud than her station warranted, but she had the manner born and was used to running an extensive household and business. If she could handle that she could manage the lands of a lord.

There was a puzzle there. A sense of connections waiting to be made. It was maddening to have half a puzzle. And, he admitted, to have his father exert his prejudices at this point in the courtship rather than the earlier stages. Rudigar had actually grown quite fond of the girl, though he knew himself to be too cold a man to truly call it 'love'.

Two steps covered the room one way and a military turn, then two steps the other way as he paced in the limited confines of his room. If only he could be certain that his father had done this because of his dislike for commoners.

Fool. Had he forgotten that every royal line had at least one peasant king or peasant queen in it? He was proud enough of blood connections to the royals. And proud enough of having been able to take the king's only sister as a wife. Blue blood. Faugh!

He stopped in front of the large wardrobe and rested his head against the wood. A fool for a prince, the King delaying the assignment of these lands which was aiding the bandit problem, the king insisting the bandit problem was Rudigar's to solve since he'd been pushing for Lordship of the area. And now this. The other things he could have dealt with in their turn.

The assignment of these lands was a powerful tool in the King's pocket. Of course he was taking his time and letting the nobles vie for it and expend their influence on this project rather than some of his others. Rudigar had counted no less than four other projects the king had snuck by his nobles due to this dispute and he was certain there were more.

No, it was the other games that bothered him. His father's games and some of the other games in court. And the Crown Prince seemed more interested in playing with wine and bards than doing his duty. If anything happened to the king...

Rudigar shook his head angrily and pushed way from the wardrobe stepping back to the table the landlord had called a desk. He drew a sheet of paper towards him and settled in to compose his response. It was time to set some of these games onto his terms rather than someone else's.

Bearskin... Gregor... ran his hand over the rough crates in the supply room that he had been rented, at a rather exorbitant fee as well. The musty scent of the earthen walls was more comforting than insulting. Honest earth had been his friend all his life. Honest earth. Honest work. He had little enough of either these days.

He closed his eyes and wistfully wished he could pray. He had gotten used to not bathing though he didn't like the state it left him. The wandering was no great hardship beyond the disgust and distrust his appearance bred, but he had need of guidance and there was little enough to be had.

The stone the Minstrel had given him warmed and he pulled it out to hold it in his hand and hold it to himself. A hint of music, or the memory of music accompanied it. Not completely alone. Not complete without guidance. But what was he to do? There was something here that needed doing and he could not move on until he had done it.

He had given quite a bit of trouble to the bandit troops that had been so prevalent in the area in the wake of the war. Too many had been his old companions in arms, though not the honorable ones like Heinrich. Men like him who had been cut loose and chosen to steal rather than seek honest work.

What of himself? Was he honest any longer? It was harder and harder to think of himself as Gregor.

He pushed away from the crate, eyes stinging in the smoky light of the lamp. He slipped the little stone back into his inner most pouch. Four years had passed. Four long years. More than half way through his time of trials, but this was when the greatest peril would come the Minstrel had said.

She told no one anything they did not need to know. That he had reasoned out. But what did that mean to him? He wasn't sure.

His Gift was Memory, and the memory that called him most was the Merchant's daughter. What little she had told him of her family's plight had struck a chord with him. Perhaps there was something he could do there to help?

He tapped the side of his nose thoughtfully, and then nodded to himself. He would have to see what he could discover tomorrow. There were people who would deal with the likes of him, and he could do much by letter that he could not do in person. Now it only remained to be seen what needed to be done. And perhaps it was good that he had spent much of the last four years in practice.

Chapter 9
SHADES OF RUIN

Dim lights shone on wet streets. The clop of hooves and the squeak of wheels across wet cobbles were a sadly familiar sound. Today Johann von Argers drew no comfort from them. The reins in his hand were also familiar, though it had been years since he last had to drive his own coach home.

The faint lights shone from the upper stories of the businesses that dotted this lane. Once welcoming, he doubted many of them would welcome a man so marked for disaster as he seemed now to be. Maker of Man and Mercy, please, let the next caravan go through.

He sent the prayer up with all the faith in him, though he had no certainty it would do any more good than the others he'd prayed since this disaster started. His eye caught the sign for the money changer and he shook his head.

At least he'd managed to avoid debt. If they had to--if this last caravan, paid for, thank the Whispering Word--also vanished he could at least sell what he owned and start over somewhere. Where he did not know. Was it any wonder that his coachman had decided to take his pay and take his leave?

The chestnut gelding danced a little around something that Johann could not see, and he clucked soothingly at the creature. Perhaps Sophia's beau had decided to.... no he wouldn't think of that. He'd decided long ago that he wouldn't sell any of his daughters to keep his business afloat no matter how amenable they might be. And even in these lands where paupers could become princes, it was an unchancy thing to marry so high above one's station. She was too much like her mother.

He set that painful thought aside and sighed heavily. The horse shied as a man stepped out of an alley with a crossbow leveled at Johann. For a moment the merchant considered trying for a gallop and running the man over, but there was too much chance that would trigger the crossbow. He could little enough afford to replace the horse or the carriage, even if he should chance to escape with his life, which he doubted. Though there might be a chance. He reined in and the man grinned.

"Seems like you're a sensible sort after all, they said you wouldn't be, too stubborn. Your purse," The man's hands did not leave the crossbow. In the dim light it was hard to tell any specifics of what he looked like. "Take it out and throw it to the side of the road on your right."

Johann snorted and unhooked the pouch from his belt tossing it strongly to the right. It made little enough noise where it fell. Paying the coachman had taken nearly all his meager funds. "You're welcome to what little is there. There's not enough to be worth your risk here."

The man gave a bark of laughter and didn't even look at the purse. "Very funny, your real purse. You merchants always have a secret purse on you. And I know that Caravan sold for a princely sum. No more pretending you have nothing old fool."

"Do you think I would be driving myself home if the Caravan had sold?" Johann shifted in his seat experimentally, and the crossbow raised a hair in return. The merchant subsided. "I do not know your source, but it seems you are deeply misinformed."

"Well then, it looks like we'll have to do it the hard way. Pity, your daughters are going to be in a very sad state without their father, even if they can sell that big old fancy house," And he drew the crossbow more tightly to his shoulder as a massive paw shot out of one of the larger alleys to be followed by a massive bear.

The crossbow bolt went wide and ricochet off the paving stones before spinning away into the night. The horse reared and it was all Johann could do to prevent the creature from bolting, not that he blamed the gelding in the least! How was a bear that big in the city?

When he could turn his attention to the world again he discovered not a bear, but a very large man (Delmin perhaps?) In a Bearskin. The man was covered in grime but his grey eyes were kind as was his voice.

"Are you harmed, good Master Merchant?" The man asked stepping a little aside to avoid the horse, which cast a long baleful glare at him. Well the bearskin wasn't likely to make the horse happy.

"I am whole and unharmed, though I think it will be long before I am able to sleep. I am glad you came along when you did Master…." Johann trailed off, the man was probably a free man. He didn't think any Lord would let his vassal out to behave so outlandishly.

"Bearskin. They call me Master Bearskin." The man reached down to pick up the discarded purse and the merchant saw a flash of silver on his right hand. Master Bearskin proffered the purse and Johan took it, ignoring the unpleasant scent. How long had it been since he bathed?

"I owe you my life. What may I do to repay you?" Johann leaned forward resting his forearms on his knees to better look at the man. Younger than he thought. Interesting, and more fit than he expected from his disheveled state.

Master Bearskin shook his head. "I ask no reward. Simply pray for me. I have three long years ahead of me."

Johann frowned, that boded ill, but the man had risked himself and bought into the Merchant's troubles. The least he could do was return the favor. "If you have no lodging, come with me. I can provide housing for you and a meal. Not so grand as I might have in the past, but warm and wholesome. I can also see a bath laid for you…"

Bearskin shook his head. "For the meal and the lodging, I will most gratefully accept. I must refuse the bath. As I said, three long years to come before this trial, this penance is complete."

Penance for what? Johann wondered, but he refrained from asking. it was certainly none of his business and he had enough troubles without borrowing any. "Then please, if you will ride? I think it will be easier for both of us."

"And I think your horse will be happier without me in easy smelling range," Bearskin bowed politely, a more courtly bow than Johann would have expected. Curiouser and curiouser, and he had never been good at squashing his curiosity. Though he could, and did, hold his tongue over his questions as the man entered the carriage. He felt it sag under the weight.

He gave the supple reins a gentle flick and the horse once more started down the street carrying them home to who knew what form of trouble.

Gregor breathed in the refreshing air of the gardens, the rich earth, the scent of flowers, and even the scent of the vegetable garden out of sight and smiled. Herbs he couldn't see added a spice and tang to the warm scent of the roses he could in the dim lantern light.

He stepped out of the coach into the cool air and let the breeze carry some of the dust he had accumulated away. That had never been against his bargain. After all, the wind blew where it blew he didn't seek it.

Even now it was off rustling the branches of fruit trees and rippling the water of the pond. The smooth paving stones were comfortable under his feet. How his boots had held up this long he didn't know. Too much of Power and he was too weary of the questions and the guessing.

The house was only two stories tall but broad, a luxurious configuration for how deep into town it was. The stone was old and so was the architecture. He reached a hand up to help the merchant clamor down from the driver's bench and hand the reins to a young man whom Bearskin took to be a groom. The young man bowed, "You'll want to hurry."

Johann frowned and motioned Bearskin to follow him, and Gregor did. It was no effort to keep up with the merchant's pace. He was fully a foot taller than the other man, and it let him enjoy the surroundings. Treasure every sensation. While it lasted. It never lasted. He set the thought aside. Better to treasure the moment than dwell on uncertain futures.

As they drew closer to the house he took in the broad, strong wooden doors bound in bronze. If it weren't for the first floor windows, this house would be most fortifiable.

He shook his head but refrained from an outward laugh at his own folly. Even four years could not remove certain habits from him. He hadn't thought he would have been suited to the life of a soldier, but it was a better fit than his current one. At least there had been purpose there whether he always agreed with that purpose or not.

Sharp, female voices echoed down the well polished wooden walls of the entry hall. He winced for the carpet as his boots tracked mud onto it. He would have to leave enough behind him to cover any damages. There would be time enough for that later. He hoped.

The merchant beside him frowned, even as Gregor took in the warm scent of the wood, surprisingly free of smoke. How had they managed that? Surely...

Emerald and fire blew around the corner in a whirlwind of fury. She barely came up to his chest, but her anger crackled through the room like electricity and he felt the bear responding. He ground his heel down upon it. This was not the time. Not the time. The woman spoke, voice musical even in her fury. "You just try and stop me, Sophia! I..."

She crashed to a halt right in front of them as she spotted her father, or at least Gregor presumed the merchant was her father. He certainly looked it. His arms folded across his chest, and his voice was dangerously calm as he asked. "And just what would your sister be trying to stop you from doing?"

Another woman came into the hall, moving with purpose but much more decorum. She was tall, golden blond with a finely boned face and eyes as intensely blue as the red-head's were green: sharper than Anna's had been and less merry. She held herself like some of the Lords he'd served under. Her voice was a mellow middle soprano, and much calmer than the Karin's had been. "Do you wish to tell him, Karin? Or should I?"

Karin blushed red as her hair and held her chin up, "I have an engagement this evening, Father, hopefully it should help the deplorable state of our house."

"Is that any way to speak in front of a guest?" The Merchant admonished. "I fear you shall have to send your apologies, in writing. Master Bearskin will be joining us for dinner. We owe him much, or I do."

"What happened, Father?" The queenly one asked, not demanding but...

Bearskin had trouble putting his finger on the tone. But as if this was of personal importance. No. He gave up trying to classify it, but it was of more importance, or perhaps a different kind of importance to her than concern over her father.

"I was set upon by thieves and this gentleman saved me," The merchant motioned to Bearskin who bowed with his best court manners. Manners he had practiced well enough to let him remain in the command tents when there were messages to be delivered that they did not wish to commit to writing.

Both girls' eyes went round. It was a startling contrast, and Gregor had to keep from chuckling. Well he was still as unexpected as ever. Maybe that would turn out to be a good thing? He wasn't sure.

"Just like Isela." The golden-haired girl turned to regard him. He was struck by how tall she was for a woman of this land, coming almost up to his shoulder. "A man in a bearskin, dirty but with courtly manners. Would you be the same Master Bearskin that two nights ago escorted a young woman home from the tailor's?"

"What's this?" Interrupted the Merchant. "What happened to Isela?"

Sophia shook her head and sighed. "The guard you assigned to escort her decided to take his pay and his leave shortly after they left the tailor's shop, leaving her to walk home alone. I have my suspicions about why he would do so in such a manner but..."

She held up a finely boned hand and made a motion like pouring out sand. The Merchant's face grew dark with his own anger. "And why is this the first I am hearing of it? You run the house well, Sophia, but this should have been brought to me immediately."

"That was my fault, father," A soft, voice spoke from the end of the entry hall and Gregor recognized the girl he had rescued. She was not as dramatically striking as her sisters, but he found her soft grey eyes even more compelling. There was compassion there and wisdom. Strange for one so young for all the three were full grown. "I asked her not to tell you. I told her I would, but I had not found a way yet that did not seem like it would bring more trouble upon you. You have enough without that."

The merchant motioned her towards him and embraced her. "You and your sisters are more precious to me than any trouble. More precious to me than all that I own. If I must, in these troubles, I will sell all this and go back to farming beans as I did when I was a child."

Isela smiled and even the red head chuckled. Sophia smiled, and dropped into a curtsy. "Pardon our manners, Master Bearskin, but we were not expecting anyone else. Perhaps you would care to freshen up while I tell the Cook to set another plate? Isela could show you a room. I fear Karin will have other things to do."

Sophia eyed the elaborate dress and the merchant nodded. Karin looked like she might protest then, momentarily, sagged in defeat. She gave a small curtsy herself. "Master Bearskin, please forgive any discourtesy I may have offered. While I have differences with my family."

Here she glared at both her father and her sister before returning her lively green eyes to Bearskin. "I would not intentionally level those on a guest. Now, if you will excuse me for a moment?"

Bearskin gave her a small bow and she took herself off down the hall and out of sight. Sophia hesitated, then, when her father nodded dropped a deeper curtsy and followed her sister out of sight.

Isela came down the now much emptier corridor and smiled up at Gregor. "If you will come with me? I will see you to the guest room. Dinner will be soon, but I think you shall have time to freshen up. Hot water can be had for the asking, at least."

"I fear I cannot take you up on that generous offer." Bearskin followed her as she led the way down the hall, and across a grandly appointed foyer, so grand he had trouble taking it all in. "I have an oath that forbids it."

Isela shot him a puzzled look, then nodded as if to herself. He found himself uneasy with the knowing look in those eyes. It wasn't the brooding suspicion or the sneering superiority, but something closer to true understanding.

Did she realize how dangerous a path she was treading? Not that simply knowing the truth would bind her to his fate. That much he would trust the Minstrel's word on, but still... He focused his attention on the path and what his guide was saying, leaving his thoughts to tend to themselves.

"I hope you do not mind that it will be somewhat simple fare today at dinner. Our house has fallen on difficult times, though we have not had to sell off what we own, yet." She spoke the last word in almost a whisper and he nodded. She opened a polished wooden door of some dark wood he didn't recognize, and motioned him inside.

Light sprang into being about him and he blinked in surprise. "What strange Power is this?"

Isela laughed, a bright and merry sound that lit her face and took her from pleasantly pretty to beautiful. "These? Elf lights, one and all. Father dealt with them in his younger days. Though he never said how he made those contacts. We are still the best source for Elvish goods, or were."

"What trouble has fallen on your house?" Gregor asked gently. "First you were set upon then your father. I cannot imagine it being a coincidence."

"No, the ones who set upon me said they were sending a message but from whom? And who was intended to read it? Father perhaps but I don't know what might have sparked it. We have no great secrets as far as I know," She hesitated as if she had more to say, then snapped her mouth shut as she seemed to decide against it. After a deep breath she answered the question he had asked. "Three years ago we mysteriously lost a caravan. It happens, we had presumed some brigands who had been caught up in the levees went back to their old ways and formed a larger force than normal. But they were never caught. The next year we lost two caravans. Last year we lost fully half of the caravans we sent. This year none have gone through."

Bearskin frowned then nodded. "I will have to think on this, Miss. I think I can help with at least some of your troubles, I cannot speak to them all."

She nodded and turned the subject. "Feel free to use anything in the room. You will not stain it. Good charms were laid over all in better days.

My mother was a fastidious type before... Anyway if you are cautious and do not deliberately destroy things most things should be quite safe from mere dirt, including the books."

Gregor's eyes lit and gave her a deeply formal bow. "Thank you... it is greater courtesy than I had dared to expect and greater than I have long received or long shall receive."

He looked down at his hands and stepped back, not trying to dismiss her but not wishing to hold her here through any hospitality obligation. She hesitated once more then stepped back herself. "I shall come for you when supper is ready. Please make yourself at home."

And she was gone, without pomp or swagger. Gregor settle himself into a chair and wondered what it all might mean.

Chapter 10
Mysteries of Hope

The merchant seated him in a place of honor to his own right with his daughters arrayed about the table. The lack of Mistress of the Household made a few factors click in the back of Gregor's brain.

A fine linen cloth was set at the table and the dishes were highly polished. The goblet he was served in was actually silver, with intricate inlays in what he thought was ivory. He tried not to squirm, and handled the silver fork with great care. He could fade into the background about nobles if he came as a servant, but this? This...

The merchant bent low to as he poured Gregor's wine. His voice was barely audible, "It takes some practice to get used to these things. No one here will think the worse of you for any slip ups. I myself was a farmer when younger."

Gregor nodded and managed to relax a little, as Sophia instructed the lone maid that served them. Then the Merchant spoke more loudly. "Today we have been granted mercy by the Whispering Word, would our most honored guest care to bless the meal?"

A pang went through him and Gregor shook his head. "I am sorry, but I am not yet permitted. But please. Share your blessing."

Isela's grey eyes flicked to him and narrowed.

"Not permitted? What..." Karin burst out and then yelped as someone, probably Sophia, kicked her under the table.

"I'm sure Master Bearskin has his reasons. What they are is none of our concern." Sophia gave her sister a quelling look and Karin looked like she might say something nasty back, but Sophia continued. "Father would you do the honor as our guest cannot?"

There was a bite in her voice, that he wasn't entirely sure was deliberate. She might be more polite about it than the red-head, but she had the same questions. Sadly their questions would go unanswered at least for now. Yet again there was that uncomfortably knowing look from Isela, and yet her expression was one of sympathy not condemnation. If she knew what he'd done. He cut the thought off lest she have some Gift that would let her read it.

The merchant bowed his head and blessed the meal and the table chatter flowed around him.

"Master Bearskin, where might you hail from, if I may ask?" Sophia's tone was exquisitely formal and Karin managed to keep her eyes in her head as she rolled them though only barely.

"North a ways and east. I have wandered much through these lands in the last four years," He shrugged and let himself savor the food.

The rich scent of the beef did not lose anything in the flavor. If this was 'simple' fare he was glad he hadn't come to see what they considered normal! Potatoes were almost expected here but there was a cream soup, rather than one in broth. Some of the best herbed bread he had ever tasted, with generous portions of butter, and a dizzying array of fruit.

"I am glad your wanderings have brought you this way, but have you no home to go back to?" Karin asked, though she rushed through the first part as if it were more curiosity eating her alive than any true gratitude.

Gregor's face went very still and Isela reached out a hesitant hand then withdrew it with a glance towards her sisters. He shook his head, "No, no home to return to. Nor any family. The war has its costs. I do not even know for certain who it was that buried them."

"North and East?" Johann frowned and seemed to be thinking. "Most likely it was Freiherr Rudigar von Neuen. He had much success in the war in those directions. He is a hard man, but just. He was known to bury the dead, foe and friend alike rather than leave them to rot."

"That matches what I was told. Would that all commanders had such mercy," Gregor said softly. "If it was him, I owe him a debt."

Sophia hesitated then nodded. "If you would care to send a message, I could see that it was delivered."

Karin shook her head. "He hasn't come calling in more than a week, sister dear. I think he may have moved on to other pursuits."

"If you could simply thank him for the service he rendered to the dead of Nevahs, I would be grateful." Gregor said softly. If he had received the first message, a repetition would still not be amiss, especially with a more reliable messenger.

Finely boned hands clenched slightly on her own goblet and Sophia nodded, sapphire eyes softer than he had yet seen him. "I will at least send word to that effect, even if he does not come to see me any longer."

Karin laughed, "Oh, he won't. After all, why should he? Now that he's seen we are as ruined as he could desire. You can't count on him to save us."

"Karin, that is enough," Johann said firmly. "We should not trouble our guest any more than we already have!"

"We've trouble enough to drown in, Father. I don't see how discourtesy to this guest will make that any worse." Karin snapped and Sophia rested a hand on her shoulder.

"Enough Karin. Do you really want to tempt your fate that greatly?" Sophia warned.

"As if you were one to speak." Karin laughed, though her eyes narrowed. "I am not the one courting so high above myself."

"Please. Sisters, let us at least have the meal in peace," Isela begged. "Let not Sight or Fate or trouble ruin that."

"Bah, I hold little stock in any such Powers excuses one and all," Karin tossed her head but did settle back down and did not look at Sophia, glaring resolutely at her plate.

"I would not put any stock in that belief if I were you. I have twice met Fate's Minstrel," Bearskin spoke, his deeper voice cutting through the silence. "What the final end of those encounters shall be, I cannot yet say. But she has given advice that has been good, and when a power of that degree speaks of the Virtues and Vices as power we call to ourselves..."

His table companions looked at one another nervously, though to his credit the merchant seemed to shrug it off with little change in attitude. Sophia's expression hardened speculatively, cold and distant. Karin's expression was also speculative, but there was an impudent smile tugging at her mouth. But Isela's eyes were sympathetic and she nodded as if something had suddenly made sense to her. It was she who spoke, "What did she say to you?"

"Cleave to your Virtues," He said simply, and the faint music of a distant flute once more spun about him. Isela's soft eyes went round as if she could actually hear the ghostly tune of his memory. He smiled at her and continued. "She also said the Virtues were subtler than the Vices, but more powerful, not less, for all of that. If she warns any of you of a Doom heed her. If not. Perhaps her advice to me will be of use to you as well, perhaps even if she warns you of nothing."

Once more silence fell on the table, and Gregor at least welcomed the distraction of the next remove. He had never eaten this well in his life, though he had been a skilled enough farmer and hunter that his family had only rarely hungered before the war--before-- He shook himself free of impending memories and concentrated on the scent of the soup. He picked up an apple, firm and sweet and let the silence play out. As usual he was more at ease than those around him, for once it wasn't because of his appearance.

When the final remove was brought, he ventured. "You mentioned troubles, Master Merchant, and I have heard some hint of it. Would you care to confide in a stranger?"

"Please, call me Johann. You have more than earned that privileged," The merchant slowed, taking a bite of bread and cheese before continuing, head hanging low. "I believe Isela has told you some of our trouble. From what the man you saved me from has said, at least the most recent caravan was sold, rather than purely lost. And openly sold as a caravan rather than as brigands might in secret."

Bearskin nodded and glanced at Isela. "And the ones who troubled you spoke of sending a message."

Isela nodded unhappily as her father once more scowled, though the scowl was not for her. "I have some skill at needle work and it has been helping to keep the household running, but I do not think we will survive should this last Caravan not go through."

"It is worse than that, my dear. In several of the caravans were certain objects. Worth nothing to sell on the open market but beyond price to the correct people. Those have vanished utterly whatever else may have happened. The owners of those objects are *displeased* with their loss," Johann looked carefully at Bearskin who nodded.

"That would be a greater trouble than I expect any would court. I suspect you have an enemy," Gregor shrugged.

"Father, tell the whole truth why don't you?" Karin came to her feet bringing one hand down on the table with a smack. "We have an enemy indeed, but that enemy has not dogged us simply these past three years, but since you let our mother die. Her death is what undid us, these losses are merely sealing that fate!"

"That is enough!" Johann snapped. "Karin you forget yourself. I know you have taken your mother's death hard, but she died years before any other trouble."

"Tell the tale your own way, Father, if it helps you sleep. But I remember well enough. You called no healer for her, and she died. Now that brings ruin on our house. Justice for justice." She whirled away, somehow managing not to snag herself on the chair or any other furniture as she stormed out of the room. Her father watched after her with a mixture of guilty, fury, and an all too familiar grief.

Sophia pursed her lips and then took a deep breath, "Please, Master Bearskin. Forgive us and forgive Karin. She was just old enough to remember our mother clearly, but not old enough to understand what happened. I remember."

"Peace, Sophia. you need not defend me, though I appreciate it. She is right about one thing: If I had called a healer early before there was any trouble with her labor, then she would have lived, but there was no sign of trouble, and..." The merchant reached and hand to her almost in supplication. She took it and squeezed.

"I remember, Father. And I remember the midwife's panic. She may be right that that was when fortune turned against us, but not because you did not call a healer swiftly enough when an easy labor turned deadly in a few heartbeats," Sophia dropped his hand, and pushed her plate away. "I should see to the other servants."

She curtsied courteously enough to Bearskin, and took herself out. Isela reached out to touch Bearskin's shoulder. "Master Bearskin. I was not old enough to remember our mother clearly, but I know this. She would not want us to mourn her forever. Neither would those you have lost wish that of you. I do not know what the future holds, but you have twice saved those of this household. Perhaps I am bold, but perhaps not. It seems the Whispering Word has brought you here for a reason. Let us at least be friends to ease the pain, even if we cannot be your lost."

He reached a grimy hand to pat hers gently, wincing a little as he left her hand smudged and dirty. "That is the kindest offer I have received in many years. But I would not impose. As I have said, I have troubles of my own, and would not add them to yours."

"I understand Master Bearskin," Johann interjected. "But Isela speaks rightly. Your path is your own, but I would be honored. We would be honored, if you would consider us should you pass this way again. If we must sell and move, I shall leave word at the Silver Smith's guild. I have friends there who will not put too much stock in appearances."

"And I have done business with that guild before. Yes. Thank you. Now, perhaps we should all seek our beds?" Gregor suggested and the others rose. He followed suit, though once more caught the merchant's eye. Johann simply nodded almost imperceptibly.

***

Ink and paper, the sharp tang of wax and copper. All familiar scents, and Gregor found himself relaxing into the accustomed confines of a clerk's office. Though this one seemed unmanned by any clerk. The high gloss wood of the shelves shone, and the baskets of paper scattered light. Yet, as he breathed deeply something was missing.

He looked about as the elflights came up in more of the room, bathing it all in a pleasant golden glow, soft and welcoming. The furnishings were more fine even than the church in his little village had been. Though he saw a small prayer book tucked away, worn with use, on one of the shelves.

That brought a smile to his face, and he bent to briefly inspect one of the elflights. Elflights! The scent of smoke was all that was missing. Of course the merchant would only need the candles he had neatly stacked on his desk for melting the sealing wax. He needed no lamps with elflights.

Nodding to himself, Gregor turned his attention to the merchant himself. The man, who was older than he had first thought, or perhaps it was just the recent troubles? Gregor couldn't tell, but for whatever reason as Johann von Argers settled himself into the large well cushioned chair at his desk, he seemed old. "You wished to speak with me, Master Bearskin? Or at least it seemed so."

"Indeed. Isela said you have lost several caravans over the last three years, essentially since the end of the War. It might be I can help you," Gregor began slowly.

Johann leaned back in his chair and seemed to think, picking up a metal pen absently to tap in his hands. "I and mine already owe you so much Master Bearskin. I hesitate to put myself more into your debt."

Gregor shook his head. "Master Merchant. Johann. I do not think you can fully understand what joy this evening has brought to me. Besides, it is not in me to turn aside when there is something I might do to help. That has been my folly and my saving grace at once."

Johann nodded. "You said you had three years remaining of your troubles. What limitations do they put upon you? I would not ask you to do something that would cause you greater trouble or cost you more than any man should forfeit."

Gregor nodded in acknowledgment that the man seemed to have guessed right. "For seven years I must wander. I must wear this bearskin and may not wash, nor trim my hair nor nails. Nor may I pray to the Whispering Word. Truth be told that has been the hardest."

"One reason you asked us to pray for you," murmured the merchant and Gregor nodded. "Then I see nothing that would hinder you from helping, but nothing that will allow you to, either."

"I have the Gift of Memory, so anything I do discover I can recall, and I have done clerk's work in the past so I can also clearly write what my memory stores," Gregor shrugged, but the merchant leaned forward, then shook himself.

"Were my house in a prosperous state and you not bound to wander, I would be tempted to offer you a position, Master Bearskin. We could use a good clerk and while I am quite efficient at keeping my own books, it is not a task I enjoy. However the clerk has also taken his services elsewhere," Johann shrugged. "Would you hear the troubles we have had?"

"I would. You mentioned missing artifacts and Isela mentioned that no caravan you have sent this year has successfully reached its destination and returned the received monies to you." Bearskin had been thinking over what the man who had assaulted the merchant had said. There was something deeper going on here, but what? He could see robbing a merchant, but ruining one? "Have you any enemies?"

"I have enemies, no successful merchant does not, but I had not thought any of them would be capable of this. You heard Karin, she blames Rudigar von Neuen, dangerous as that might be," Johann shook his head. "I do not think it is him, but I cannot think who else might care that much. Yet his reputation for ruthlessness does not carry to casual destruction."

"And if he is courting your daughter, then having your house prosperous enough to bring advantage to a noble family would be in his favor," Gregor suggested, and the merchant nodded.

"This I have considered. I can only think that it was the artifacts, curious as they were, that were the true targets. Honestly, the first one to vanish happened before the war, though not in my hands. Its loss was why I was hired for the rest. I thought I had enough defenses." He shook his head sadly and stared down at the bronze pen before once more laying it on the desk.

"How desperate is your case?" Gregor asked softly.

"If the next caravan fails to go through, we are undone. The final artifact is in it, and much else of value. We might be ruined even if it returns should it not sell so well as we anticipate, but we would be in better case for starting over," Johann looked up at his towering guest. "But I fear there is less you can do about the finances than you can do about the missing caravans."

Gregor smiled and simply reached into his pockets and began to pull out silver. Handful after handful he brought out. "This is the other piece of my bargain: that I should never want for silver or gold. I think my foe would be displeased with the use to which I have put his silver."

The mound of coins glittered in the elflights and the merchant's eyes were wide with astonishment. Well that suited Bearskin well enough. Perhaps the man would re-evaluate his chances of helping. Gregor pushed the pile towards Johann. "Will this make a difference?"

"My Lord, I even I cannot tell you with certainty how far this will go by eye. If you will give me but a moment." And the merchant pulled open a drawer and extracted a scale and set of weights. He swiftly and skillfully sorted the coins and murmured something over them. Gregor hid a smile. Not that he blamed the merchant for his purity spell. Gregor would have cast the same in the merchant's case. It was a simple enough charm.

The scales themselves glowed faintly as the coins were lowered on them. The merchant sorted and counted, though there were enough coins that it took him some time. When he was finished he lay down his pen and pushed away from his desk, a very solemn expression on his face. "Master Bearskin, I tell you truthfully, this could buy all I own. I cannot rightly accept it without some form of recompense."

Gregor hesitated then raised his right hand to show the ring he wore. "Then perhaps, you would be willing to take one Gregor Bearskin as your partner three years hence? I can promise he is a hard worker and will gladly learn all you can teach. The war left him with nothing and he will have cause to seek a new trade."

The merchant looked from the coins to Bearskin then back to the coins. Then he lifted his face to look in Bearskin's eyes as he had not since they began their discussion and what he saw there seemed to decide him. A yearning for hearth and home, and a hope to provide for others what he could not have for himself, perhaps? Or perhaps that was some of Bearskin's own folly. He knew his motivations well enough, he would not suppose another might read them so clearly.

Once more the merchant spoke, but this time his words were slow and careful. "I think a Junior partner might be a healthful thing for the trade. I am not getting any younger. While this is much I have put more into the business over the years."

Gregor nodded and smiled, "And Gregor Bearskin, while able to learn, would still have much to learn about the trade. It is reasonable he should not come to the business a full equal, but, perhaps, as a friend."

"A friend who will be gladly welcomed and to whom I will be ever grateful," The merchant smiled it an impudence that suddenly took him from old to young again, "And perhaps he shall be an eligible young man when he does show his face. and my business shall not completely pass from my bloodline when I am gone!"

Gregor chuckled. "I would ask you draft the contract then. I know the language well enough. But there is a great difference between reading and copying a contract and writing one."

"Would you care to wait, as Gregor Bearskin's representative, or will morning be soon enough? Even I must take some time to draft these correctly," When the merchant picked up his pen this time it seemed much lighter, or perhaps he did. Gregor wasn't entirely certain.

"The morning shall be soon enough. Though I may ask your help in estimations of coin values before I leave. I fear I have made something of a fool of myself by underestimating their worth." Gregor turned to go then hesitated and looked back over his shoulder at the merchant. "One last thing, Merchant."

Johann kept the pen, but his expression was suddenly less merry and more serious. "Yes, Master Bearskin?"

"If your men with your caravan should happen to see a large brown bear keeping pace with them, tell them to ignore it, pay it no heed. Do not hinder it unless it offers them violence." Gregor turned back to the door, pushing it open and going through before the man had a chance to respond.

Johann shook his head and pulled a fresh sheet of paper before him. He had jotted the coin weights down by the scale, the conversion from there was simple enough. But if he wished to find his bed before midnight he had best begin the contract now.

Chapter 11
DEEPER BINDINGS

The scent of roses wrapped itself about him. Fruit and other sweet flowers mingled with that low, rich base as Gregor wandered the Merchant's garden. The grass gave a gentle cushion to feet more used to rocky paths or hard roads. Tall hedges of some flower he had never seen, towered above even himself, also draping flowers. The song of a nightingale drifted towards him in the light of the moon, caught by the gentle breeze, that seemed to dance about his spirit and carry away the strain.

There was no hint of a flute to rival the nightingale's song, for which Gregor was grateful. For all he appreciated that lady's help, there were times and pleasures that were best on their own. For the first time in four years he encouraged his Gift, soaking in every moment of the peaceful night painted garden. Silver light drew color out of everything, red roses seemed a melancholy black. Soft gray leaves rustled in harmony with the nightingale. The moon was kind to him tonight, it left only a sleepy loneliness rather than a brooding menace.

He would treasure this while he could. His Gift would keep it clear.

A soft noise behind him and he turned, seeing the old soldier stop at the edge of the hedge row, and Isela stepped further in. Gregor simply waited for her then offered her his arm as he had two days earlier. As then she took it with no hesitation in spite of the grime. "I had not thought you would be out this late, Miss."

"I had not thought any but myself cared for the gardens on a night such as this. My sisters find them depressing under the moon." Isela looked about her a small smile on her face.

"And you? How do you find them?" Gregor asked, the odd note in her voice striking a chord within himself, even if he could not say why.

She smiled up at him, face lighting, until her grey eyes rivaled the luminous moon. "I find them lonely. There are many things to find here for those with the eyes to see it."

Gregor looked about him and shook his head. "I fear I only see a sleeping garden. Alive and green. Restful at night. It eases my soul in a way I had not thought it would ever be eased."

"Come with me." She cast a glance at the soldier, Nathan, Gregor thought was the man's name. The man tailed them at a discreet distance, giving them the illusion of privacy without leaving Isela unescorted. She grabbed Gregor's hand and led him gently through the high hedge maze to the very center.

"This is one of the secrets Father has, but doesn't understand. There are others. This one was our mother's." Isela led him up to a smooth marble pedestal shaped like a column from an ancient building. Atop it floated a sphere of light. Color played within its depths like spider webs at dawn. and it shed a gentle light of its own, returning color to the washed out garden. Indeed, the colors here were almost painfully vibrant, and he didn't think it was just the contrast.

"What is it?" He asked in awe. He'd heard of such things but never had he hoped to see one nor had he discovered their purpose.

"Sophia calls it a star stone. But I don't think it is. It knows us." Isela stepped closer and motioned Gregor closer. "Does your Gift tell you nothing about it?"

Gregor shook his head sadly. "No, my Gift is Memory. None of this will I forget, but I cannot remember things I have never known."

"It reaches across the veils," she said softly. "I would give much to know where mother acquired it."

"You have the Sight then. What does this do that you can See?" Gregor cocked his head down at her. Amongst the Delmin, Sight was a treasured gift. Trained as much as the tribe could manage, or if they were scattered, as much as they could arrange from outsiders.

"It wards us. It reaches across the veils and creates a place of safety, of calm. It cannot force the calm, but the only trouble in this place are those mortals bring with them. I think our mother may have been more than she pretended. I only remember a little. I was very young." Isela looked at the sphere, holding up a hand near it, but never quite touching it and Gregor nodded.

"Sophia would be the oldest of you, then?" He asked thoughtfully.

Isela nodded. "And I the youngest. Sophia was ten when our mother died. Karin is only a year older than I am and I was but six years old."

Gregor reached a hand to rest on her shoulder and squeezed gently. "I know loss. You have my sympathy."

She reached up her hand to pat his. "And I know loss as well. So you have mine. Mother may have had other Gifts, but her harp went to Karin. And anything else she would likely have given to Sophia. With all the treasures going missing from our caravans I have often wondered why no one came here seeking this."

"Who would know of it? Unless your father has shown it to guests when he entertains." Gregor looked down at the woman beside him and the light playing across her soft features making her seem almost otherworldly.

"The gardener knows but he is a dear friend of fathers and has not deserted us, beyond that? I do not know. He does not bring guests here commonly. Unless Karen or Sophia have brought any here, I think it remains unknown, but such things are not easily kept secrets. Like Karin, I have my suspicions about who is behind our doom, unlike Karin I do not think the hand is mortal," She shivered a little.

"What do you See?" He asked gently even as he had seen his father ask his mother, even as he had asked Anna so long ago.

"I see fire deferred. I do not know what it means but the war is not resolved. The fighting has ended, but the cause is not yet answered," She blinked and shook herself free of the vision. "The Veils are clear. Even the Sidhe avoid this place. It is like the sphere only tolerates mortals. I do not know how it would react to elves."

"Neither am I inclined to try and find out," Gregor admitted, then turned the subject. "I must soon begin my wandering again. Would you object if I came to call once more?"

"I would very much like that Master Bearskin." Isela looked up at him and smiled. "Perhaps Father could be persuaded to take an apprentice if our troubles should pass."

Gregor breathed in the cool night air, rich with the scent of ripe fruit and the roses and the tang of the herbs. The hum of the orb's power reached his ears. Whatever it truly was, but in all of that, he looked down at the gentle woman in front of him. "I think I shall be able to help with some of that. Should Gregor Bearskin come calling some day, look for the mate of this and you shall know him and me."

He took out of his pocket one of the beads Anna had given him, and offered it to her. "I ask no promise simply wait and see what the next three years shall bring, if a stranger has such a right to ask."

Isela reached out for the bead holding it up to examine the carvings. "I have never seen a Delmin bead before. Yes, Master Bearskin. I will await you or this Gregor Bearskin. You have served my family selflessly, how could I do otherwise?"

"I hope there would be other reasons to wait for me in time," He made no promises, nor expected her to make any. "Should waiting be no longer an option nor a desire. Leave the bead at the doorstep. I will find it."

She nodded and smiled. "I have no suitors, but perhaps I shall get to know one of you well enough for such things. Time will tell."

"Time will tell indeed, Now, I think we should both seek our beds m'Lady," And once more he offered her arm, and she accepted and he felt an unfamiliar sensation creep into his heart: Hope.

R udigar von Neuen ran his hand over soft, smooth fabric. Calloused fingers savored the feel, even as his mind buzzed. This time his surroundings were much more palatable. Though the old fool who had governance of this poor excuse for a fortress had certainly not assigned him the best quarters. It was only to be expected. Four years was not long for a city to forget their conquest.

He picked up the fine crystal goblet and sipped his wine absently, tasting the vintage's sharp richness only reflexively. Another room. Another series of letters, papers, and maps and no closer to the answers to any of his questions than that.

He strode to the window and pushed aside the heavy amber colored curtain with his free hand. "What do you think, this time, Beren?"

He didn't look over his shoulder. He knew where the man would be. It was one of the things he valued about his companion. Though those things were, themselves, legion. Good help was to be treasured when it was found, and Beren had been without price. He would have to think of a way to reward the man properly.

"I think we have lingered here too long, m'Lord. I think the Bandits have moved to other places." The man came to stand beside him, though a little to one side, where he could be properly spoken to without seeming to claim equality with his master. Rudigar nodded.

"We should move on soon, but I am not so sure we have been here too long, I have just received very interesting news in one of our other inquiries." Rudigar passed the newest missive he had received to the man, breathing in once more the rose and lilac perfume that scented it. Her perfume. Damn his father. Damn his foolish pride.

Beren took the letter and read it quickly, starting slightly as he realized who it was, and then nodding. There were no intimate details in it that might embarrass, but its news was interesting. "Do you think she would arrange an introduction?"

Rudigar shook his head. "I would not ask her to, not with the letter I must send her next. But we may be able to satisfy both our lines of inquiry at once."

"What do you see my Lord?" Beren asked promptly, and Rudigar turned slightly away from the cool drab stone of the window to regard his valet, his most trusted subordinate, with ice-blue eyes. Beren simply returned the regard as few had been able to do.

"I've not the Sight and you know it well my friend, but the connection is there. I do not think our Master Bearskin is with our elusive bandits, he's foiled their game too many times, but if he has become friendly with the good Master Johann, then there's a chance he will take a hand in their troubles and we might use him to find the bandits. I doubt there are two such skillful bands in these territories." Rudigar turned back to give the square his regard. The scents of market day wafted up on a gentle breeze, not so hot as it had been. Evening was coming to a close and the tang of fall was starting to hint in the air.

"Yet, if he can handle a dozen brigands himself, it might be wise to approach him with caution, whatever word he sends." Beren proffered the missive back to his master and von Neuen took it and tucked it carefully into his pouch. This one he intended to keep: to remember her. He was unlikely to find her equal amongst those his father would deem acceptable.

"Caution is always advisable when dealing with the dangerous. But I think the risk in this case is worth it. I suspect he will trail the Caravan and then we will trail him." Von Neuen leaned forward until he could feel the breeze more steadily rather than snatches of it. There was a connection here but he couldn't see it. He wasn't sure what it was, but it was there. "Send word to my father, that I have a lead on my mission and will not be able to return to the capitol until that mission is complete, but I look forward to seeing him there when I arrive."

That should keep his father guessing at least for now. Beren nodded and pulled his heels together with a click. "And for the lady?"

Rudigar shook his head. "That one I will write myself. She deserves that much from me."

Beren hesitated then turned. But he caught himself and looked back. "My Lord, I would not close all doors in that direction. Stranger things have chanced, and she reminds me of someone from the Court though I cannot think who."

"You've been around the King's Court longer than I, if you think of who, tell me. I've too much kin in that court to proceed carelessly," Rudigar pushed away from the window. Duty called, as it always did. And he was duty's slave. It seemed fate was unwilling to change that.

He heard the door close as Beren went about his own mission. Yes, he would word this one carefully. His father deserved the blame. He doubted he would have much hope, no matter how carefully he worded this. Ending a courtship was never pleasant, and resuming such a thing would be near to impossible even with the most gracious of words. Such was fate dealt him and he would deal with it as it came.

Chapter 12
THE HUNT

The bracken clung to his fur, the scent of berries and herbs invaded his nose. At any other time he would have been tempted to browse, but for all the bear was more massive than the man he moved more quietly this way and had fewer troubles with the wild life. He spent a moment of gratitude for all the practice he had spent over the last four years.

He lifted his heavy head, and pointed his nose upward inhaling deeply of the chill wind. New scents? His ears twitched as the caravan creaked and rattled along the road. The guards chatted and complained. Sore feet. Rough roads, and some complaints of boredom from the youngsters.

Bearskin almost snorted at that, and at their commander's response. Old soldiers appreciated boredom. The alternatives were always worse. So the merchant had retained some sensible guards.

Great paws laid themselves gingerly amongst the leaves. Once more the breeze brought him new scents, stale beer and the tang of something else that he didn't recognize. Something that tingled in the back of his throat and set him on edge. They were four days out from Argers and the next town was several days off.

Beady eyes narrowed as he tried to guess the range between himself and the next narrowing of the road. Sadly, he wasn't quite that skilled with this form, but that sheer wall of granite and the ravine the road ran through struck him with unease. This was ambush territory and in bear form he could not shout a warning, not and have it understood.

He sniffed the air once more and then the grass, easing his way between the pines. Spruce and larch brushed his fur with their branches.

He scented rabbit and grouse, both holding very still he suspected, lest the large predator in the area find them for lunch. But it wasn't them he was hunting.

The scent resolved: Men. He had trouble distinguishing colors in this form, though he thought it had more to do with his understanding of what he was seeing than the bear's ability to see. But he could spy three forms with some bright badge on their shoulder and crossbows in their hands.

He crouched and considered leaping, but if there were more about...

He skirted the crossbowmen, and one glanced back over his shoulder. Bearskin froze still as a statue. The man subsided and the bear breathed a sigh of relief at least in his mind.

The caravan rumbled and rattled up the road. Bearskin's ears twitched as he heard the rustle of leaves and the scrabble of feet against rocks. There were more but where?

There! One man had just stood and opened his mouth, and Bearskin threw back his head and roared before lumbering towards the man standing. With oaths and curses the men poured out of the tree line.

Two of the crossbowmen wheeled desperately trying to sight on him. One shot went wide, the other nicked his skin and ruffled his fur. The third crossbowman was made of sterner stuff. He held his position and sighted on the captain of the caravan guards.

Bearskin twisted himself about in mid charge lashing out with a paw just as the crossbowman pulled his firing lever. The bolt lodged itself in the captain's shoulder rather than his throat. A burning pain lashed down Bearskin's arm.

He glanced down to see a spear sticking into his shoulder. The back hand of his swipe took the spearman from his feet. The leader was shouting but Bearskin couldn't understand. It wasn't a language he knew which sent alarm bells somewhere in the back of his brain, but the Bear was more in control than he was. He could not think of that yet.

The spear thudded to the ground as he brushed past a tree, and plowed himself once more towards the leader. The tang of blood and fear assailed his all too sensitive nose. And something else, something that was only too familiar. Battlefields and powder wagons. Bearskin lashed out a paw and the leader went flying. His pistol flew in the other direction unfired. A clatter of battle behind him.

He wheeled and barreled forward once more plowing over ambushers who had come at the caravan from the other side. The guards had formed a small hedge of spears, but they were terribly few and the merchants were cowering in their wagons.

This wasn't their kind of fight.

It was one Bearskin knew only too well. Something familiar tickled his mind but he could not yet catch it. The men were running now. The fools! He gave chase, bellowing his fury. His head snapped up. Music? But the sound was gone. Had he imagined it?

He watched the men go and lifted a paw, then set it back down. No, not yet. They fled. He would not pursue them to their deaths.

His chest heaved and suddenly he hurt. He bled from more than just the spear wound. He sat on the ground and closed his bear eyes and turned his attention inward. Moments later Gregor opened his eyes, human again, still bleeding. He could feel the Minstrel's little stone, warm against his skin.

Wearily he made his way back to the caravan.

"Halt! Who…" The guard, painfully young, too young to have fought in the war hesitated when Bearskin stepped out of the woods and pulled himself up to his full, formidable height. But he pulled himself together and tightened his grip on his spear. "Who goes there?"

"I am called Master Bearskin by many, lad. Is there any way I can help? The last of them ran off." Gregor gestured back in the direction he came, "pursued by a large bear."

The boy looked at Gregor's shoulder where the spear wound still showed, and his side that had been pierced by arrows and swords, all of which showed bloody. "Of course Master Bearskin. If you know anything of treating wounds we'd be grateful."

"Gladly, though you'll have to provide the hands," He held up his own: filthy, with claw-like nails. "I'll likely do more damage than help but I can share the knowledge I have."

The youngster took him back to where the wounded were being treated and Gregor wished he dared show them his treasures. But he remembered what the field surgeons had done and remembered how they had answered his questions when he asked of their trade. Perhaps there was something he could do. It was up to him to at least try.

Several hours later the stench of blood had grown old, and the wind had carried some of it away. The bandits were stacked to one side of the road, and a crude cairn laid over them. Mostly out of courtesy for any who came after, but it was a grim edifice against the pleasant greenery of the woods. The wagoneers were tending their beasts. Fortunately, they hadn't lost any though the horses whinnies were still somewhat distraught, even this far from the blood.

"While I'm grateful for your intervention, Master Bearskin, I fear you're a bit unconventional for my tastes." The Captain of the Guard stretched an arm that would heal and thanked the youngster, who'd turned out to have the steadiest hand with a sewing needle of any of them. "Were this the war, I'd welcome it. But the war is over and this kind of trouble..."

The man shook his head and Gregor nodded, "Understandable. I have come far since the War myself. Are you and your men going to be able to finish this journey?"

"If we have no further problems, we should make good time, even with the wounded. Thanks to your knowledge we're in better shape than I expected, but..." The man shook his head and shut his mouth.

A smile quirked Gregor's own mouth. "Let us just say you were told to ignore any bears you should see that did not cause you trouble, yes?"

The man's head snapped up and his blue eyes narrowed as he once more examined the bearskin, its wearer, and the scene. "I think I do begin to see, but that does not change matters, nor our problems. Such as what we shall do with the prisoners. I do not have the guards to watch them."

Bearskin nodded. Four of the bandits had been alive when all was said and done. They had been treated once the caravan had seen to its own wounds, but now that they had, simply turning them loose in the wilderness would be madness and slitting their throats would be murder.

Bearskin thought for a moment. "Do you think you can make the next town safely?"

"Unless they find a lot more friends very quickly, we should make a town by the end of today if we push after dark. But we won't be able to with them." The Captain once more indicated the prisoners.

"Then bind them securely and leave them with me. I think they will give me less trouble than you," Bearskin smiled. "And perhaps I can leave them with a town's constabulary and save you the trouble."

"I would dearly love to know who hired them," The Captain muttered.

"Well, I may see if I can find that out." Bearskin stepped away from the wagon and the horse seemed to relax a bit. Not that Gregor blamed the horse.

The captain watched him step over to the men in question and kneel beside the least hurt of them. The sharp tang of the forest still mingled with the scent of human blood. A scent he'd hoped never to smell again. "Do you understand me?"

He spoke Athiric, the trade tongue shared in this part of the world beyond just Almarc and Bayr, and the bandit nodded slowly. He responded in the same tongue, his pronunciation atrocious. "I understand. Speak slowly please."

"I will keep this simple. You are my prisoners. I am taking you to the next town where I will give evidence. The caravan will also give evidence. If you hope to avoid being hung for brigandage, you would be wise to speak of who hired you," Gregor straightened. "And do not think of running. I can and will catch you if you do. Bears are notoriously hard to outrun, and we Delmin take much from our totem."

The man shifted uncomfortably and the wagon shifted slightly behind him, wheels creaking against the movement like a whimper. Gregor simply shook his head. They didn't seem common brigands to him. Or at least not just common brigands. Sadly they were made of sufficiently stern stuff that they simply turned frightened looks on one another and said nothing.

The captain strode over, waving off one of the drovers who went back to his beasts. "We need to leave soon, Master Bearskin if we are going to make the town before it is too late to travel no matter how hard we press."

Gregor nodded. "Go. I will take care of these. Tell the town I will be behind you and if they have an honest Lord tell the guards of the attack and that I will be following. If it seems the lord is corrupt, well, I've dealt with that before."

The man nodded, "Unless the town has changed in the past year, their Lord Mayor is a good man, though not all his councilors are so honorable."

"There are always those," Gregor agreed and grabbed the first of the prisoners by the shoulder and hauled him to his feet. The second followed, and soon all the prisoners were in a line and he busied himself about their bonds, making sure they were not tangled and led them well off the road.

He could handle four. Hopefully they wouldn't try to mob him that would end poorly for everyone involved, including him.

The horses stamped their feet, and the drovers flicked the reins. With a creak and a groan that reminded him of the caissons, the caravan began moving again. The churned up mud and crushed larch scattered and splattered about, but it was honest dirt and he'd never minded that.

He eyed his prisoners carefully and, once the last wagon was past, tugged at the rope. Without them he could have made the town well before the caravan, but he had other duties. He hoped he wouldn't regret them.

Chapter 13

THE BEAR AND THE BARON

R uddy soil, slicked black with some substance that Rudigar von Neuen's nose identified as blood, scattered about the King's Road, or what he presumed passed for the King's Road in these parts. This had been part of Bayr and he had not been impressed with their roads in the war. He was less impressed now. But it left more evidence than cobbles would and that was some small favor. Not that his father was likely to think of it that way.

He ignored the champ of horse bits, and the stamp of their feet, as well as the salt-tang of their sweat. They'd ridden hard to follow the trail they'd found only to arrive too late. Curse these bandits.

"What do you seek, my Lord?" Beren stood off the side of the road watching the woods warily. The rest of their company had remained mounted, save for a single scout who was canvasing the woods still.

Von Neuen stood and patted his own rouncy and the neck before turning towards his servant. "Evidence. They gave a good account of themselves here, but..."

His eyes fell on the heaped stone grave. The caravan had moved on, the ruts made that clear. They had done so under their own power and along their original path. Now it was possible the bandits had simply seized it, but he didn't think so. Something told him there was an added element here, and he had long since learned to trust his instincts in such matters.

Beren stepped in close and lowered his voice so the men couldn't hear. "What do you See, my Lord?"

Von Neuen shot him a look and shook his head. "There was an extra element here. Something different. Something... off. What I can't say; the ground is too scuffed. I have seen at least one bear print, yet there is no bear carcass. Should a bear have involved itself in this it is likely all would have turned on it, bandit and guard alike. So what happened?"

A rustle from the tree line brought von Neuen around hand on sword hilt. But he dropped his hand as the scout he had sent out stepped into view. Von Neuen nodded and strode over to the man. "What did you find?"

"Whatever the beast was that was here, it did not behave like a bear. Though all its tracks were that of an enormous bear, the kind I've heard of them having in Rodyan. Judging by its stride I'd say twelve feet tall when it stood on its hind legs," The scout shrugged. "It was remarkably discerning for a bear. I found tracks on that side of the road as well."

He waved over across the road. "And it seemed to target our bandits and only our bandits. Then the tracks simply went away as if the bear had vanished into thin air."

Von Neuen nodded thoughtfully. That fit with his hunch about something else going on. But what did it actually mean? That was the question. "How many escaped?"

"I counted five tracks, but they were muddled so there may have been more. I can confirm if you want to take the time?" The scout cocked his head at von Neuen. The man had been determined to catch these brigands, but also to protect the merchants along the road. Those goals seemed to be in conflict now.

"Mark their direction, and we'll double back if there is the luxury. Was there anything else unusual?" Von Neuen turned sharp eyes on the scout who shifted uncomfortably.

"There was a set of tracks from the same area the Bear vanished that headed back towards the caravan rather than away from it. By the weight and size, I'd say the man was very large himself. Probably the size of the raiders from the north, or a Delmin." The scout hadn't intended to mention that, not with von Neuen's reputations for dealing with people who brought him incomplete answers but...

Von Neuen simply nodded, then gave a ghost of a smile as the man relaxed, easily guessing his thoughts. "I do not punish a man because I do not like his news. You've clearly done the best you can in the time I have allowed you. Sadly we have little luxury to chase all over for this crew. If they have fellows and run into them, they will likely fall on the weakened caravan, especially since the bear seems not to have followed them. They can't count on it saving them a second time. Tell the men to prepare to ride out."

The scout bowed and trotted back to the knot of still mounted men and von Neuen turned back to Beren. "I wish we had gotten even one of the bastards alive. Though, perhaps the caravan will have a prisoner they leave at the next town."

"No need to wait for that," A voice came from the opposite side of the woods as his scout had gone.

This time von Neuen drew his sword and he saw that Beren had as well, but the figure that stepped out of the woods was strange to both their eyes. Filthy dark hair that was probably brown, but it was difficult to tell, hung over a boldly carved face. Amber eyes regarded them frankly. A bearskin draped over all his tattered clothing and his fingernails came down in tattered claws.

He held in one hand a rope and attached to the rope were three men, all wounded, looking bedraggled and hardly in any better condition than the man leading them. Over one massive shoulder a fourth was slung. and von Neuen couldn't tell if that one was breathing.

"Peace. I mean you no harm. You asked for Prisoners. Well, I have them. I had intended to lead them to the next town, but this one," he jostled the one on his shoulder and it moaned. "Decided he would try his luck in an escape. It's been a lively time."

"I see and you would be?" Von Neuen lowered, but did not sheath, his sword.

"I am called Master Bearskin by most, m'Lord." And the man cocked his head at von Neuen as if he actually expected a courteous response.

"Freiherr Rudigar von Neuen, on the King's Business." Von Neuen sheathed his sword and stepped closer. "I have heard of you Master Bearskin."

"And I have heard of you. I have faced you on opposing sides of the battlefield in the war," There was no liking in this Bearskin's eyes, but neither was look or tone unreasoning.

"I fear I do not recall your face, but I hope you were one of my more honorable opponents. It is unusual that both of us survived," von Neuen remarked dryly. He could think of a few of his opponents in that war that he had let live. He frowned thinking but set the thought aside. There would be time for it later.

"My face is not in a state to be recalled at the moment," Bearskin answered mildly giving the line of prisoners a jerk to settle them. "But I would thank you for the service you did for the dead of Nevahs. It was more than most would do."

"So the letter said, and I would thank you for the aid you have given that family." Von Neuen returned, declining to mention the first thanks that had been tendered to him, for now. "All I did was what decent men ought. The people of Nevahs had never harmed us, and were not our target. It was only right."

The man in the bearskin nodded slowly and von Neuen could not read his expression only that there was pain in it, but an old pain. The man shook himself, much like a bear and the man on his shoulder cried out. Bearskin instantly settled. "This one needs attention by a doctor. I know some of those skills but it is as someone remembering instruction not the skill of practice or intimate knowledge. And I would turn him and these others over to some lawful authority."

Von Neuen nodded slowly. "We will take them off your hands. Have you questioned them?"

"Somewhat, and I have a lead to follow once the caravan is safe and safely home. If you would follow it. Meet me in Eislathen three weeks from now." Master Bearskin glanced at the prisoners and offered the rope to von Neuen.

Von Neuen smiled and motioned for Beren to take the rope, while he stepped around the man. "I may take you up on that Master Bearskin. I have heard much of you and would hear more. If the King grants me these lands as I think he shall, or even a portion of them, and you seek employ, I could use a resourceful man."

The man in the bearskin laughed, a hearty deep laugh though there was a bitterness in it von Neuen couldn't quite understand, and that irritated him. He was used to understanding. But the man continued. "It is tempting, m'Lord... but I have three more years before me before I can choose any permanent course. If you are granted these lands... rule them with the mercy you showed the dead of Nevahs and you will do well. Now by your leave?"

With no rope in hand the man bowed and then returned to his full height. Rudigar was a tall man for the Geroth but he barely came up to this man's shoulder. Well. He wasn't going to be intimidated by mere size. Even the largest could fall. "Until Eislathen, Master Bearskin. And... a message for the Lady... tell her the fate was none of my choosing..."

Master Bearskin nodded slowly. "I will tell her that, until we meet again, m'Lord. Virtue guide you... and pray for me."

"I doubt my prayers will be of much assistance," Rudigar von Neuen muttered as he watched the figure walk away. Beren was already securing the prisoners. He had work to do, and a long ride before the next town...

Chapter 14

EISLATHEN

Darnasku was well behind him and the rolling green hills of the high plateau of Eislathen lay before him. The land was rich and green, even so late in the year as this. Golden wheat and amber barley nodded in the gentle breeze and fresh loam coaxed him onward, deceptive in its welcome. Gold and scarlet tinged the distant trees, setting him ill at ease.

Ordinary forests always struck him as strange. The Dead Wood was what he had known. He shivered slightly, but controlled it before any but Beren noticed.

These woods lived, not sustaining an unnatural life from raw magic like the Witch Trees of the Deadwood. Glowing black veins of power and... he turned his thoughts aside to the living highlands before him.

The town itself was a model of its kind. Stone walls. Stone houses. And likely stone hearts of the inhabitants. Mountain folk tended to be stubborn at the best of times, Eislathen more than any. Well, the Dead Wood taught its own brand of stubbornness.

Rudigar von Neuen wheeled his rouncy towards his men, "We'll seek lodging here tonight. My coffers will cover it."

He paid little heed to what they thought of the order. They followed that was all that mattered. He'd made certain they were tended to, and...

The scout from the ambush site maneuvered his palfrey forward. He smelled of herbs and earth, in short like a peasant, but Rudigar had come to trust the man's judgement and insights. "This land is strange, My Lord."

He spoke the title seriously and Rudigar nodded in acknowledgment. "It is. We are growing closer to the Dead Wood. I am surprised things seem so ordinary here."

"To the eyes they are, but if you ask the land..." The man trailed off and shrugged casting a quick glance over his shoulder.

Rudigar chuckled. "Peace. I do not share my father's view of magics. Power permeates the world. We would be fools not to understand the powers that affect ourselves."

The man nodded slowly but Rudigar could tell he was not convinced. He turned ice blue eyes on the scout. "Report what you see. I'll tell no one, especially not my father, the source of your insight."

"As My Lord commands." The man bowed. "There are threads of power here. The earth pulses with it. A black thread passing eastward and somewhat south. That one is strong. Green and powerful strands form a web over the plateau which is likely why it is so fruitful. There are other strands I cannot follow any more than I could understand the bear. Though there is the tang of familiarity here. I would not be surprised to find him."

"We were supposed to meet here so I am not surprised you sense him," Rudigar acknowledged. "There is more here than meets the eye and more than simple caravan raids would justify. Have you seen any signs of our nominal quarry?"

"No, My Lord. They have vanished as thoroughly as the bear did though without quite the excuse." The Scout smiled and Rudigar nodded. He didn't often encourage familiarity, but the scout was clever enough to discern what the vanished tracks meant. The bearsark were not unknown in these regions, though they were vastly uncommon in the Geroth. The Delmin... well he did not know. But the northern barbarians had often used such in the forefront of their raiders.

"Keep your ears open in the city. Leave the politics to me. Find me as regrettable and overzealous as necessary when you speak to their people. My reputation has its uses," Rudigar actually smiled and the scout shuddered for there was no humor in it and it was a cold and bitter thing. Rudigar saw the speculation in the scout's eyes and kept his satisfaction to himself. There were lines to be walked here and so far he had walked them well enough. This town would be another challenge to see how well he walked them again.

He raised a hand and his squad fell in about himself, his valet, as arms man in this case, and the scout. They would see if Master Bearskin had ferreted anything out or no.

The ride to the town was dusty and the road ill kept even by local standards. The guards leaned on their spears and chewed whatever vile substance the locals chewed for fun. The tallest of them stood, spat, and approached as they drew near the gate.

He would have thought a town with so orderly and well maintained a wall would have an equally orderly and well maintained guard, but apparently their mercenary masters had let slip their discipline. He cut the thought off as the man drew near.

"Now who might you be your loftiness?" He looked up at Rudigar from the ground to Rudigar's height on the horse. Rudigar let the sideways insult slide for the moment. They were not his vassals yet, and he was simply here on an errand for the King. The King. Whose reign was unlikely to be long if the court had any say in it.

He set that thought aside and coolly regarded the speaker's spear, which needed sharpening. His armor, whose scales needed polishing, and his helm which had no fewer than three dents in it. Either it was second hand or the man was tougher than he looked.

"Freiherr Rudigar von Neuen. On an errand for the King." He chose, as had become his custom, the least of his titles. It had seen him in better stead through his wanderings than trying for greater honors. Odd that it should be so, at least to him, but he was not one to ignore the reality of it even if he did not understand it.

"Oh for the King is it. I see," The sarcasm dripped so heavily that Rudigar wanted to offer the man a rag to clean it up with. Or at least warn him not to step in such deep puddles.

He shrugged keeping his tone calm and reasonable, or as near as he could manage, "Yes, the King. We have been hunting bandits and brigands in the region, and they have burned several towns. Now if you would care to continue your practice in rudeness, we might continue; otherwise, inform your commander that we are passing through and have no business in his town save a night's rest. And please direct us to the inn."

The directions were simple and straightforward, though the manner of the man giving them did not improve. He could sense Beren's growing displeasure, but Rudigar was not surprised. Eislathen was one of the Landfrei cities--cities that answered truly to no king. Had there been an Emperor in the last few centuries, he could have called them to task, but there was no emperor. As most of the Landfrei were highly profitable, most Kings preferred to leave them be, and garner funds from them more indirectly.

It was unsurprising that such a city would be involved in the illegal trades. What care had those without loyalty for the law or the well being of others? But he kept his contempt to himself, at least for now. There would be time enough to teach this city manners when the king assigned lordship.

Beren trotted up beside him once they were well on the road. Rudigar had not needed to glance over his shoulder to know the gate guard was sending a runner to his own superior. He'd have been more the fool than Rudigar had thought if he had not. "Peace Beren."

His companion at arms snapped his mouth shut on whatever he'd intended to say. There was nothing the man could say that would affect the outcomes here. But they would have to be cautious. Such cities did not bend to their lords easily, not even the lords they chose for themselves.

The inn was well maintained, and he saw at least four other inns of various grades in the same area. Well this one was proper for his rank. He suspected Master Bearskin would be at one of the others. So, that would be a complication but an expected one.

The building was stout enough to defend at need though mostly of wood. At least the wood was thick enough to burn slowly if the building were set alight and the roof was slated rather than made of wood which would aid its case. The court was substantial and he caught a hint of an open grassy paddock that might extend out behind the Inn. It was hard to tell. If so it boded well for his men's horses, as did the orderly arrangement of wagons to one side of the court. The paint was fresh.

The area clean. Yes. It would do adequately. The Innkeeper seemed to be a man who understood the business. Rudigar approved.

He might not approve overly greatly of peasants, but neither did he share his father's contempt of them. Better one who knew his work and did it well than a fool. Besides, nothing would get done without the peasants. There could only be so many lords or things became hopelessly complicated.

A groom came out to meet them and a price was quickly settled on for the entire troop. It seemed a well enough run place, and they weren't going to deplete his coffers too much. He had only brought so much coin with him. At least his men knew they would be paid when they returned home so he hadn't had to concern himself with a pay chest. Their expenses were tempting enough to brigands as it was.

The innkeeper bustled forward and Rudigar bowed. A large, tusked man stood at one corner. Ogir? Here? Then again this one seemed peaceable enough so perhaps he wasn't the raider his kindred so often were. "Meals for my men and myself. We have been in the field so whatever is standard and usual will be sufficient."

"Of course, m'Lord, ah… would you be the king's man who has been hunting bandits out this way?" The Innkeeper bowed obsequiously. So at least some people here understood how the world actually worked without foolish ideas of independent operation. On the other hand it was particularly galling to be known only as the 'king's man'. He would let it pass this time.

"I am, for the moment. Has he sent word?" Rudigar kept his inquiry polite. That could be one reason for the designation.

The Innkeeper shook his head. "Not from the king an acquaintance of mine who goes by Master Bearskin was asking after you. I owe him much and…"

The man trailed off and wiped his hand busily on his apron, as if trying to avoid too much familiarity. Well Rudigar could appreciate that effort. He despised easily familiarity even from his fellow nobles. "I have heard of Master Bearskin. If you know where he is, tell him I have arrived and would have council with him. Preferably in a private room."

Guilt mingled with relief in the Innkeeper's face as he bobbed in acknowledgment several times. "Yes, m'Lord. I'll let him know. You'll find most of the town knows him one way or another. If he were more presentable..."

The man trailed off embarrassed and Rudigar simply nodded. "I can see that, but I am not above doing business with a man who looks a bit unkempt."

Now there was an understatement! but Rudigar plowed on. "He and I have some overdue business indeed. Our enemies seem to be mutual."

The Innkeeper bowed. "As m'Lord commands. How discrete do you wish this to be?"

"Make sure there are no ears on us in the council, beyond that. We meet in an inn." Rudigar shrugged and gave a faint, but genuine smile which startled the innkeeper into reciprocating.

"Even so, m'Lord. I will see you have your own serving maid. My daughter is trustworthy enough," He bowed deeply and seemed to withdraw a degree from the conversation. "How many men have you with you? I do not think I have private rooms for so many."

"I have ten men with me. My Man at Arms and I shall share a room. The others are soldiers. Barracks are not unknown to any of us. Especially after this long in the field. I will be glad of your pallets or beds, after these months." Rudigar kept his tone largely indifferent. So the man was more clever than most. Perhaps it would be worth cultivating him as a contact. It would save him trips to these parts.

"As My Lord commands. I shall see to the rooms at once," the Innkeeper used that as a dismissal and Rudigar chose not to take offense. It wasn't the way of his father's lands, but in these parts they seemed to value dispatch over subservience.

He was finding himself fond of that. Yet one more thing not to tell his father. All the complications this mission entailed. He turned to Beren and began making arrangements of his own. It would be well for some of this to be public. Let them see what their potential Lord was like.

E islathen had changed since he was last this way... Bearskin inhaled deeply the scents of the city, the pungent aroma of the spice merchants. The homey stench of the stables in the sun. The faint whiff of the tannery on the breeze. The smells were the same.

Truth be told so were most of the sights. The stone cobbled roads. The wood and stone houses. The welcoming stained glass windows of the church gleaming golden in the setting sun. The sounds were different though. Merchants packed up their booths with little shouting and fuss. No one called to him to try their wares, even though he'd been through here before and they knew well enough what his pockets carried.

Merchant after merchant looked away and he shook his head.

"Master Bearskin!" Called one tall, lanky fellow with a shock of honey colored hair. His nut brown face disappeared into a veritable cavern of wrinkles as he smiled, and his gray eyes were almost completely lost in the folds. "I had not expected to see you back. It is my absolute joy and delight to see you here."

Bearskin smiled at first, then glanced over at one of the other merchants who was glaring at the fellow approaching. He drew himself up to his own full height, and the scowler looked hastily away. "Master Liemshir. I would have thought you would be at your shop. What has you out and about this early in the evening?"

The jewel merchant waved that off. "You, to be honest. I have been keeping an eye out for you many a day hoping you'd pass this way again. You're a difficult man to track down when there's messages to deliver."

"This is hardly the spot..." Bearskin demurred for the moment. "Ears listening..."

"Bah, let them listen. Few enough of them don't know, though. Let them gossip the whole town will know in an hour. Freiherr Rudigar von Neuen has arrived in town and he and his men are staying at the Crowned Hearth, and you have been invited to discuss a few things with him. I'd like to ask you to come by my place either tonight or tomorrow morning. I have information about a few things for you."

Bearskin debated, then lowered his voice. "My friend, is it about the queries I've been making?"

The man nodded and then laughed. "Of course I'll have you. I'll not let a little dirt get in the way of what you have done for me and mine."

"Then I would ask you join us tonight." Bearskin's voice was low and the man gave a small hand sign of agreement but shook his head vigorously.

"No, my friend I really do insists. If there are those here too cowardly to offer you proper due, I and mine know how to honor a friend when he comes to town. I'd offer you a place to stay if I thought there'd be the lease chance of you accepting. But..." He shook his head. "I shall see you there."

His eyes flicked down the foreigner's road where the inn in question resided and Bearskin nodded ever so slightly and raised his own voice. "If you insist. I shall be grateful to eat your food and come in as a friend and guest rather than a servant or embarrassment. It is a treasure not to be lightly cast aside and I would be a fool to do so."

"It's settled then!" The merchant patted Bearskin on the shoulder, heedless of the grime and set off in his own direction. Well that would be interesting enough. He hoped the man wouldn't get himself into too much trouble over this. For now he had a few traps of his own to lay.

He stepped up to one of the last merchant stalls open: a seller of meat pies, likely catering to people who were on their way home with their day's wages and wanted something more than could be cooked on the meager hearths most of the common folk possessed. "Peace friend. I am only looking for traveling supplies. I hope you'll forgive my friend. He has his ways about him and I would not impose upon you."

There was a light emphasis on the last word as Bearskin took in the stall, good sturdy wood not one of the rickety structures he was used to seeing. Amateur craftsmanship not much better than he, himself, could to but solid and workable as someone whose profession was other than carpentry could make it. The place was also cleaner than he was used to even here and he stood just far enough back not to sully it. The golden brown eyes of the shop keeper flicked from him to the counter and then back to the bearskin and he nodded, Bearskin thought in thanks.

"I have many pies left over for the day and the working people have mostly passed. I should have what you desire if you have funds to pay for it... Master Bearskin?" His voice was accented, and the rhythm of his words was odd, though not unpleasant. Bearskin found himself nodding along. The man stepped up to the counter and into the light. Truly black hair and skin as bronze as could be without being made of metal. Southerner here? That was unusual indeed.

"The only thing I may truly count to my own name is a surfeit of funds, which you know if you know me for Master Bearskin." Gregor smiled taking the sting out of his words as he added the anomalies together. "I take it you are new to Eislathen?"

"I have come here to seek my fortunes in the last year. I have had troubles on my road north, but such do the weavers of destiny decree and what may man do about them?" The man shrugged. "Bandits strike where they strike."

Bearskin nodded then shook himself and Gregor responded. "I may be able to help with that. But first. I need supplies suitable to travel that will last for many days in heat and strange weather."

"I know this weather for we have the Black and Silver Waste in my own country. My pies are made to withstand such. They do not command the prices I would have expected but..." He shook his head. "It is enough and I am better off now than I was when I arrived."

"This is always to be preferred. I will take enough for two weeks travel. I do not mind if they grow stale as long as they do not grow poisonous," Gregor reached into his pocket as the man began to stack pie after pie on the counter. They were of a sort he had not seen before, unraised crust rather than even quick rising. A very hard shell, yet the smell was savory. He waited until the man had finished stacking before he laid his handful of shining silver on the table and the man's eyes went round.

"This is most generous. If you will forgive the scale and the spell? I am still learning your valuations." The man bowed. "And you need not fear these going bad. As long as the outer shell is not broken they will keep for as long as a year. It is a secret my family knows. Like the making of hearthstones only less common."

"Use whatever scale and magics you think necessary. I have grown accustomed to it in my travels," Gregor waved the concern away as his eyes flicked from alley way to alley way. There would be trouble tonight if only he could tell where, but that was not one of his Gifts. If he could consider the bear itself his Gift. Now, for the moment, he was most himself. But the world was changing about him and he did not like it in the least.

The shadows were lengthening and the silence that had haunted these streets was no longer hindered by the day-to-day noises of business. It seemed a thing alive. Well they were close to the Dead Wood and that was never a comfortable place to contend with.

"My Lord Bearskin," He fumbled with the title, as if it was one he desired to give but wasn't sure was correct. "Pardon, I do not know how to address a man of such obvious wealth and... this would purchase ten times what I have here. I do not have enough stock to make good on such a sum please..."

He divided the coins and seemed rather distressed. "It is our custom not to accept money until the sum has been bargained over. I have discovered here that such things are different, is this one of those things?"

"No, my friend. It is not. But you have had misfortune. And I made no joke nor lie about money being that of which I have surfeit," Gregor kept his tone very formal. "What you have here will serve me very well indeed in my mission. I am hunting a thief. And am desirous of preventing another war. Yet I have the means of helping those along the way. If you would accept it, I would be grateful."

The man bowed deeply. "I will keep your business to myself."

"That is not necessary." And Bearskin lowered his voice so only the man could hear him. "In fact if you could spread word that I was asking after the Forest Heart I would be quite grateful. Though this does not compel it. This is freely given with no string or requirement beyond what will pay for the food."

The man simply stared at him then nodded slowly accepting the shining pile. "You are most generous Master Bearskin. I see the truth in much of what I have heard about you. I will do as you say in regard to these funds. Are you certain there is nothing I might do for you personally? This will mean much to my family."

"Pray for me. I have somewhat more than two years in peril. Your fates and our Virtues walk with you where you go." Gregor bowed politely, hoping he had managed to get the depth right. He had not dealt with more than two southerners in his time in the army and wasn't sure they were even of the same people. They had been very closed lipped.

"Even so it shall be. The brightness that shines in all souls shine upon you and the fates ever move in your favor," The man bowed very deeply indeed and Gregor smiled sadly. He had little desire to gain these people's admiration but... He let the thought trial off and finished stowing the food in his pack, turning his feet towards the Crowned Hearth. There was yet much to be done.

Chapter 15
PIECES OF TROUBLE

W armth wrapped around him and Rudigar stepped out of the cold streets and once more into his inn. His. Well, in the sense he was residing there for the moment though the landlord was likely to dispute the possessive. He set the thought aside and bobbed his head to the Ogir bouncer who smiled a tusky smile and raised a hand slightly in greeting.

The strains of a harp drifted his way from the direction of the hearth. The tune was a complicated one and one he was not familiar with. He flicked a glance in the direction of the harpist and took in the red hair, the harp, and the slightly pointed ears. Elf or half-breed he expected, but if she was still here he would see about inviting her to court. She was an excellent musician and deserved much better than this pitiful place.

He stepped on the thought. The Inn was clean, almost scrupulously so, and even if the heavy wooden tables were not fancy they were well maintained and well cared for. The metal steins and clay mugs were well made and their bottoms were not artificially thick to trick customers into thinking they had gotten more than they truly had. The food was simple, but the tantalizing smells had been taunting him since his men had arrived.

The men had all eaten and he had reminded them they were on duty and not to gamble their supplies away. That should at least keep things to a dull roar.

He ran his hand against the smooth, varnished wood of the bar and tried not to shiver. It was not so silky as court or his father's manor would produce, but here, it seemed wrong. He could not see the Deadwood, but it lurked. It haunted his mind and he had little doubt it was involved in these troubles.

"This way, m'Lord," The innkeeper bowed, and flicked a glance to one table that seemed to contain mercenaries. They were loudly gambling over something but there was something off about them. Something Rudigar could not pin down. Their leader was a tousled fellow who seemed too ordinary for words.

Too ordinary for words.

Rudigar nodded to the innkeeper and motioned for him to lead the way. He would say nothing. The more a sorcerer knew of one, the more power they had. That much he had learned in the war. Curse his father's abhorrence of magic as a useless peasant superstition. Curse his father's abhorrence of anything that didn't confine itself to the nobility. It left Rudiger with some painful holes in his education.

The Innkeeper led him through a doorway near the end of a short hall of the ubiquitous golden wood. "If you will wait here, your guest will arrive momentarily. My Marianna will take your orders."

He hesitated and Rudigar snorted as he found his seat, a pleasantly made thing of well treated wood and comfortable, if plain, cushions. "Out with it, man, I've never punished the messenger for his message."

"Master Bearskin has another he would add to the proceedings. He says there may be useful information the man possesses that will be of interest to you both. He has also asked me to tell you that the only thing he has in surfeit is funds so if you would do him the honor of allowing him to pay, he would gladly do so for courtesy of your time." The innkeeper bowed and Rudigar inclined his head. That last had sounded almost like a direct recitation. Well if Master Bearskin had money to fill the cannon with, he'd let the man show it. At least for now.

"I would not dishonor a man by refusing his generosity, but should he underestimate his funds, please do not embarrass him and discuss with me after?" Rudigar arched an eyebrow and the Innkeeper actually looked startled.

"My Lord, that will be no issue at all. Of that I can assure you. I will fetch them in." The innkeeper bowed, leaving Rudigar to puzzle over that little tidbit. Though, it fit with some of the other things Rudigar had heard about the man. Tales that he left silver about as if it were air to be freely breathed, acquired, and let loose. Asking only prayers, as he had asked Rudigar to pray for him.

I do not know if you truly listen, or truly exist, but this man his worthy of more than he has been given. Watch him. Or if he is false show him to be false swiftly and with surety. Rudigar lifted the faint prayer, knowing his eldest sister, with all the surety of her twelve years of age, would have been appalled at his temerity. Questioning the Whispering Word? Why it simply wasn't done!

In spite of all the times in the holy book where it clearly had been done, and the Word had taken no offense.

Rudigar was no great hand at discerning Power from Power, and it was unwise to deal with powers one did not know, so he left Powers to others with more discernment. He doubted very much that any other Power would be audacious enough to intercept something sent directly to the Whispering Word, so his prayer should be safe enough, whether that Power chose to listen or not. It could not hurt.

His thoughts carried him through as he fingered the wood of the arm of his chair. With the grain, rather than against the grain as so many of his father's pieces were. It seemed more appropriate that way. Easier on the finger in spite of hints of roughness under his finger. As if the silkiness of his father's pieces had been an illusion. He allowed himself to consider that possibility in the few seconds he had before his guests arrived.

Bearskin came first, then another man tall for the region, rangy and lanky rather than bulky with a bustling energy that Rudigar felt himself responding to. He seemed not much older than Rudigar until he smiled and his face became almost nothing but wrinkles. Older than he first looked then. But it was Bearskin that largely held Rudigar's attention.

The man tended to draw the eyes away from anyone he accompanied. Dirty. Disheveled. His amber eyes rested evenly on Rudigar, and the Freiherr, son of a duke, found himself thinking of the man in terms that would be more fitting to an equal than the peasant he had claimed to be.

He came to his feet and motioned to the two chairs at the table with him. "Please, my guests. Have a seat. I am well acquainted with you, Master Bearskin, or as well acquainted as most might say possible. Would you care to introduce your companion?"

Bearskin inclined his head and the lanky fellow once more smiled his wrinkly, cheerful smile. "Freiherr Rudigar von Neuen, please be known to Master Fynn Langmeyer. He is one of the local jewel merchants in these parts and has always had unusual connections."

"You do me undue honor, Master Bearskin, and I have heard of Freiherr von Neuen who goes by his lesser titles when he could independently claim Junerzong of one fief, and Edler through his father. I have been curious and gratified by his humility," Fynn bowed deeply and took his own seat to Rudigar's left, and Bearskin to the right.

"I had expected this to be a meeting between myself and Master Bearskin, but there was some implication you had word that would bear on both of us. I suppose you have had the miss fortune of interacting with our current illusive crop of brigands?" Rudigar cocked his head at the other man and wondered, briefly if he should have brought Beren with him. He discarded the notion. The other man was too ticklish about his Lord's dignity and Rudigar had brought his sword, so it wasn't like these two would take him quietly. He didn't think Bearskin would try. Which implied his friend would not either.

"I may. I know I have completed some inquiries into some missing caravans and antiquities that Master Bearskin had asked about." Fynn flicked a glance to Bearskin who nodded. "A certain Johann von Argers was entrusted with the care of half a dozen artifacts of great significance. None of them reached their intended destination. The first thing to go missing was the Heart of the Forest. It was that which precipitated the war between Bayr and Almarc. It has not been recovered which was why Almarc offered Bayr so generous a peace settlement."

"No proof they actually were responsible for the loss," Rudigar murmured. "I take it the others were equally significant?"

Both Fynn and Bearskin shook their heads, but it was Fynn who continued, "None so legendary. But each an artifact of great Power and significance to something, even if their significance was extremely local. None of them has been heard of again."

Bearskin interrupted briefly. "Have you interrogated the prisoners?"

"To a degree. They had little enough to say. Only that they had trade this way to offload black market goods. It is not uncommon in the Free Cities," Rudigar shrugged and made his statement simply one of fact not of condemnation and Fynn sighed.

"It is, sadly, true. There are many great advantages to be in a Free City. There are also disadvantages. Freedom has its prices and not all of them are pleasant," Fynn's tone was Philosophical, but Bearskin looked grim.

"I have tracked the goods to here. Here they were sold. The monies went into pockets other than Johann von Argers, who thought all the caravans were lost. I have made a list." He pushed the list across to Rudigar. There was more there than just von Arger's losses. And Rudigar wondered at that.

As he read he found himself nodding. This was a wider pattern, though his beloved--no the lady he was courting. He would not give her title other than that. Her father was involved up to his gills, though likely as a dupe not a willing accomplice, but there was another pattern here.

"I see. Have you considered these? If I may mark it?" Rudigar flicked a glance to Bearskin who nodded.

"I have a spare." Bearskin shrugged. "I can read, I can write. and the Gift of Memory is also mine."

"That will be of use if we must bring this to the King rather than deal with it ourselves." Rudigar commented absently, ignoring the look Fynn was giving him.

"I have no great magic, but It seems to me your villains have deep hooks in Eislathen. And I want them gone." The man's voice was grimly determined. "I love this city and would not see such scum abuse her."

Rudigar steepled in his fingers and paused for a moment. "I will speak freely here, I find the free cities to be disorderly, lawless, discourteous, and havens for every reprehensible deed known to man. Would some-one bring them to heel, I would be quite pleased. But that is not how they function, nor could they be tamed without destroying something fundamental to the reasons one would desire to tame them. Any more than one can take a mule and make it a horse. And even if one could it would destroy the value of having a mule in the first place. That these were brought here to be sold does not surprise me."

Fynn leaned forward angrily, but Bearskin caught his shoulder. Whatever he would have said was interrupted by the serving maid. She briskly took their orders and left with efficient dispatch. That was at least something. She had been modestly polite which was something else quite proper.

Rudigar looked to Fynn and met his eyes, ice blue to warm brown. "I do not say these things to condemn your city. That is not my place, nor, even if the King grants me these lands by right of conquest, will it be my place. I say it because such passion and dedication deserves an answering honesty. I would not deceive you and pretend to love this place and pretend my concern for it is for itself.

"Eislathen must, over all, take care of itself. I am here on the King's Business hunting those who have been a thorn in his side in this region since the war ended and now, with master Bearskin's information, since before the war itself began. This close to the Dead Wood, it is a perilous place to be. And I see your prosperity hanging by a thread. Your Vices are strong, but I cannot see any Virtues, and that is a dangerous place to be when meddling with things of Power. "

Bearskin's hand tightened harder on Fynn's shoulder as he forced the other man wholly back into his seat. "It could have been more diplomatically put, my Lord. But I will not argue with the sentiment. Instead I would counter with a word given to me by a Power: Virtue is more subtle than Vice, and its power is greater not less because of that."

Fynn flicked a glance at Bearskin, surprise seeming to interrupt rage and Rudigar took advantage of the distraction for the moment. "Which power, if I may be so bold as to ask, and the conditions of your burden do not forbid it?"

It was a delicately as he could refer to whatever curse Bearskin stood under. The man looked down at dirty hands and closed his eyes. Rudigar waited, whatever the man said next would bring several of these patterns and connections into focus. At last Bearskin looked up, "Believe as you will. It was Fate's Minstrel who so advised me when she sought to turn me from this doom. She said if it fell upon me, all hope was not lost. But cling to my virtues for they were subtler than Vices."

He waved a hand rather than repeat the whole saying, and Rudigar and Fynn both nodded. Rudigar chose his words with care. The tale rang true enough to his ear though to his knowledge he had no Gift of Truth reading, but he knew men and this did not seem as a lie to him. A lie might have come more easily. Outlandish as the tale was. "I see, and I can see why you have not spoken overly much of your interaction with the lady. I will not say it is an easy tale to believe, but believe it I do. Was there other advice she gave that you would care to share?"

Bearskin shook his head. "We passed some words, but other than giving me something I am only to use when I am certain the time is right..."

He shrugged, and Rudigar suspected there was more to it than that, but he could hardly blame the man for keeping his own council on this matter. It was unchancy dealing with Powers, especially this particular Power. Instead Rudigar turned the subject back to their quarry. "Well if she has aught to say about the enemies we pursue I trust you will relay that as well?"

"I most certainly will," Bearskin said softly.

"Then I think I can return to my point." He looked to Fynn. "Perhaps my opinion of this city could have been left aside, as it seems to have detracted from my point. Which is, it seems the Vices, unique. No, I'll not say that for they are present everywhere, but common in the Free Cities are allowing these brigands unusual latitude. Normally in other cities if they were to hide such great and bold thefts they would have to bring the local lord into the conspiracy and that would leave the King and any other noble a great deal of latitude to apply pressure. Not so here. Your black markets are impenetrable by the normal means of the rest of the Kingdom and much that must be hidden else where is done with defiant openness here."

Fynn nodded with manifest reluctance. "It is so, and people of good heart and good conscience must try and curb such things. We do have laws here. But we prefer not to bring their enforcers down more than we must. The law is a club. All too often it sweeps away the innocent as well as the guilty. Please realize, not all free cities are as Eislathen. Our system is strange even to the other cities. Our council squabbles continuously and gets little done and we prefer it that way. It means they are not interfering with us.

"Most of the other cities function as if they were their own little kingdoms, with the lord as king of his own tiny realm. There these bandits would likely have to behave more as you would expect, but if the lord sheltered them you would have less recourse. Here, unless the whole of the council is sheltering them, one councilor or another may be persuaded to act against them."

Rudigar blinked twice and felt his eyes widen and mouth draw into a frown before he could stop it. That did put a different complexion on things, though it seemed to make things far less tidy than he would have preferred. On the other hand it was not his city. He must always remember that.

He bought himself a few moments of time by taking a drink of the most excellent ale the serving girl had brought. He usually preferred wine or mead, but this was bold, with a hint of apple or... He set it aside. He would ask after the source of the Ale at another time. He would enjoy its delightful strangeness for now. "Have you any Councilors you might entrust with this information? I will make sure that the King knows that the town is helping. I know he cannot affect your free status by normal means; however, it might ease relationships."

Fynn grimaced and drummed his long, callused fingers on the table as he thought. "I can think of one. The Lady is no great friend of mine, but she is scrupulously honest. And that means much at such levels."

"I would value such a person myself. Honesty is a luxury many cannot afford, and a risk few are willing to take," He left it cryptically, then returned the page to Bearskin. "Do you see the pattern I have marked?"

Fynn looked over towards the page and Bearskin turned the page so the other man could see it. For someone with the Gift of Memory, a glance would be all that was needed. Fynn looked puzzled. "They all seem to be fancifully named, but I see no other pattern."

Bearskin frowned hard, "Pardon me, m'Lord, but I seem to recall something akin to these three." He made another mark on the page. "But under slightly altered names. We have the Heart of the Forest, that we know. You have here the Minstrel's Star. And there The Nightingale's Silver. And Here the Bear's Cloak."

He spoke very slowly amber eyes flickering between Fynn and Rudigar. "We Delmin have lore. About the Silver Nightingale. And the Whispering Star, which one of the old Priest's books said was also called the Minstrel's Star. And the Bear's Cloak. Or just the Bear as we call it. These are not artifacts but things in the heavens. Yet if these are artifacts might they call on the heavenly things for Power?"

"That is not the pattern I saw, but it makes some things make more sense. What is the significance, to the Delmin, of these things?" Rudigar cocked his hand, and Bearskin seemed to take the pause where the serving maid brought their food gratefully. Rudigar let him think and began to eat.

At last, after a few bites of his own dinner, Bearskin spoke again. His voice soft and trouble. "When the Bear touches the Whispering Star we of the Delmin hold the Feast of Stars. It is a feast of reconciliation and redemption. It is a time of great significance and great power. The tale behind it is too long to tell here, but if these truly match the tale itself. What could it mean?"

"And the Silver Nightengale?" Fynn asked gently. "Where does that figure in?"

"The same place the Star's Soul figures in. In each case on a particular Feast of Stars, different for each one. Those Heavenly Powers put an end a long standing bloody feud. In one case the Silver Nightingale restored one of the fallen to life and true health as the Whispering Word granted a boon, but that was before the Dead Wood became dead and the old lands of the Delmin lie in that wood. I do not know how it could possibly be of significance today." Bearskin looked up. "What could they want?"

"In our tales, these four items, with the Heart of the Forest were somehow instrumental in preventing the corruption of the Dead Wood from spreading. Perhaps you are unaware, but the 'Neuen' lands skirt the edge of the Dead Wood on one side, and the Halvarsand Empire along our southern border." Rudigar paused and they all nodded. "I think we have a hint. This has something to do with the Dead Wood. I hope it is not someone trying to harness that place's foul power. That never ends well for any involved or any unfortunate enough to be within three counties of the fool."

"Yet, that gives us another avenue of approach. I shall contact Councilor Heithru, and give her the particulars. Whatever she thinks of our odds of catching the bandits, I think she will bend her formidable talents to finding these artifacts. She no more desires the Dead Wood to expand than any other," Fynn tapped the blunt end of his fork on the table thoughtfully, before returning to the roast.

"What talents might those be other than perhaps wisdom and political acumen?" Rudigar asked.

"She has the Sight, which shall be of immeasurable use to us I think." Fynn shook his head. "Is there ought else we should discuss?"

Bearskin smiled. "I think it is appropriate that the last caravan with another artifact has made it through and the goods have been delivered to their rightful owners. Including a particular piece of crystal and gold that we have not talked about. What may come of that piece I do not know."

"Crystal and…" Rudigar blinked twice and let out a low whistle, forgetful for once of dignity. "Fate's Wheel?"

Bearskin nodded, and Rudigar opened his mouth then shook his head. "Better I not know who that went to. My father would spend considerable effort to pry the information out of me should it happen that I knew."

"Has he magic to know what you do and do not know?" Fynn asked in startlement.

"He knows many things that I would give much to discover how he acquired the knowledge." Rudigar said grimly. "I have thus far managed to keep knowledge of this away from him. Part of that is I have not gone home these many months. It as always at home in the presence of his witch that he discerns the most."

"Witch? Is she a true witch? or does she ape the part? Or are you just unfond of her?" Bearskin asked sharply, and Rudigar took no offense. Witchcraft was a punishable offense in all kingdoms, including Almarc.

Or at least most witchcraft. Power thieves were never particularly popular. They tended to bring the wrath of the Powers they stole from down upon them and everyone around them.

"To the best of my knowledge she truly is a witch. She does not seem to function as the mages I have known do. Nor does she seem to be using a Gift, and there is much of wickedness in how she applies her powers whatever their source. She is also my father's mistress and was before my mother died. I am reasonably fond of my step-mother. She did not attempt to cast myself or my brothers aside in favor of her own children when they wed," Rudigar considered. "So there may be something of all three in her. I have not the Power or Gift myself to truly say, only that it is a title that she has taken to herself though she does not flaunt it."

"Then something to be wary of," Bearskin acknowledged but Fynn watched Rudigar intently.

"Given your family's proximity to the Dead Wood and what you just said about your father, could there be some involvement of his in this matter?" Fynn's tone was flat, and his eyes wary. Such an insult to a noble would be the cause of a duel in many places, and Rudigar's reputation as a swordsman was formidable.

"I do not know. It does not fit the pattern but I cannot say why. I hope that I shall be able to chase that thought to the front of my mind or find evidence that proves it does fit the pattern. I will say this is within his temperament and intelligence, but I do not think he is sufficiently foolish to attempt to control the Dead Wood. I could see him attempting to seize the artifacts to present them in court, or more likely have me present them in court to gain prestige at having 'recovered' them, but if so he would have done so by now. The midsummer court would have been the ideal time for such things." Rudigar mulled the thought over. "Midwinter would be the next best time, And if he had been waiting on the Wheel that will be when he does it. I will make discrete, very discrete, inquiries. Whether he is involved or not we cannot allow him to catch wind of this."

"And if he should be found to be guilty of these crimes?" Bearskin asked gently, and Rudigar looked at the other man and saw sympathy in his eyes. This one at least had grasped the full implications of the situation.

"I shall turn him over to the crown's justice and hope that the King is willing to have mercy upon those who were no witting part of his schemes," Rudigar said softly. "Especially my sisters. They would have no part in this. The oldest is but twelve."

Both other men nodded, but it was Fynn who spoke. "And so you take deadly insult better than I, my Lord. Might we turn to the food since the conversation has become enough to spoil anyone's appetite if we continue?"

Rudigar surprised himself by chuckling. "By all means, let us do so."

Chapter 16
DEADLY FOES

Bearskin sat perched atop a great rock that jutted near the poorer districts of town. The stone's roughness had been mellowed by years of wind and rain and it was comfortable enough for him. He had not had the heart to tell either of his dinner companions that inns no longer welcomed him. Not even the Crowned Hearth had had space for him. Or at least space that he would accept. He would have frightened the man's guests away.

The Bearskin weighed on him and Gregor closed his eyes, picturing before him a pair of soft grey eyes and reciting her letter. It was too dark to read easily even with the moonlight. In this his Gift truly was a gift. Even if some misfortune should take her physical letter from him, they would always be his.

The fall flowers and the scent of nuts in the woods tickled his nose and he found himself grateful for the meal at the Crowned Hearth. it was becoming harder to keep the Bear in check, but he would fight that battle. He would not lose himself to the Bearskin. He only had a few small years left. He would need to write to Isela and Sophia again.

He had seen the Caravan back to the first safe town, and he didn't think any of those men would betray Master von Argers. The one question that taunted him was who had sold the previous ones? Had the bandits taken over the caravans and sold them here themselves? The ones he'd caught had not been involved in those strikes. Did they use different people each time?

It was a puzzle and for once it was a comfort not to have to worry the problem alone. Von Neuen had been trouble for his units on the battle field. He, himself had crossed swords with the man twice. Not that he expected the man to remember him. His greater reach and strength had been largely what saved him. And he had chosen not to take the man's life when he could have war or no war.

Was this his reward now? Was this one of the things the Minstrel had meant about the subtlety of virtues? He didn't know, but he also wasn't going to count on it to actually continue. He would take any blessings that came his way and neither ask for nor expect anything.

His ears, much more sensitive than they had been four years ago, picked up the faint cries below and he almost ignored them. Von Neuen had been right about one thing, this city allowed bandits to thrive and he could not save everyone, but...

He pushed off the rock and propelled himself through the stench ridden refuge strewn streets. That voice was familiar. He skidded around a corner on the grime. A cry! A loud one, pained.

Fynn. This was where Fynn would be going home if he had spoken to his councilor acquaintance. He stretched his long legs as far as they would go. He must get there in time. A grunt of triumph. There were words in it, but words, Gregor could not catch.

A growl escaped his throat as he rounded the last bend and he roared. His vision shifted and for once he did not fight the change. He had few enough friends in the world. He would. Not. Lose. Another.

"Quick strip him and let's get out of here." One voice, gruff and worried reached his ears. "They say..."

Bearskin's form lumbered into the poorly lit square. Fynn lay on the ground bleeding, but he did not smell dead yet. Bearskin lashed out with a paw and felt it connect with the gruff one's companion, the larger of the two and the man went flying into the sturdy stone of a building.

He reared back as the other man lowered the spear he had not seen and stabbed at him. The man jerk sideways as a crossbow bolt took him in the shoulder. Bearskin once more lashed out, but pulled the punch this time, targeting the man's arm to knock the spear aside.

Out of another street charged... Von Neuen's man at arms? Bearskin had little time to register that as the armsman finished the work he had begun.

Bearskin turned on the bear within him, forcing it back into its proper place. He was a man he was not a beast. The Beast was useful to him, but he was in control of it, not it in control of him.

He gritted his teeth against the pain. For some reason it never hurt to become a bear, but returning to human? Was pain and growing more and more painful.

He wondered if that might not be the ironic end of the Devil's Bargain to become nothing more than the beast he had slain when it all began? Well he would fight that as he fought Old Scratch and the bear that had been set on him.

When he opened his eyes, he was human again and the armsman was kneeling beside him. "Are you injured Master Bearskin?"

His tone was courteous enough and he was brave enough to approach after seeing the full measure of Bearskin's curse. Gregor gave him full credit for that. "I am uninjured. We must see to Master Fynn."

"He's in a bad way, but yet lives." Beren pressed his hands to the wound.

Bearskin hesitated, then thought of the gift he bore. He fished in his pouch, "I will need this back but it should aid him. It has helped me when I have been injured."

The smooth, green stone glowed faintly and Beren's eyes narrowed. "Where did you get that?"

"Powers move in mysterious ways. That was given unbidden by some-one who sought to turn me from my folly. Ask your master who. I'd not speak the name here. We've enough trouble without adding Powers to the pot," Bearskin offered the stone to Beren who nodded and took it. The glow dimmed but did not go out. So, it seemed to work best for him?

Bearskin stood as Beren held the stone against the injury. A sound of feet attracted Bearskin's sensitive ears, and he stepped out to meet the guards coming down from a side street as if chased by the wind. Or fleeing the biting stench of the chamber pots in the alleys. Their leader raised a hand and the group halted in easy sight of Gregor.

"Master Bearskin, we heard reports of brigandage." The guard was short, even for the locals, and broad enough to hint at some dwarf blood in him. His hard, brown eyes flicked from bearskin to Beren to Fynn.

He glanced over his shoulder, "Marcus, tend the wounded. You've got the bag."

The guard broke ranks and ran forward with a satchel. Gregor recognized the symbol of a healer's bag and the clean, pungency of the herbs. He turned his full attention back to the lead guard and shrugged. "I heard the fight but was too far away to stop it before Guildmaster Fynn was in the condition he is in. I downed the first one and Freiherr von Neuen's armsman took care of the other."

"Downed the first one, hmmm?" The sergeant eyed him thought fully. "Your usual way or did you do things the way the rest of us do."

Bearskin shrugged. "My curse has some benefits."

The man nodded. "Then if you will wait here. The mayor and council will not be pleased. The Guild's Circle will be less pleased, especially if he dies."

Marcus worked with quick, deft fingers and Beren kept a hand on Fynn's shoulder with the stone concealed in it. How he should know that Bearskin didn't want his treasure known, Gregor had no idea, but he was grateful. He would have to properly express that gratitude at some point. How he had little enough idea.

The Sergeant approached the Armsman.

"Can you give us your account, Master..." He trailed off with an arched eyebrow.

"Beren, Companion at Arms to Freiherr von Neuen. Truth be told, I was following this man. My Master has been tracking some very dangerous bandits. They have reach and scope far past any we have dealt with before. He felt it best if someone kept a discrete eye on the man. Unfortunately I do not know these streets as well as I should like for such work and he got too far ahead of me to prevent this. By the time I had caught him up, Master Bearskin had intervened, and I flanked the one with a boar spear before we could add another body to the count." Beren's voice was grim and the Sergeant scowled at the mention of von Neuen.

Bearskin wondered at that. The Sergeant and his men were never less than ready for their duty. Did they have some issue with Von Neuen's task here? Or was it, as Fynn's had been, the implication that the city itself was consorting with that grade of trouble?

"I see. Next time you want someone watched, come to us, Master Beren, you or your master. I do not like that the King of Almarc thinks he can intrude where we have let no other King intrude, but that is hardly your master's fault. I know what he could claim that he has not has done him some favors at least in my end of the guard." The Sergeant shrugged and Beren nodded.

The young guard, Marcus, looked up from his bandaging. "I think we should get him to a proper healer now. He'll make it, though my Gift isn't strong enough to do more than keep him alive to get him to proper help."

"There are worse gifts to have," Gregor said stepping forward. "If you do not think it would do him harm, I can carry him."

The Guard eyed him and firmly wrapped Fynn's cloak over the wound. "Carry him with the wound outward and his cloak between yourself and him. I think we can manage. With such an attack I'm not sure any of us wish to have our hands occupied should someone try a second time."

He looked to his sergeant who nodded and spoke next. "We'll show you both to the healer, then I think there will be people who want to speak with you in more detail."

Chapter 17
Next Moves

Spice, exotic and southern, wafted in as the Councilor entered the same wood paneled room in which Rudigar had met with Fynn and Bearskin. She was only of average height for a woman, and Rudigar found himself comparing her to Sophia.

They had similar bearing, but little else, physically, in common with one another. She was dark where Sophia was golden bright. Black of hair, bronze of skin, with eyes the color of fine amber. Slim and elegant she lacked Sophia's vibrancy. Perhaps this is what Sophia might have become if she had been raised in court?

Rudigar somehow thought not. There was a coldness to Councilor Haithru that Sophia lacked, though she had often tried to mimic it. A fool's errand. She had other strengths that would serve her better than coldness.

He took a bottle of wine from the table and poured them both glasses, sipping his own with a slight smile before offering her hers. The lady chuckled, a surprisingly merry sound for one who seemed so solemn, and paired with a smile that softened harshly elegant features and drew wrinkles to the corner of her mouth. He revised his estimate of her age up some years and wondered at her youthful appearance.

"Freiherr von Neuen, word was given me that you would discuss matters with me on the King's Business, and that it may have bearing upon the shameful attack on good Guildmaster Fynn." She took the seat he pulled out for her and he settled himself between her and the door so she knew herself safe from external threats, but on the other side of the table so he did not threaten.

She nodded with appreciation for the placement and it was his turn to smile. It was good to have a skilled counterpart in this game. Though he hoped it would not become 'opponent'.

"Yes, there is another involved party, but he is not commonly fit for polite company by most measures." Rudigar shrugged and sipped the wine thought fully.

The lady inclined her head, "Fynn's 'Master Bearskin'. I have heard his name quite often and the town owes him a debt. People in the town more so for his generosity. I have often wondered at his game."

"I have only guesses, my Lady. What I know is he is Delmin by blood, and has been laboring under a curse for some years. Five now if my count is accurate, but no fewer than three. He has yet two years, give or take, remaining on whatever trial has been set before him. He has never divulged the details only that he cannot bathe and cannot pray, and seems to ever wear that bearskin as his primary garment." Rudigar shrugged. "I also know him to be a strange, but intensely honorable man."

"That is how Fynn described him." The lady fingered her glass thoughtfully before taking the smallest of sips almost out of courtesy to him rather than desire for refreshment. "Yet, Fynn is gravely wounded and it is yet unknown if he will live."

"My Companion at Arms was there. He said it is likely the man will live, though he will have a rough road, and should someone try and tip the scales the other way it would be easy for them," Rudigar kept his voice carefully neutral. He should have expected it. Well, he had expected it, but he had expected to have better time for it.

He'd also truly expected the main attacks to be directed at himself, after all he was the outsider. He was the one no one would grieve over if he simply went away and never troubled these people again.

The Lady once more nodded, "Yes, though I wonder at his presence there."

"I had him following the Guildmaster. We have been pursuing some resourceful, clever, and even more unscrupulous than usual bandits. That is actually why I requested your presence. Guildmaster Fynn spoke highly of you. He said you both had the Sight and were scrupulously honest. Though on the last, I am not sure if I should salute your courage..."

"Or shake your head at my folly," The Lady actually laughed this time. "You have a streak of stubborn honesty yourself, Freiherr."

"In this matter call me Rudigar. I would prefer not to stand on ceremony. There is too much to be done and the town resents me enough as it is." He shrugged he had expected it. "As strangely dual a personality as this town seems to have."

"It does have something of a dual personality," Lady Heithru took a longer drink of her wine as if to collect her thoughts. "First, I will tell you what I know. Anything I say you can take to be true to the best of my knowledge. I can be deceived, but it is not easy to do so. You see my Sight is paired with Truth. I am honest through acceptance of the inevitable. I will not attempt to corrupt my own gift to play the usual games of politics. So I attempt to use those rules to my own advantage. So far it has served me well. But honesty is no Virtue in one who suffers pain when they lie."

"The Fae would seem to disagree, I find your position the more honorable." Rudigar raised his own glass to her then nodded slowly and thoughtfully, "What do you know about the artifacts Fynn discussed with you?"

"I know they were sold here, in the in-between market," she looked long into her glass and sighed. "It is... a bridge between the legitimate market and the more illegal markets. I know your von Argers was not party to those sales, please relay that to your King. It was not he who did this, and I have long sought the identity of the ones who did. Those are not artifacts to be trifled with."

"No they are not, and finding who is behind this is my own purpose, a purpose in which Master Bearskin had been of great assistance," Rudiger considered the patterns before him. "I wonder if we have not been asking the wrong question."

"My Lord?" The Lady cocked her head to one side in a quizzical gesture.

"How did Master von Argers get these artifacts in the first place? I know the first he carried came from the hands of the King but the others had been, supposedly, lost to history or stolen. So who gave them to him? And who was he supposed to send them to?" Rudigar mused.

"I have a list of who they were supposed to be delivered to, all here. And all the men they were supposed to go to were at the auctions and lost them handily, but the seller refused to believe any evidence of ownership. There was a petition before the council, but the individual was gone each time and always seemed to be a different person," The Lady spoke slowly finger tapping her wine, eyes narrow and Rudiger watched her carefully.

"Seemed to be?" He asked gently as the pattern seemed, to him, to be falling together.

"I saw two of them. here was glamor involved, but I never got close enough for long enough to pierce the glamor. My gift is know so that may have been by design on the part of these people. Which means I can aid you much if you catch them but they will likely be avoiding me how ever they may." She looked up and her amber eyes were troubled.

"I do not ask the Free City of Eislathen to fight these battles for Almarc," Rudigar began slowly. "But if your Council would help me bring them to justice, or more likely permit me to operate in regard to this matter, within your borders."

"And deal with the guards who would rather you not look into this at all?" She asked with a small, smile, this one showing just the hint of teeth.

Rudigar raised his wine and savored the rich flavor, casting aside the memory of who had introduced him to this particular vintage for a time. His hand stroked the grain of the wood in the table as he thought, responding to the questions, explicit and implicit, with care. "Indeed, though I would not draw too many conclusions based on their actions. The ones who greeted us were slovenly and seemed more interested in perfecting their rudeness than doing their duty."

She nodded, with just as much care. "I think I know the ones of which you speak. They have been troublesome. Under other circumstances, I might suggest that some of the auctions we discussed previously had happened when those individuals had the watch, but their families are quite lively to deal with when it comes time for a full Moot of the town."

"We have such even in my father's lands. Perhaps especially in my father's lands where sloth is punished, true, but there is no reward given for hard work," He shook his head and laid his glass down with a determined clink.

"But not your own? I know you hold lands in your own right through your mother's line," she let the question trail off but he nodded.

"It is so, I do not reward easily, if the rewards were easy to attain would they value it and strive for it? But I reward work done beyond what is expected. I punish those who do not do the work expected of them, and attempt to ensure the peoples under my administration are cared for well enough that they are capable of the tasks they are set," He shrugged. "I do not claim it any great virtue. It is simply the care any shepherd has for his sheep or any farmer for his lands."

"So you view your people as nothing more than cattle in the field? To sow and thresh and work?" She once more cocked her head at him, but here eyes had narrowed, and he considered her frankly. With her Gift, she would know much he chose not to reveal but this he had never hidden.

"Even as I treat myself. It is my task to see to them, or appoint able overseers to care for them when I am not there. They render their work to me. I protect them from brigands and bandits. I see they have food, as much as is possible, in lean years. I do not feast when my people hunger. I do not lightly ask them to take up arms when it is my place to raise up at least basic forces to guard them. I see justice done amongst them and see those who would abuse justice also punished. Is it so different here than in all the other lands?" Rudigar let a touch of his exasperation show at that.

She tapped her finger against the glass and the nail made a rhythmic ring. Her Amber eyes met his. "I am from Madrin, we view things rather differently. People are not cattle to be herded. They are to be led as individuals."

Rudigar shook his head and gave a short bark of wry laughter. "No wonder it sounds odd to you here. People can be led as individuals, as I have led men into battle in ones, in twos, and also by the hundred. Did

I lead those men individually? Mind you I've never faced the Madrinin in battle, neither do I wish to. Your people are quite, quite mad."

"We would say it is the rest of the world is mad. Our borders have been free for countless years, and no one has successfully managed more than raids against us," She raised her glass to him.

He simply shook his head. "It is beside the point. The world is different here. They look to me to lead. I expect them to follow. That is all. I say to one go. He goes. I say to another come, he comes. I tell the housekeeper at my estate 'see that this happens' and she ensures that it does happen. My opinion of them is, usually, unimportant to the matters of efficient running."

"You are not so heartless as you like to present." She held up a hand when he made to protest. "I'll say nothing. I think I may understand why. We know a little of your father's lands."

"Then you will know the wicked side of these obligations, lords who manipulate skillfully, and pretend to fulfill their obligations to those below, but mostly use them up, cast them aside and find others who will do their work and start all of it over again. Including his sons if he is so inclined." He raised his own glass to her in a salute. He had not intended to tell so much.

She nodded and stood, "I think we have finished our business here. I will give you what information and aid I can. You have the council's support in the matter of hunting these wolfs-heads down and destroying them. Only in this matter, but it is a beginning. We shall see what manner of man this King who would be above us sends."

"May I withstand all the trials this sends my way. Do you mind if I give this information to Master Bearskin?" Rudigar quirked a brow at her and she shook her head.

"I anticipated you would. He will move well in places you cannot. Heed him. There is steel in his soul and it does not bend easily, either to hate or loyalty, though beware his temper," She finished the dregs of her wine and returned the glass to the table.

Rudigar returned to his notes and poured himself another glass, letting her see herself out. If she was truly Madrinin, she would not appreciate too much cosseting.

"Rudigar von Neuen. Honorable son of a dishonorable man."

Rudigar's head snapped up and she stood at the doorway, door open, but he was somehow certain nothing she said would reach any ears but his. Her eyes seemed to glow like coals. Something about her blazed in a way he could not define, but he could sense the connections about her. And he simply waited to discover the meaning of her words.

"Your path holds many traps. Shun expedience and do not surrender that which is dear to you simply for your father's sake. There will be joy in your future if you let it come to you, but it will come through trial. Trials you must choose to face, rather than turn aside to the more common path."

The lady shook herself and seemed to return to a more normal aspect, connections fraying, and for the first time von Neuen wondered if there was more to those connections he sensed than simply intuition and logic. He knew well enough what had just happened. He bowed, more deeply than their relative stations warranted. "The Sight speaks, I listen. I shall heed your words as much as mortal man may."

She nodded, "Whatever the Sight told you, I think you shall do well. I am good at taking the measure of a man, and there is something noble in you, even as there is something indomitable in Master Bearskin. This tangle needs both of you."

Rudigar nodded. "By your leave?"

And the lady bowed and stepped through the open door, and Rudigar had a fleeting glimpse of the Armsmen than followed her. He gave a brief prayer for the Lady's safety. They were near to losing one ally, they did not need to lose a second. But there was work to be done and he could not be everywhere. Best to leave the Lady to her own measures and see to his own tasks as best he could.

Chapter 18
ENEMY VEILED

Rain washed all scents from the air but its own, and the sodden smell of the bearskin, too close to his nose to be washed away. Yet today he did not attempt to use the Bear's form to protect himself. His ears strained for more mundane sounds through the muffling drum of the fall storm. Distant thunder rippled towards him, too far to be a proper peal, too far to see the flash in the hazy gray cloak of the forest.

Bearskin--Gregor-- he reminded himself. The less he thought of himself as Bearskin the better as far as he could tell.

The wagon tracks carved clear ruts even in the steady rain. It wasn't torrential, but in these lands it was hard to tell if it would stay gentle, for mountain values of gentle. He paused to rub his calves. Six days following horses on his own two feet had pushed even his endurance. If they hadn't had the wagon he wasn't sure he could have done it.

There was something odd about how they were pushing their mounts. He wouldn't have thought the horses could maintain the pace. Horses were faster, but it was easier to push men than beasts beyond normal limits of endurance. Even the horses drawing the wagon had been pushed. He was surprised they had not foundered.

The trees persisted in slapping him in the face with their wet leaves, as if somehow offended by him. Well the feeling was mutual. He ducked low under a branch (no easy task at his height), and once more knelt to examine the trail. No, there was something decidedly odd going on.

For once he wished von Neuen was here. He could use the man's courage and more his wit. For all his own Gift and intelligence, the other man had a wealth of knowledge that Gregor deeply appreciated and could not replicate, but he had not seen him since Eislathen. Rumor had it he had been called back to the capitol. Gregor had hunted this last year alone.

One hand flicked a scrap of fabric from the rut and he frowned. Bright saffron greeted him as he let the rain wash the reddening mud free. Below the mud had been dark and rich almost black. Rich enough it made the farmer that he had been long for a plow and ox. Here it had turned to something redder, more clay like, and yet mixed.

It was almost as if the soil here had been made rather than simply being. There was no place sand could wash in, and no sign that the trees that grew with such abundance contributed their annual fall foliage to the soil.

He shivered something stirring in his memory, but he'd been chased by too many legends to sort out what it might mean. There were tales of places where Powers had created the conditions of the earth itself, but those were unchancy places at best. His quarry was riding through as boldly as if this were their home territory. It may well be.

Gregor made himself consider that possibility. They were getting near von Neuen lands, and the Dead Wood. Neither option was overly appealing to Gregor. He didn't think Rudigar von Neuen would be behind this, but the man had been open about the quality of his relatives.

Gregor rubbed his shoulder and considered the scar beneath. There were advantages to being Delmin and head and shoulders above most opposing soldiers: few could match him for reach, fewer still with the boar spear that had been his usual weapon. Yet it had been von Neuen of all of them that had marked him at their second meeting, then not taken his life when he had the chance.

He didn't think the Almarcan Lord recognized him. He knew he'd marked von Neuen as well, but what did honor and mercy on the field of battle translate to in such games of intrigue? Was Rudigar von Neuen capable of such feats of duplicity? Could he have orchestrated this? And then been put in charge of catching himself?

Gregor made himself face the notion squarely even as he returned to the tracks, this time the horse tracks beside the wagon marks. The prints of the horse were different than the ones his memory supplied from von Neuen's horse. But Lords often had more than one horse. Yet he had had few remounts when they had met in the woods and when he had come to Eislathen. In addition he had ever dealt fairly with Master Bearskin, even though he had little reason to trust him.

Warmth once more came from the smooth stone the Minstrel had given him. Fynn had healed enough for him to reclaim it before he had left Eislathen on this errand. Von Neuen was tangled up in it somehow. That fit the bits and pieces: the course of this wagon, the scrap of fabric.

Though there were many lords who had yellow hues in their heraldry, but this was a bright color, one he'd only seen once or twice. Once on von Neuen's tabards and once on Baron Hochritt's arms. His own former Lord had always tried to display above his station. How he'd afforded such things Gregor had long wondered.

He dragged his thoughts back to the task at hand. What was wrong with him? He tucked the scrap of fabric in a pouch and trudged after the wagon marks. He was gaining on them, slowly. Too slowly. He didn't dare shift to a bear and trail them by scent, even though he could change at will now. It was harder and harder to become human again. Especially after Eislathen. Yet...

And yet...

Rain dribbled down the back of his neck between himself and the green greatcoat that he tried very hard not to think of most days. How beholden was he to the Devil? No. The Minstrel had said no more than he allowed and he would not allow more than the letter of their agreement of hold on him. No more.

He clenched his teeth and wished he dared pray, but that would wait. One more year. He slipped a hand into the one pouch he always hid and clenched both stone and bead in his fist. And touched the letters Isela had sent him this last year. He had promises he would rely on, made to him and by him. He must see through. He must.

Isela's words returned to him: fire deferred. The cause of the war must be resolved. Was he on the trail of that cause now? Which of the legends he remembered was the key? He kept his eyes busy as he turned to the far past rather than avoiding it. Weary as he was, perhaps it was something that should be avoided no longer. Especially if the trail led to the deadwood.

Chill wind carried dying leaves past Bearskin as he crouched by the trail. He breathed deeply the decaying scents of fall foliage, and the wind brought also the scent of berries. He closed his eyes listening hard, counting the birds. He knew little of what they were beyond here a hawk, there a pigeon, and another too small to eat but with a beautiful voice. He treasured their melodies, rough of soothing. They were his alarms.

The trail had looped back again and he could find no place where the tracks continued and no sign they had been concealed. The ground was still soft, though not as mud splattered now that the rain had stopped.

The air promised frost. Gregor wasn't sure if it was wet enough for snow. Storms here blew up with a suddenness that seemed unnatural to him. Nevahs had always been sheltered from the more violent storms.

He scrubbed sweat out of his eyes. Sweat that chilled him the moment he stopped moving and gave the wind a chance to get its teeth into him. The tang of blood reminded him of his last close encounter with the party. Just a scout, but they were putting out scouts so they suspected someone might be on their trail. That didn't bode well for him, and not just because the scout had been good enough to cost him his walking stick. There were at least a dozen of them and only one of Master Bearskin.

The Bear in him snarled, and he stepped on it firmly. He needed the senses but didn't dare risk shifting. Not here. The Dead Wood was close and now they were actually on the northern reaches of Neuen Rittermark, Rudigar von Neuen's lands. Yet the party seemed determined to skirt the edges of them, unless Bearskin had completely lost his bearing and positioning. Which was always possible, he admitted to himself. Until he'd taken the Bearskin he'd been no great traveler.

He strained for any sound that might give him a clue to where these men might have gone. Any sound. Any...

The birds.

Bearskin flung himself into the bushes and nearly impaled himself on a spear. The leaves exploded outward and he wrenched himself sideways grabbing for a stick, anything that he might use for a weapon.

A quick thrust from one of the ambushers' spears put an end to that line of thought. He could little afford the attention!

He backpedaled as another spear thrust came at him. At the third he reached out and snatched the spear shaft, pulling with all his considerable might. Even in human form he was still a powerful man. His wanderings had not made him less so. The spearman had come with the spear and Bearskin heaved that end of the spear around.

The spearman shook free and tumbled into some of his fellows. Bearskin flipped the spear around and lunged at the first man on that side of the line, making full use of his height and reach advantage. A glitter from his right caused him to duck left, only to find himself being herded into waiting spears on that side.

They were getting around him. He couldn't afford to be surrounded! He doubted they were interested in taking prisoners.

He cast the spear backwards, catching it near the head and was rewarded with a grunt of anguish from someone trying to sneak in behind him. He grinned savagely and swung the haft about, darting through the opening.

What should have been the opening.

More spears waited him. It wasn't a dozen. It was closer to two. He swung the spear around once more to clear space before settling into his old stance from the melees, but what could he do against three ranks of them?

"Well, well what have we here? We seem to have found a rogue bear," The voice was vaguely familiar, not like someone he had heard but like someone with a voice similar to one he had heard. But whose?

Grey eyes flicked up towards the approaching noble. No one could mistake him for anything else. Whether he was or not was another question. Tall, relatively speaking, on an excellent chestnut horse, with dark hair and startlingly blue eyes. He was also dressed entirely in saffron and scarlet: von Neuen house colors, with their heraldry to boot. He reined in his horse and paused a moment, and the sunlight caught the contrast of the bright colors and the darker features. Bearskin thought the effect had been deliberate.

"What? No words? I am disappointing Master Bearskin. I've heard so much about you, then I suppose one can't expect a beast to speak," The man shook his head and the slight tail that bound his hair bobbed. Bearskin's eyes narrowed but he did not release the spear.

"I've not been truly addressed. Would you care to introduce yourself properly since you seem to have the advantage of me." Bearskin's eyes swept the ring of spears.

The man laughed, and it was not a pleasant laugh. There was an echo of something beyond the familiar in it, and Bearskin tried to suppress a shudder. He'd heard that laugh in Old Scratch when they made their bargain. Yet he didn't think this man was another disguise for that. He was too solid for it.

The dark head leaned forward, though frowned a little when he realized how little he towered over his captive when he did so. "My name is not important. Call me what you will. It is not important. Especially as you will not be about to call anyone anything very soon."

"Very well, do you prefer traitor, thief, or fool?" Bearskin ignored the men about him, though did not forget them. He wasn't sure he could make a hole, but it was possible. Yet his battlefield instincts were telling him that this man was more dangerous than the spears. He just wasn't entirely sure how.

Intensely blue eyes narrowed, and shimmered green for a moment and Bearskin watched very closely indeed as the man scowled at him. An illusion? Or something else? The man sat back up and looked down his long, straight nose at Bearskin. "You speak very boldly for a prisoner."

"The man cornered has little left to lose so might as well speak his mind regardless of who he might be addressing," Bearskin smiled. He couldn't force his shoulders to relax, but he kept his tone casual. It seemed to irritate the lordling further. "Do you have a title you would prefer over those?"

"I suppose 'Imperial Majesty' is a bit too much to expect just yet," The man sighed heavily, but his eyes never left Bearskin, and Gregor refused to rise to the taunt. The man shrugged and continued. "You will call me simply 'my Lord'. It is simple enough to satisfy your desire for defiance and close enough to accurate to keep things polite."

Gregor smiled, "Then let us get down to business before I see how many pieces I can take out of your men. What do you want with me?"

"You amuse me, and there is much use I could make of you." The man's fingers began to move in a complicated pattern and Gregor watched it closely, committing it to his Gift. He felt a pressure on his mind, and dug in his mental heels.

The man frowned and Gregor met his eyes defiantly, feeling a melding of powers though what it meant he could not say. There were few enough books on magic in the world and none of those available to those without the Gift.

He had not yielded to the Devil. He would not yield to magic.

The man's frown turned into a scowl and his features blurred into something. It was gone too quickly for Bearskin to consciously catch them. But they were familiar, very familiar. "I serve no master I do not choose."

"Then you will die," The man said simply and motioned to the spearmen who lowered their weapons.

"Then you'll never have the Wood," Bearskin called out. "You don't have all the artifacts."

The man held up a single hand and his men halted, spears much too close for Bearskin's comfort and he could smell the beer on some of their breath. The lordling cocked his head. "How do you know I want the Wood?"

Gregor smiled, "Now that, m'Lord would be telling, but you haven't been overly clever about it, have you? Just look at the pieces you have taken."

The man nodded slowly and considered. "Bring him with us. We can take his head later if it is convenient. Or if he tries to escape. Even a bear's hide is no use against a well aimed spear."

Bearskin shouldered his own weapon, and one of the men stepped forward to take it. He shook his head.

"No, this one I'll keep for now. There should be enough of you to handle me if I try to use it, but I'll not be marched to my death without some chance of fighting back." He met the eyes of each of the guards, and a few looked away. The rest simply sneered at him and he smiled.

Chapter 19

A SECRET OF THE WOOD

Black. Black leaves. Black sky. The sun shone a dull and angry red as if the wood had tainted its light. For all Gregor knew it had, yet he was himself. The Bear was quiet here. Almost as if it were afraid.

For his part he welcomed the chance to think clearly. A nightingale sounded distantly and his 'host' swore with creative fluency. The Silver Nightingale. Bearskin wracked his brain for the proper legend. While his Memory would supply anything it would not help him make the connections he needed here. Yet one of the artifacts...

He bit his tongue and cut off the thought. His host had been fiendishly accurate in his guesses of Bearskin's thought. Though Gregor had noticed that falling off once they crossed the threshold of the Dead Wood.

The eerily white wood of the Witch Wood trees, traced through with a luminescent black vein, called to him and he refused to answer that call. Decayed wood, decayed leaves, and mushroom's bounty reached his nose and twined about the back of his throat in a vile taint.

A dark castle, bright to the eye but dark to his spirit, rose suddenly out of the stark veil of the woods. The black leaves of the Witch Wood contrasted sharply with the pale luminescence of the marble and alabaster fortifications of the castle itself. The stark white of the Witch Wood stood paler than even the beech it resembled. Yet the castle itself was whiter than the wood. Whiter than the moonlight, and Bearskin had an uncanny suspicion that had there been snow it would have been whiter than the snow itself.

And yet all that whiteness seemed to cast shadow rather than light about him. The sun could not pierce those shadows. He doubted when the moon rose its honest and pure light would have any better fortune, for all its light fared better against illusion and deceit. The Sun was too straightforward. The moon understood that which was hidden and so could reveal it. He shook off his thoughts as his captor's path directed them to the castle.

"Such is the Keep of the Woods." The lordling had fallen back to where he could once more easily speak with Bearskin. When they entered the wood he had taken the lead. Gregor supposed he was the only one who could surely lead them to this keep. A thought to keep in the front of his mind, though it was the back of his mind that seemed to have the best reliability in this matter. Well better to use all of his mind just in case.

He let his thoughts natter along for the moment. Keeping them largely innocuous. If his captor could read thoughts... He cut that thought off and continued down the mental rabbit trails he'd been stalking. The castle itself looked to have been pulled out of the mountains that housed the Dead wood, from the stone of the mountains itself.

"It was," The man on the horse responded to the unspoken thought. "Though even I do not know who so commanded it. As far as I can tell it may be older than the Empire of Illysia."

Gregor started at that. "Before the War of Veils?"

"I see you are well read," There was a hint of mocking approval in the lordling's voice. "Sadly, I cannot show you some of the defenses this place has to offer. Your status as my prisoner protects you."

Gregor simply smiled at that and said nothing. Let the other man guess. The illusory eyes narrowed at him and Gregor focused on thinking of nothing at all or more, when nothing was truly impossible, the feel of the till under his hand. The smell of the freshly turned earth. The taste of fresh rain in the air. Filling all senses but sight with the past that never would be again. That past was buried and his captor could not harm it by plucking it from his mind.

The lordling looked away and gestured expansively to the castle. "Behold, Moonstone Castle. Here you will die, Master Bearskin, because I have no intention of releasing you."

Gregor threw his head back and laughed merrily. "Oh Master Traitor, another has been working his hand at my death for six long years. What makes you think you are more skilled at such things than he?"

"Who is this enemy of yours?" The lordling reined his horse in and they paused before the bridge though there was no moat, nor was their any stream to feed it here.

Gregor waited as the noise of the portcullis being lifted ceased to ring in everyone's ears. The party began to move into the courtyard and Gregor looked up at his captive. "My Lord. Are you sure you want the answer to that? You may discover you serve another master than you think for I have heard the echo of his voice in yours."

"I serve only my own will. Name your enemy and perhaps I will send him your head as a gift," the lordling bent down as the portcullis was dropped behind them.

"Old Scratch bid me live as you see these seven years. If you think you can best him be my guest. My own fate has yet to be judged. He does not have my soul yet, and neither will you my 'Lord'." Gregor set his eyes to the doors of the keep with great determination. "Neither will you."

Chapter 20
Captive of the Castle

The melody of birds drifted to his ears through the open window. Bearskin had been used to the woods, but the sheer volume of birdsong here seemed strange to him. His room was comfortable enough, the soft sheets, better than the homespun he'd lived with his life through. There were velvets on some of the cushions but he'd been courteous enough to the cleaning staff, poor beaten things, not to touch them. He knew what he shed, even with the rains that had kept him cleaner than he bet Old Scratch had counted on.

He breathed in the scent of lavender and rose. The rose from the open window. The tang brought back memories of Anna using the rose water from her own roses to sweeten some of the cooking when berries were not available, and the fresh scent of spring cleaning rosewater had been used to freshen winter stale blankets.

He breathed deeply and tried to relax. Relax. He hadn't relaxed since he had been in Argers with Isela's family. Before then? Before the war. He spent a fleeting moment to worry over Heinrich. Not that anything was likely to give that man trouble! But still they had been friends.

Bearskin set the thought aside as he always did. There was little he could do for Heinrich, and he had been determined not to draw the other man into his troubles and now? No, that was one decision that still stood. He would risk no soul but his own.

Voices drifted down the corridor and he held very still, this castle was strange. Nothing worked as it ought, and if the castle realized he was listening the trick of acoustics might end.

"I want the merchant ruined, Ambrosius, and you have failed in that," it was a voice Gregor didn't know, but then the other voice spoke in one he knew only too well.

"My Lord. I have done everything possible. Who could have predicted that our captive would have existed, much less come to the merchant's aid?" The name. the voice. they finally solidified in his head. Baron Ambrosius Hochritt. His own nominal liege lord, at least before the war and he had written off all vassals in conquered lands.

"Yet has our prisoner saved him, and the last of two artifacts needed have been denied me. Our bargain is not concluded. I will take charge of the prisoner, and you may go. See the Star Stone and the piece that was lost in the last Caravan are properly rendered. That is the only way you will regain your lands. Now go," The second voice commanded and Gregor could almost see the imperious wave of his hand.

He felt little sympathy stir in his heart for the lord that had cast him aside. All for having the ill fortune of being bound to lands that had been conquered. And yet, if he had remained bound he would not have had this chance at freedom. But that had not been of his Lord's motivations: to keep his vassals free of enemy control. He had simply cut his losses where he could. For that Gregor could grant him little sympathy.

He was surprised to discover there was little enough animosity there. His former Lord could go his own way and Gregor would be about his own business. They need not conflict. Though they need not align either. If his Lord chose otherwise, that was another matter.

He tested his memory and things shifted and flowed. The words of the conversation remained the same but the tenor of the voice shifted strangely. What magic was in this place that it could tamper with even his memory? He leaned back, the cold stone of his prison room grounding him. That sense did not shift as he sifted through his memory. The tones change in his recall and in this matter he trusted his Gift over his senses. There was fear in Baron Hochritt's voice and a menace he did not understand in the other. Who was the other voice?

That was where the secret lay, he was certain of it.

"Master Bearskin?" A voice sounded at the door to his make shift prison.

"Who calls the cursed?" Gregor answered. Let them wonder at that for now.

"The master of this castle would have words with you." There was a note in the man's voice Gregor had heard often in the servant's voices here and he considered his response.

Rising from the bed he came to the door and opened the small window that allowed the occupant to view any servants that might be coming. "The master of the castle or your master?"

"They are the same." There was a note of anguish in the man's voice and Gregor nodded.

He held the blue eyes of the man for a moment then smiled, almost in pity. "Tell the master of this castle I am currently at his disposal having nothing else pressing, and..."

He hesitated. "If you can receive something under the door?"

The man, a relatively normal sort for this region. Middle brown hair, blue eyes, skin darkened by sun rather than breeding, nodded once and tried to keep astonishment out of his voice. "I can. My Lord?"

"Then this is for you, for your duty, with no strings attached. You and yours have been kind and generous to me here." They had been seeing to his slovenly self with rare dispatch and courtesy.

He pulled three pouches from his pack. He'd been collecting them over his years of wandering and filled them with a handful of coin each. All silver. Less difficult for such as this servant to explain than gold. Though more difficult than copper. "They come under the door. One is for you and you alone. Do with the others as you see fit. You and the staff of the castle have been kind to me. I would return that kindness."

The man pulled the pouches from under the door and looked up in astonishment. "My Lord."

Bearskin shook his head and smiled. "No. Trust me in this matter. And if you, as everyone else I have gifted seems to say, want to do something for me. Please, pray for me. I am in sore need. Here and now and deep into the future."

The man nodded. "I must take you to my current master."

"I would ask nothing else. If you come free, there is a certain mer-chant in Argers who has a partner Master Bearskin." He shrugged and left the matter there. The man nodded understanding, then bowed and backed away from the door. Gregor did not expect to see him but it was a hope. And hope was all he had these days.

Chapter 21
DUELS OF WITTS

Gregor waited. His chair was leather and unlikely to be soiled beyond repair from the bearskin and, truth be told, himself. He was none too clean after these years even with the rains. For the first time in years he felt the grime. He smelled his own stink, redolent of rotting leather and unwashed human. He tasted the foul sourness of his own breath and saw the long and twisted claws that his nails had become. And yet, he was unconquered.

His enemy had gained a measure of control but he was yet himself and that could not be anything but a grief to his enemy. Time had passed. He had, he judged he had a year or so remaining. This place distorted his sense of time, but he had time. And time was on his side not his captor's.

The door creaked open and Gregor's grey eyes flicked upward. He did not rise, and the man who greeted him simply nodded. He was ordinary. Hues of brown, pale as the people on this continent tended to be, but otherwise disturbingly ordinary.

Gregor forced himself to stillness. If he were going to create a disguise this very sense of the ordinary was one that would suit. He thought of the Minstrel's bead and set the thought aside. This was not the time for that. Not yet. This was another's task. He did not know how he knew, but instinct had been his guide, and reason backed it. He would give away no more than he had to.

"You're a bold one. Why do you not stand in the presence of your betters?" The voice was aristocratic and polished and Gregor simply cocked his head to one side. Had the man really not disguised it? It was hard to tell.

Gregor smiled and looked up, only slightly up. The man was short especially for the lands of Almarc. "I have seen no evidence that I am in the presence of my better. I am in the presence of one of my captors but that does not make you my better."

"Oh really? If I could have caught you would that not make me your better?" The man smirked but it did not touch the man's eyes. Those remained cold and snake-like. Calculating.

Gregor stayed where he was. He felt the Bear stir, but did not respond to it. There was more to this than he was willing to put into words. Or even thoughts in this place. "No, it means you had a momentary advantage. I have seen war. It is not always the best general who wins. Sometimes the best general is simply surprised. Should you prove yourself my better I will acknowledge such, but when it takes two dozen spearman to capture a lone, unarmed man. I feel I can say with no reservation that I have not yet met my equal. Or do you think such as the normal balance of things?"

The man gave a bark of laughter, though it seemed feigned to Bearskin. He was not yet willing to call the man on it. Not yet. He would wait. The strangely nondescript features smiled at him. "No, they were simply there. I could have taken you with less. Would you care to dispute it?"

"I would," Gregor stood towering over the man. "What would you do to me here? What can you do my diminutive host? What is to prevent me from walking out that door?"

"There is the matter of my armsmen," The man showed no concern as Bearskin loomed more than a foot over his own height.

Gregor snorted. "Men you terrorize by you position who bear you no loyalty in the slightest. Do you think they would honestly support you if there was another who proved himself stronger?"

"Do you think yourself stronger?" The man asked and Gregor felt something shift about him. What, he could not say. He watched the man carefully, but gave no sign but wariness that he had felt it.

Gregor shook his head and chose his words with care. "Stronger than you? Perhaps. That remains to be seen. I have not tried your strength. Stronger than the man who brought me here, yes. Were it him or me,

I would win without hesitation. One on two dozen? Those are fools' odds. And I am not yet wholly a fool. Though I have had my moments."

"Oh really?" The man leaned forward as if he were truly interested in the response.

Gregor threw back his head and laughed. "Show me a man who claims he has never had a moment of folly and I will show you either a liar or a fool. Which are you, my Lord? Liar or fool?"

The man glowered at Bearskin who simply regarded him steadily. He touched a spot on the wall and a panel slide aside, he took from the cubby that was revealed a carafe of wine, and two glasses, and smiled up at Bearskin. "Would you join me for a drink, Master Bearskin?"

"You first, my host," Gregor wasn't about to call the man 'my Lord'.

The nondescript man put both glasses on the table and poured from the pitcher. Something wavered about the edges of Gregor's vision but he couldn't quite catch it quickly enough to understand it. Then the man approached him, a glass in each hand. The distraction must have lasted long enough for him to put the pitcher down.

A mocking smile met him as he reached for the glass with one hand. The other fell to his lap near the pouch with the Minstrel's gifts. He felt the green stone warm and watched his host's features blur as they touched. A flash of another face was briefly visible, darkly aristocratic, then it was gone. But it bore little enough resemblance to von Neuen. They might be of the same people, but that was all that could be said.

Bearskin raised his glass and cocked his head at his host who sipped from his own glass. Bearskin considered, then took a drink of his own. If it was poisoned he would trust to the Minstrel's Gift. Perhaps, perhaps he would learn something.

Fire spread from his throat to his stomach. The glass slid from his fingers even as the pouch under the bearskin and greatcoat burned against his skin.

Bearskin awoke in the same room, flat on his face. The uneven softness of the carpet pressing into his cheek. Voices spoke about him, though he dared not pick his head up. He could smell wine, and his mouth tasted like he had been eating raw rat again. Though this time he didn't think he actually had been.

His memory supplied the rest. The Wine. His captor. One of the voices matched the nondescript man who seemed to command the castle. The other he did not recognize.

"Take him to a more secure room. I'll not have him somewhere he can readily escape from. He's strong enough to break many of the doors down." The voice of the nondescript man was no longer superior or condescending, but sharp and commanding. "If you can, strip him to the underthings."

"My Lord," The second voice, the one he did not know, spoke with what seemed to be great care. "You saw yourself that the bearskin would not come off. It is as if it is fused to his skin. And it laughed at our knives. Which mirrors the reports of those who survived his interference with your commands."

A foot tapped near his face, and Gregor cracked an eye open ever so slightly. The boot was well polished, and well made. He'd dreamed of owning such boots. Boots made to the wearer's foot not just cobbled together without regard to left or right foot, and only a general nod to the size. These even had proper hard soles for riding. He closed his eyes again, lest he be noticed.

"Secure him then. I do not like that my draught was as ineffective as it was. There is something else going on here. It stinks of other Powers, and I do not wish the Dead Wood to try and command or call on those Powers here. Only put my own guards on him, do you hear?"

The second voice was silent for some time. "I will have to use regular guards until such time as I can assemble your personal guard. They are currently scattered as you..."

"Of course I recall the errands I sent them on. I am not a fool like the idiot from Bayr, but by the time he wakes my own guards. Loyal guards. Must be watching him, do you understand?"

"I understand completely, my Lord," The voice was stiff, and Bearskin focused on keeping his breathing even. He'd never stayed in bear form long enough to try and hibernate, but if he could keep his breathing that way... Slower.

Footsteps resounded down the hall and hands grabbed each of his arms and pulled. He let them haul him to his feet, focusing on staying limp and unresisting for now. It was harder than he had expected.

The instinct to support his own weight was strong, especially with what they were doing to his shoulders, but he turned his mind away, focusing on a cave and a winter's rest. It was easier than it should have been.

Which meant whatever had been in the wine had been strong enough that it was still working.

He felt the thin leather of his boots, worn almost through in his trials, scraping on the floor. The men hauling him grunted and he inwardly smiled. There were some advantages to being as big as he was that he hadn't considered. The two men approached where Bearskin remembered the stairs being and laid him down.

He obligingly flopped where they left him and cracked an eye, taking in the room, and the men, at a glance. There was too much of this castle between him and the exit to make a run for it here so he made himself wait.

He'd become accustomed to waiting in the last ten years of his life. One of them grabbed him under the arm pits and the other grabbed his knees and both hauled. He hoped they didn't have too many flights to go as his back and posterior scrapped and occasionally bounce on the steps.

"Careful! His Lordship doesn't want him awake," the voice was lighter than the soldier's had been (Younger perhaps?) and unfamiliar.

"Bah, the draught the Lord gave him should have him out for at least a day, even at his size. Vice Fungus and Witch Water don't leave much room for mistake."

The unfamiliar voice let out a low whistle. "I'm surprised he's alive."

"His Lordship knows what he's doing when it comes to potions. Just you remember that. We've got to get him to the dungeon. At least what ever happens to him won't be our responsibility."

Bearskin felt the one holding his knees shiver at that. Then the unfamiliar voice spoke again. "No. We're not loyal enough for that, and for once I'm grateful. I don't want any part of that."

"Which is probably why we're not counted loyal enough. Bah, put him down here. I've the keys to the dungeon block."

Bearskin felt himself leveling out and then twisting around before being lowered. He counted slowly to five and then heard the jangle of metal clinking together: the keys. Then the scrape of one against something and a click.

"It's open let's..."

Bearskin tensed and lashed out with a hand knocking the unfamiliar voice, who was indeed the younger of the two, off his feet. Bearskin lept to his own, just in time to dodge a kick from the elder of the two. He reached out a long arm and relieved the man of the keys, while reaching out with the other to lift the youngster by his belt and heave.

The boy went through the dungeon door with ease and Bearskin sincerely hoped he hadn't killed him, but he had other concerns. The elder paused and glanced about.

"Shove lightly Master Bearskin... and good fortune in the hunt."

Bearskin hesitated then obeyed. He gave the man a shove. This time he heard the skitter down the steps, not many at all, and a complaint from the bottom. Taking a moment he re-locked the door. It would be inconvenient for them, but they were alive. Why had they let him go?

He set the thought aside and turned down the hall. If he could only find something familiar.

Chapter 22
Escapes

Gregor threw himself into an alcove and attempted to wedge himself between the statue it housed and the wall. He held his breath as heavy footfalls tromped down the hall in an approximation of unison. Echoing and reechoing. Dust clogged his nose and his mouth, strange and sharp. His nails dug into his palms as he held himself as still as he could manage. While there were advantages to his size in two on one, there were disadvantages when trying to skulk about and hide. Especially in a place like this.

No murmur of voices accompanied the footfalls, and another scent wafted into his little retreat. A cloying scent that was only too familiar now: witch wood flowers. He wouldn't have thought the Dead Wood would have so many, though witch wood tree was the only tree that would grow here. He had expected it to never flower in so cursed and corrupt a place.

He felt the pull of the magic, whatever thing it was the Witch Wood trees grew on and fed on and fed. It called to him. He dared not shift, but the bearskin about his shoulders felt five times its normal weight, heavier even than the day he put it on. Silence trickled by, echoing with the sound of imagined feet.

Gregor permitted himself a slow breath. One. Then two. Still no more feet came down the hall. He opened his eyes and stepped out into the corridor. For once he held the bearskin close about him. Heavy it may be, but it was a burden he could not be shut of. What profit a man if he escape the dungeon but lose his soul? He suppressed a chuckle at the thought.

Though.

Though. His feet moved even as he turned the new thought over in his mind.

One corridor. Left. Then two right.

The whole place felt like Scratch. The slick wheedling malignant feel. Two more left.

Was that what was wrong with the Dead wood? It certainly seemed to be what was reaching out for him.

Three steps down. A left turn.

He ducked through an open door as his ears detected foot falls. Dust and ash from lamp oil assailed his nose, but the room was unlit. He edged his way back into the room cautiously, and a hand clamped over his mouth. Gregor stepped back and ducked throwing his assailant off balance and forward. He had only a vague impression of a tall, lean form that bounced like some insane ball to its feet.

"Clever, but," The form shut the door with impossible silence. "I assure you unnecessary."

Flame sprang into being in the man's hand, for the figure was more or less male, though more beautiful than any man that Gregor had ever seen. "I have been waiting for you, or someone like you for some time now."

Gregor straightened and blinked. The stranger matched him inch for inch and the gracefully curved ears told him the man was either elven or Sidhe. What would they be doing here?

The man smiled and bowed. "You're as quick as I was told. As for why I am here, do you really want to know that?"

"Yes, though we've little time and others were coming," Gregor countered, keeping his voice low. Feeling every inch of the dirt and dust compared to the immaculate form of his assailant.

The man nodded understanding. "They will not hear us. I have Power enough for that, but I have a task I need your aid with, and you have no reason to trust me."

"Certainly not when you grabbed me from behind," Gregor pointed out. The carpet under his boots was thick and easy on the feet. There was a heavy wooden desk to his right and the door to his left. Little enough room for someone his size to maneuver, less for the bear to come out to play. Could he take a Sidhe here?

The man shook his head as if reading the thought. Who knew, perhaps he had. Gregor tried to think more quietly, but stilling his mind was not a skill he had ever excelled at.

That thought seemed to bring a smile to the man's mouth, this one merrier and less mocking than the last. "Yes, you are more hopeful than I had been led to believe, but I wouldn't have believed her if she'd told me the truth. Now, why are you here? Other than escape, you could have made that easily by now."

Gregor considered and stepped back to a more normal stance, if the man wanted to talk rather than fight he could at least do him the courtesy of hearing him out. "There are certain things stolen that are here. They should be returned to their rightful bearers."

The man nodded and frowned this time, though it seemed a frown of thought. "Then she was right indeed. I have something for you, guard it with your life and get it to the King. Not to your Merchant friend. I think your von Neuen is honest enough, but his family is not. He must understand this only goes to the King and none other."

Gregor's eyes narrowed. "The king of Bayr or Almarc?"

The man started, as if that had actually surprised him. Perhaps it had. "Why Almarc? Or do you want the war to start all over again due to that fool of a baron?"

"I've scores to settle with the baron myself, but I'd not see that war repeated. And my scores are secondary to other concerns," Bearskin didn't actually expect to exact the proper vengeance for the treatment his lord had meted out to the vassals who had fought and bled for him.

The man regarded him for a long moment more and then dug into his cloak, though where the pocket was Gregor couldn't tell. Knowing the fae, that was likely by design.

Gregor's hand flashed up instinctively and he caught a heavy bag. It clinked and clattered, surely not coins? No, it thrummed in his mind with Power. Was this? He cast the thought aside. This strange interloper might not be the only one who could read his thoughts.

"Clever man, now. Remember what I said. That goes only to the King, however you must get it there. Do not give it directly back to the merchant or it will be taken once more. There are traitors there much closer than he would find comfortable. Witting or no. Now." The man strode past Bearskin, or at least that was the feel. It seemed almost as if he was suddenly by the window, but Gregor could remember him passing, though he didn't remember seeing him pass.

"I will see it gets to the king. I have a guess who the unwitting traitor may be," The middle daughter if he was any judge, but that was a different trouble.

The man at the window simply nodded and touched the shutters which sprang open. He swung up onto the sill and Gregor found himself watching stupidly.

"Who are you?" Gregor asked as he cradled the precious bag to his chest.

The masked figure smiled as he stepped into the shadows, but his voice echoed as much in Gregor's mind as much as his ears. "Simply a superior Thief, my friend. Simply a superior thief."

Cool stone pressed against Gregor's forehead. The bear stirred, and he fought it down. It had never been so clear before. The need to barrel through these halls trampling everyone in his way, but that wouldn't get him out. That wouldn't get the parcel to the king. That wouldn't save anyone, least of all himself.

He could smell the forest. The back of his throat burned. Was that the Vice Fungus they'd drugged him with? Could that be why the bear was so hard to control. Why the rage was so close to the surface after so long silent?

He'd always had trouble with his temper, but never like this. He braced his back against the stone. The alcoves had grown fewer. That meant he was nearing the entrance but it made it harder to make any progress towards it. Patrols had increased as had ordinary foot traffic.

How long had it been? His time sense said only an hour since he had left the study, and yet the shadows had shifted dramatically.

It was the Dead Wood. Nothing was sane here. Possibly including himself, but he wasn't going to give in to that. Sane or insane he had a task. He would not give over. Not when life started to promise a purpose. If he could return these things...

He cut the thought off. The Elf had been able to read his thoughts, would anyone else here? He also dared not stop thinking entirely. The bear was too near the surface if he slipped...

He took a deep breath and listened hard. No one. Pushing out of the Alcove he made a dash down the hall. Dangerous if anyone was watching out of a door, but he was conspicuous enough that even a sedate pace would fool no one, not with the bearskin that was still his burden to bear. The hall dead ended and as he approached the cross-hall he heard steps.

Flinging himself backwards he pressed into a door way, closed, face to the door and the bearskin out. It was dark furred, and the wood was dark. Perhaps... just perhaps...

"Thankarat, what brings you this way, you're usually holding council?"

The voices seemed to be coming from the junction of halls. The first one was deep and amused, the second less so. "His Lordship has lost a prisoner. He resisted his Lordship's favorite poison and woke up a day early, took his escorts by surprise and locked them in the dungeon. Have you seen anything? He would be trying to escape though I suspect His Lordship has set the castle to confuse him and muddle the ways."

The first voice let out a low whistle. "No, I've seen nothing, but I've been back from my patrol only these last five minutes, and have just come from stabling my horse."

"Well, Dunstan, get back to your men, and get them assembled. If he makes it out of the castle we'll need to make pursuit and your unit is the only one back yet."

"Who was the prisoner that his Lordship is unwilling to simply leave him to the Dead Wood. Or does this one know its ways?"

Gregor held his breath and closed his eyes, focusing all his thought on the conversation behind him, committing it to memory voices, names, all. He set aside all thought of the wood pressing into his cheek. The splinter digging in to his finger and the smell of dust and horse coming from the hall, probably the man who'd just gotten back from patrol.

"It's that Master Bearskin fellow that has been a thorn in our side. Almost more than the younger von Neuen."

"Bah we have hooks in the man's father, even I know that. He's of limited threat."

"You may know it," Thankarat snorted and Bearskin thought he heard a tap on a breastplate. "But if the elder von Neuen even suspects, our agent is likely to die, and that will cause quite the disruption to his Lordship's plans. So keep the thought to yourself. More than the Elves can read minds, and just because most Gifts are being forgotten about doesn't mean they can't be used."

"Have you forgotten why I'm here and in his Lordship's service?" There was a bitterness in the man, Dunstan's, voice. "I will get my squad assembled. If he makes it out we will find him, though I'll be setting some others about here to making sure he doesn't make it through the gates."

"Very good, and don't forget what his Lordship has done for you. For all of us."

Bearskin could almost feel the threat in that statement. Done for them or to them? With Vice Fungus potions, Gregor wasn't willing to guess on that point, but...

He cut the line of thought off and focused on the hall. One set of boots sharply retreated, a second set of boots turned down his own hall and Gregor held his breath as he heard a scratch of a pen, then something fluttered and the boots once more walked away. Gregor gave a ten count and stepped back from the door, as he did his eyes flicked to the floor. A scrap of paper lay there in plain sight. Who had paper to leave lying about? Obviously whoever kept this castle had more means than simply the estate. He could have seen someone simply taking the place but this spoke of connections.

He picked up the sheet, written in charcoal, as the field messages in the war so often had been, were a few short phrases: Left corridor, second right. Small door by the stable. Tell the gate guard 'Tikwa'. He will let you through. Pray for us all.

Would that he could, but there were others he could. He knew the man's name and he quickly ducked down the corridor. So there were others here who shared his curse one way or another and were hoping to win through. Well if he could do aught for them he would, but first he had other tasks to see to.

Chapter 23

DANGER IN THE DEADWOOD

There was no smell in the Dead Wood, only a lingering sense of malignant decay and... absence. He had heard only a single bird since he had begun his journeys. After the snatches of bird-song he had heard in the castle he had expected to find some bird out here. Not so.

The woods were unnaturally silent. And not the silence that fell when clumsy men tromped their way through the wood and wild things hid. His throat was dry and that sense of decay clung to him.

He had not felt this watchful a silence even after a battle in those few moments before life went on when everything went still for just a moment. No, he glanced to and fro and darted to another tree. Not that hiding would do him any good here. The vice Fungus glowed faintly purple, and the leprously white trunks of the Witch Wood, white only here of all places in the world, glowed themselves from black veins of power.

He had heard many legends of the Dead Wood, but none seemed to say what it was. The pouch on his belt pulsed with power almost as if in response. But he had to keep moving. There was no cover here. Nothing lived enough to hide behind, especially for someone of his size. At least that meant he had some visibility and there had been no pursuit.

Not that any was likely to be needed to give him trouble. His eyes darted left and right and he struck west. The Dead Wood was on the border between the Halvarsand Empire and Almarc, but it was narrower east to west, so he would be more likely to come free this way.

He ignored the rumbles in his stomach. No one ate Vice fungus if they wanted to live life as anything but a toad and any stream he was likely to find here would be as contaminated and twisted as everything else.

He desperately wanted to pray, but he dared not. He would trust to the Minstrel's gifts. This was not the time for the bead though it felt close, but how?

He placed his feet carefully. The carpet of black leaves, undecayed as far as he could tell in spite of the smell and lingering malaise, was unbroken. He had already narrow avoided two places where the earth had collapsed into deep holes, and the leaves had completely covered the gaps.

He adjusted his course cautiously but when he glanced once more at the sun he found he was off from his course significantly. Was even the sun twisted and bent here? Or was it merely the appearance of the sun?

He recited his memories from the castle over in his mind. The light had been strange there, too. But if he could take no direction from the sun what could he take direction from? There was no road. The men who had brought him here had simply led him to the castle. The Woods had looked much the same to him. There was nothing for him to remember and recognize to find his way out.

But stopping was death, so he kept on. He would trust. Was this the fullness of his doom? He hoped not. He would not yield. He had promised Isela he would return to her. He had not returned in time for Anna, he would not allow that to happen again.

One step.

Two steps.

A dozen more followed. Step after step, ever seeking westward. He would not yield. What if he was going in circles? He lowered his eyes and did not look toward the sun. He held one hand slightly ahead of him. He would take his course opposite of his shadow.

What if he was wrong? He had much knowledge. His Gift meant he learned things easily, or at least learned information easily. He had learned very young that knowing a thing and understanding it were quite different.

Was this something he had failed to understand?

He admitted the possibility. The shadows grew longer and he quickened his pace. No one willingly spent the night in the Dead Wood. While there were no things that haunted it by day. Night was another story entirely.

Yet if he had to spend the night, well he would see if there was a moon tonight. The moon's light was more steeped in illusion than the sun's and oddly it revealed things that even the sun could not. Perhaps.

Perhaps.

He walked on and the sun sank lower and lower and his shadow grew longer. And then he found the truth of the saying: There was no twilight in the Dead Wood. For one moment the light was that of evening with at least an hour before the sun set and twilight began and then there was darkness. The full darkness of night.

He almost panicked. The bear reared up in his mind demanding control. He could track such things. His nose would lead them out and Gregor turned on the bear. This was not a place for such things. It was a trick.

Gregor clenched his fists and his filthy nails bit into his palms. No! He would not yield. he would not yield to the devil. He would not yield to the Master who tried to claim the Dead Wood. He would not yield to lords who abandoned their men. He would not, above all, yield even to himself. Not to that part of himself.

He knew his vices. He knew Wrath to be among them. And the bear seemed to feed on Wrath. He would. Not. Yield.

He opened his eyes once more, deliberately unclenching his jaw as the bear retreated once more into some part of his mind. The moon had risen while he fought his silent battle, and there in the blackness of the fallen leaves was threaded a silver path beckoning him on. He glanced up and the Whispering star stood in the sky, framed as the heart of the bear. He set his feet to that silver road.

S weet scents floated past him and Gregor's head snapped up. These were the first scents he had caught since leaving the castle: jasmine and rose and other flowers he did not recognize. He breathed deep of their sweetness, the heady intoxication flooded through him. The silvery path of moonlight had broadened to a highway, and before him lay a door of shimmering silver, blued by the moonlight. Runes gleamed brightly and on each upright of the door sat a nightingale, as silver as the door.

When he came within three of his own arms lengths of the door each nightingale raised its head and burst into song, a song he had heard before but could not wholly remember, which meant... He nodded to himself and stepped up to the door. Perhaps this was the way out? Perhaps? He did not think the Minstrel would trick him, nor that any could duplicate her music.

But the Runes flared to life as his hands reached for the door.

Enter here to find your doom
A path of hope or endless tomb.
Some be lost and some be saved.
Hope be all that sustains the brave.

Bearskin nodded slowly, well he knew he'd run risks here. He would not yield to whatever Veil was beyond this door either.

Yet he must go through it, or turn back and take his chances with the wood. Turning back had not been his way either. This did not seem, to him, to be the time to start.

Squaring his shoulder under the bearskin that seemed to try and drag them down once more, he put his hand firmly on the door. It sprang open before he could touch it and a swirling road formed on the other side. A road through impossibly green hills under a sky that seemed to be carved from lapis lazuli.

Once opened the door must be entered.

He stepped through from the hazy, shadowed gloom of the Dark Wood to that impossible sky.

The air curled about him with intoxicating perfumes. Rich regal roses, sweet jasmine, and a deep purple smell he had not smelled since childhood and the wisteria trees about the old mausoleum at the church had died. All mingled with a thousand smells he could not isolate and some he was sure he had never smelled before. But which Veil had he passed through?

He carefully followed the road. It was unwise to stray too far and that silver thread that had led him here seemed to follow the center of the road, bright as moonlight even in this day-lit land. Or perhaps not day-lit. His eyes swept upwards and the sky, while blue and bright and dotted with the purest of white clouds, seemed far closer than it ought, and not in the ways of clear days. As if it were simply painted.

Stooping he reached a filthy hand to the grass and ran his fingers over its smooth, silkiness. The rich tang of loam was missing and his hands could not penetrate that thick carpet. Indeed it seemed like a true carpet that only imitated grass. He had yet to see the flowers his nose told him were somewhere near. It was all green and blue as far as his eyes could reach, flat and calm.

Yet, he could not see as far as he thought he ought. Save straight ahead, it was like being in some great hall that simply echoed the real world. Which meant Sidhe, but unfriendly or ambivalent? And did it matter?

He stood once more and set his feet to the path this time watching warily left and right. He could see no seam in the sky or the grass, and did not dare look behind him, that was unchancy in Fae lands. Truth be told it was unchancy anywhere with or without power. Looking back could mean you gave an arrow time to gain, or could mean you spotted an enemy before he ambushed you from behind. Yet the Powers seemed to take looking back as doubt and weakness and for now it was not a path he would risk.

He thought to wish for a weapon, but he disciplined his thoughts, reciting some of the focusing exercises that the old priest had given him to use when his mind scattered in too many directions.

The sky rippled as if it were made of fabric and a breeze had passed over it. Curious. Had it responded to the thoughts? Possible. He tried to think more quietly though he had no notion how, focusing on keeping what he thought inside his own head. It was at least a profitable attempt, even if it failed. More profitable than speculation.

Pace after pace, mile after mile the road went on and on. It seemed to have no end. No change. Not even the scents. Perhaps it was an illusion?

The whole world seemed to ripple and the silver thread he had been following glowed almost too bright to look at as it cut the brilliantly painted scene in two and seemed to dissolve the pieces.

Bleak stone replaced grass and a dull sky like the rise of a thunderstorm, though Gregor could see no clouds nor any lightning. The air thickened and the scents of flowers turned cloying and sickening except, through it all, threaded the scent of the rose and the jasmine and the wisteria, faint, but piercing the sickeningly sweet poisoned air with a thread of life. Something here resisted. Perhaps this was not how this place was meant to be?

He drew his eyes down from that leaden sky and faced squarely ahead where a circle of stones glowed grayly in the ominous light. Brightness came from beyond them. Shifting and shimmering, casting odd shadows and seeming to be caught by the shadows. and Bearskin nodded to himself. Following the silver thread, he stepped into the circle itself.

Chapter 24
CIRCLES

"I have waited long for you." The dull, grey voice hammered at Bearskin's ears, even as his eyes cleared from blinding brilliance that the circle had inflicted on him. Here the scent of wholesome, sweet, if intoxicating, flowers grew stronger and, as his eyes cleared he saw before him a tall figure, lea, seeming neither male nor female. Impossibly thin and shrouded as if in shadows. Or perhaps it was made all of shadows.

Behind it, casting all the scattering light and overwhelming the dim light of the stones was a creature: sprightly, with huge cat like ears and a face that seemed to be merry, even as it looked up from its weeping. A cage of ebony imprisoned it and it seemed afraid to even touch the bars, or reach through to touch the faintly luminous stone pavement.

"I am sorry to have disappointed you. But what has that small one done to be so caged?"

The little creature looked up and shook its head, its ears flopping from side to side as it did so, almost comically. It waved its arms before its face as if trying to warn him off. Gregor filed that away for later.

"It has trespassed and will not yield its control as one who has trespassed must." The shadowed being answered and he felt its regard turn more fully to him. Though the thing didn't seem to have a face, only a shadow under the cowl without even eyes. Or if it had eyes they did not glow as he would have expected.

Gregor folded his arms. "Trespassed where and by whose authority do you enforce that law?"

"This place is mine now. This one therefore trespassed," The gray voice said soothingly and Gregor saw the tendrils of shadow reaching out to him and held up a hand.

"You have no power over me. I am a guest in this place, a traveler seeking only hospitality and directions, not to impose."

The shadows hesitated and stopped short of him. Hospitality laws were sacrosanct to the Fae... and they knew how to twist them, but he would do what he could.

"You are welcome to the hospitality of my house, stranger, but mind you do not violate guest right, or you will suffer the fate of this creature. Worse, as I see you stand in conflict with my master." The Shadow gestured to the bearskin. "Give first your guest name."

"I am called Bearskin," Gregor said with a smile. And the shadow turned sharply towards him, but made no reply. Two could play the game of truth and misdirection.

"Very well, Bearskin, please leave while I deal with this problem," and the shadow swiveled to face the cage, jumping from shadow to shadow, each space cast by one of the bars of the cage. So truly a shadow creature then.

Bearskin's hand fell to his pouch and he nodded to himself. "My Host, I must ask, as a stranger here, what control must this stranger yield? I would not commit an offense that would require such a forfeit of myself."

He stepped forward, standing in one of the broader patches of light where no shadows touched. The figure spun at him and hissed. "I was invited in, those who invite me in give me hold. He must surrender the last of his hold on this place. He invited me so this place is mine."

"I see," said Gregor thoughtfully, "I have no place to invite you my Host, yet it would seem he has also invited me. I passed through the door, and it swung open of its own will. Does that mean it is also my place?"

The shadow drew itself up to a towering height gathering the shadows of the place to itself, yet avoiding the faint light of the standing stones. Gregor nodded to himself. His hand slipping into his inner pouch and grasping one of the objects there. It was time for this.

"It is my nature to take that which I am invited to. It is not in your Laws, human, nor the bargains you have made to give you power to steal my Lawful dominions," The voice echoed and re-echoed from every shadow. Gregor held up one hand and inclined his head, as if in apology.

"Then would you accept a guest-gift as a reconciliation? I invite you to take it, though only it I may give." He opened his hand and on it lay a carved Delmin bead. "These are symbols of reconciliation, among other things, amongst my own people."

"You give me part of yourself? Excellent." The creature reached forward to the edge of the shadow and Gregor extended the bead into its reach and out of the light. The fingers of shade closed about it, and the bead flared.

"What? Have you no idea what you have done?" The shadow flung itself backward, striking the light and then shattering as the bead flared in its hand, driving all darkness away.

Brighter and brighter it glowed until there was no place of shadow in the whole of that small kingdom and the scream of the shadow creature had faded to nothingness in the light.

Spots danced before Bearskin's eyes and when he opened them, the world had changed once more. Neither painted greenery nor desolate shadow land met his eyes, instead an over grown and tangled garden wilted before him, solidly real at last. Wisteria, rose, and jasmine tickled his nose and the flowers nodded at him, even as the leaves drooped and sigh over their archways and trellises. The air tingled about him as if in a thunder storm and he felt the coppery charge of electricity in his mouth, yet the lightning never struck and the thunder never peeled.

He turned towards the little creature in the cage and knelt by it. "Will iron harm you? I must cut these bonds somehow."

"No iron scores on flesh of light. I do not fear the metal's bight. Cut away, my bonds to rend, and I shall ever call you friend!" The creature's ears flopped in time with its little sing-song rhyme. He took in the appearance of the creature fully for the first time. Rolly-polly body and graceful arms and legs, like nothing he had seen on a living creature. Huge head, almost as big as its body and seemingly made of two big eyes that looked up at him merrily.

Its little mouth smiled at him and he found himself smiling back. Those almost catlike ears twitched upwards as he drew his knife and flopped to the side as it turned to watch what he was doing.

The chords were tough and the knots strong, but they were of common rope. The little creature, surely it was some sort of fae, must not have been as strong as the faerie were wont to be or it could have burst the cage. But his knife made quick work of the ropes and the door swung open.

"Thank you friend, my freedom for. You have opened up the door. Here then I will grant a boon, what would you then be shown?" The creature crawled out and two tiny wings he had not seen fluttered, and it rose into the air, scattering light in every direction. The light seemed to dance about it tangling and untangling. No weaving and spinning, only in more fanciful patterns than Anna had ever managed.

"I have come this way seeking the truth of the bandits that have plagued Almarc. I know my own lord served their master. It seems to center around the merchant who carried various precious artifacts, yet I cannot read this mystery," Gregor shrugged. "My own fate rests in my hands, but I have reason to care for the merchant and his family and would ask you tell me anything that would help them."

The creature cocked its head this way and that, almost as if it were distressed. "It is no easy thing you ask. A shadow lies upon this task. Your thought is right, the truth is bound in the merchant's plight. Do not look to present day. The past it is that guides your way."

"You are fae indeed do you all speak in riddles?" Gregor asked, folding his arms in front of him. The creature spun merrily but settled in front of him.

"I speak in riddles as I must do. Yet, I would relieve my debt to you. That which you seek can still be found, through bargain's end beneath the ground." The creature flew about him inspecting him carefully.

"The larger truth is not for you. Others must see that task through. Tell the New Lord and the Maid. 'A mother's plight, a soul betrayed.'" The creature's head snapped up and a rumble shook the ground. Urgency entered the sing-song little voice.

"Now with that you must leave. Or to this place you will ever cleave. I would spare you that dire fate, so leave with blessing before it's too late."

And light spun about him and twisted and twined and he found fabric in his hand, but the rumble in the ground increased and he turned towards the path he had followed here. Only to find the flowers no longer wilting, but rather growing towards the path at an alarming rate. Dropping his dignity he ran, long legs pounding the ground, and his feet protesting the treatment as stones cut into them. But he ignored them. Would the door be there?

Vines thick with roses and thorns curled about him, and there was a hissing voice in their depths that he did not understand, could not risk the time to understand. It called to him, begging, threatening. He shook them off. They could not seem to grasp onto the bearskin so, for once, he pulled it more tightly about him. Hearing the snarl of his bear in his ear, he ignored that too. He didn't have time to shift. Now where?

There! he veered slightly to his left as the greenery obscured the path, but the door had not yet been barred though wisteria grew up over it. Jasmine bushes lunged in front of the door and Bearskin lowered his shoulder and bolted through, the vines twining around his ankles and his arms, and he wrenched free and plunged into the door.

Chapter 25
TWISTS OF TIME

Black leaves shifted under his shoulder as it hit the ground and the scent of the flowers cut off as if they had never been. Gregor rolled to his feet and the dim, eerie light of the Dead Wood met his eyes.

No wind blew. No leaf rustled. Silence ruled. And yet... the dimness did not. He looked down at his hands and held up the cloth thing that the light sprite had woven for him.

A cloak, a long cloak of shifting sunset hues fell before him with a soft swish of fabric, loud in the immense silence. As it unfurled, the lazy scents of summer flowers drifted out of it to wrap around his soul.

He closed his eyes against the dimness and breathed in that scent, feeling the smooth softness of the fabric, unlike anything he had ever touched. He stroked it with a single finger and, to his surprise, the dirt simply shed off of it did not exist. Perhaps it didn't. Perhaps it was truly made of the sunset. Gregor did not know. But he folded it carefully. And folded it. And folded it. And folded it yet again. Until it was the size of a gentleman's folded handkerchief and weighed nothing more than that. He tucked it in the same pouch that held the Minstrel's green stone.

Had she been the "she" the thief had spoken of? Thinking of that he checked the inside of his shirt and relaxed as he felt the warm pulse of the power against him. Hopefully it would be enough. Hopefully. If he could get out of the Dead wood in time. If he could find von Neuen. If. Too many ifs. Why did he feel his time was so short? He should have until spring, but there were no stars in the Dead Wood to give a sense of time, only dim light that pretended to be from the sun, and black night lit only by the fungus.

He shuddered. Best to be gone before that! Something tickled his ear, and he looked about. Nothing. Again, then he realized it was not a physical touch, rather it was a sound. The wood had been so silent it seemed strange to hear, and it took him a moment to identify it: A thrush, singing its lonely heart out. Without thinking his feet started towards the sound.

Could it be a trick? Possible, but he had little to lose. He was, as far as he could tell, no where near the clearing with the door and there hadn't been a single bird in this wood since he started his journey. He had little to lose. Though he'd been there before.

He took a deep breath and simply followed the sound. The branches of Witch Wood trees seemed to stoop low to catch him, though at his height they did not have far to stoop. They pulled at the bearskin he wore and he reached a hand up to keep it firmly on his shoulders, quickening his pace.

He trod vice fungus under his booted feet and a foul stench assaulted his nose and drew his eyelids down. He shook himself and pushed on. He must keep moving. The thrush's song chattered on, almost an invitation, though Bearskin... Gregor doubted the invitation was for him. He'd rather be turned out wherever the thrush was, than stay here waiting for his fate to come to him.

For the first time, nettles and thorns rose to block his way and he pushed through them, though, as in the world beyond the door, these sought to twine about him. As there he pushed on, dragging the bearskin down. Then he thought of the little sprite's gift. Once more he drew the cloak out of his pouch and slung it over the bearskin robe.

The nettles and thorns recoiled, and the thrush's song rose. Gregor lengthened his stride. He dared not run. Those who ran from Powers were caught by them and he did not wish to give the Wood any more power over him than he must. Vines coiled down to try and catch his head, shying away from the cloak but the rest of him was, apparently, fair game.

He ducked away from one sudden loop, shuddering at the noose-shape it made. He didn't have time to ponder where these came from. He must keep on. he must not let them slow him. Surely he was getting close. He must be. It seemed like hours since he had first heard the thrush. Perhaps it had been for now the thrush was joined by another song: the nightingale. Evening. Evening must have fallen.

Yet, he still dared not run. To run was to be hunted. To run was to yield to the pursuer. He would not yield. He would not yield. Another sound assailed his ears: a low growl, like a wolf only deeper and more savage. So that was the form his doom would take. Well the wolves would find him no easy task. Not even spirit wolves or the great black wolves who were as cunning as men.

A flicker of light caught his eye and he slightly altered his course. It didn't seem to be a mote the way the Charwood of Riola was supposed to have, nor a fairy light. It was a warm light and he made for it.

And suddenly found himself under the clear sky with the setting sun a bit to his right and a broad plain before him.

G regor closed his eyes against the impossible green and breathed in the rich, free, spring air.

Spring? His eyes snapped open once more as he took in the verdant landscape before him. the road and the sparse tree trunks were the only brown before him. A thousand shades of green, birches bordering on gold. Fresh-leaved oaks, bright and joyful, not dark and cool as they would become in summer. He took a moment to fold up and carefully store the spun light cloak, and started to jog down the road, taking it in. He must find out exactly where he was and when.

If it was spring, had he missed? Was he late? How much time had he lost in the Dead Wood?

Bird songs chirruped at him, a few of the day song-birds chirruped sleepily and found their nests. The Nightingale sung on, and seemed to argue with one of its harsher voiced cousins a few bushes down. His eyes swept the road, alert now for any sign of trouble. Was this why they had let him go? Or was there some other mystery behind it? If months had passed, why not years? Yet if years had passed he felt certain he would have had Old Scratch calling by now. Or at least waiting for him when he won free of the woods.

"I'm right here, my friend," The familiar wheedling voice. "You're late."

Gregor shook his head. "No. You're early. I'd judge it's not near enough summer for our meeting."

There was a good bit of bluff in him, but he hadn't backed down before he wouldn't back down now. Old Scratch threw his head back and laughed. "Very well, I'll give you this round, but you've little enough time to get to Nevahs for our meeting. So what will it be? The Kingdom or your soul? Start the war again or be mine forever? Or do you think you can make it to Nevahs from here in a bare two weeks and still get those baubles to the King before the War starts all over?"

Gregor's eyes narrowed, "We shall see Old Liar. You've lied before, why would you not be lying now to get me to abandon my quest?"

Old Scratch shook his head and caught hold of the bearskin carrying them both aloft well above the land. "Behold the Armies of Almarc Assemble. I can fly you to Bayr if you desire to see their forces."

Below him arrayed in tent upon tent, row upon row was a military camp, bigger than any he had had the misfortune of being in during the war. Perhaps this is what they would have looked like all assembled in one place? Gregor didn't know. But he could count. He also wasn't going to do that with his currently company. He felt a tremor through the Devil's arms and nodded to himself.

"I don't need to see Bayr's forces. I know their army well enough," Gregor said keeping his voice as calm as possible and trying very hard not to think about what would happen if the Devil let go.

"So you do. Now, what do you propose to do? Your von Neuen is out chasing my bandits every which way he can. He'll be of no help and the King is, himself, a month away. You'll never be able to do both. Even if you give in to the bear and let him run for you."

So he knew about that. It was good to know. Gregor watched the camp to the last as the Devil lowered them through the sky and back to the ground. Gregor straightened and turned upon Old Scratch, surprised to be looking the man in the face. He hadn't looked anyone in the face in years, not without craning his neck downward and them craning up. He didn't remember the Devil being so tall.

"So, Gregor Bearskin, who would try and rob me of my due, you have a choice before you. You have two weeks before our meeting in Nevahs. Nevahs is a week north of here. The King a month south. What path do you choose?" Old Scratch leaned upon his staff and smiled like a nasty little boy.

Gregor closed his eyes and took a deep breath. His doom indeed. Odd that it should come in spring with the life returning, and the scent of the earth in his nose, and the taste of the future in his mouth. But was there really any choice?

What profit a man if he saves his soul, yet those he cared for forfeit life and possibly their own souls? The castle had showed him at least one enemy, a hidden foe, was doing much as the Devil did. He had long determined he would hazard no souls but his own.

Yet could he truly prevent this war? Would the King even let him into the court as he was? If he met the Devil, perhaps he could solve the rest of the riddle. Perhaps. There was a way around this. Perhaps he could use what the Devil would give him to gain an audience and end the war before it became too deep?

He felt the powers beneath his shirt. And the lesser powers that had been gifted to him. And still more his own small Gift. A memory of a garden, and a memory of the poor light sprite. No. That sort of trickery was the Devil's game. He would not play it the Devil's way. He would warn the King and then would see to his own soul whatever that fate might bring. He opened his eyes and looked the Devil full in his spiteful face.

"Old Scratch. Go to Nevahs. I have work to do, and we shall see what we shall see in this game of yours. But be warned. Even if you win this bargain, I am Delmin, and we have never been easily led or controlled. Have a care. Now, I have work to do."

And Gregor turned his back on the Devil and continued down the road.

Chapter 26

CAMPS AND CONSPIRACIES

The clean scent of pine permeated the little copse Bearskin had taken refuge in. It had taken a day to get near the camp he remembered and he smiled. The Devil apparently hadn't counted on his Gift, or hadn't thought it would make a difference. Well, the more the fool he.

He breathed in the pine, the sap sticking to the back of his throat, yet it was preferable to the alternatives. Living and fresh, unlike the mud-trampled monstrosity of a battlefield.

His fingers dug into the dirt. They were dirty enough there was no worry of making them dirtier, feeling the rich loam of the ground. It was good land here. Good land. Worth saving. He only hoped Old Scratch wouldn't try and use him to undo all the good returning these things to the King would do.

He shoved away from the tree and stood. There was far still to go. He couldn't afford to rest for too long. His body ached. He had no idea when he slept last. He hadn't since the Dead Wood. But even he would have to sleep soon, and better that he should make the camp. Even if they threw him out it was safer on the fringes of the camp with the followers, than out in the wilds. The bear called him, had been calling him since Old Scratch had left.

He would not change again. Not until this business was concluded. Perhaps it would not be a difficulty once he was shed of the bearskin. He set the task aside and put one foot down on the hard packed dirt of the road, and then the other. One foot in front of another. He had yet a very long road to go.

Horses! Hooves pounded on the dirt surface of the road, though Gregor couldn't see them around the curve of the little wood. He stopped where he was and simply waited. Better to be out in the open if they should be soldiers. Spies do not walk up to camps openly. Nor do enemies typically travel alone when facing armies.

A mounted troop came around the bend a moment later in a well-ordered formation. The man at their head was unfamiliar. Little hope that it could have been von Neuen, but he had other cards to play. The noble held up a hand and reined in his own mount to stop the troop. "Stranger, this is a poor place to be wandering."

"I am not wandering, my Lord. I am here seeking someone." He had secured the artifacts more carefully about his person, though he hadn't dared risk securing them to either the great coat or the bearskin. Who knew what would happen then? "I've no quarrel with Almarc nor am I seeking one."

"Then are you not of Almarc? What is your name stranger?" The man leaned forward and nudged his horse, which trotted forward though only a few places, snorting and stamping as it scented the bear.

"I am called Master Bearskin. It is a name known in some parts of Almarc, and some parts of what once was Bayr. I stand as a Free Man beholden to no master, neither have I sought to become master over others. I would go my own way," Gregor answered carefully, now it wasn't only the fae who spoke in riddles, but he wasn't sure who knew what about him.

The noble's eyes narrowed. "I have heard of Master Bearskin, but he went missing in the fall and none have seen nor heard from him since. Perhaps you could enlighten us on what became of him?"

"The bandits I sought with one of your lords had more help than expected. Even I have difficulty when I am the one ambushed by a dozen spearmen not doing the ambushing," Gregor said wryly. "As for where I have been: the Dead Wood. Though where within it, not even my Gift could say."

The man let out a low hiss and nodded once, reining his horse around. The beast was only too glad to get away from the scent of bear. Gregor didn't even try to hear what he discussed with his men before one, an older man with what looked to be sergeant's rank on his shoulder, trotted forward. His horse was no more pleased to be near Gregor than the other, but also seemed to take it more in stride.

"If you will come with me, Master Bearskin, I will show you to the command tent, while the patrol continues. I hope, for your sake, you're more forthcoming with the commander than you have been with us. He is not a patient man, nor does he tolerate games when it comes to battlefields. Bayr has stolen a march on us without declaration. Claiming, after the fact, we have unjustly accused them without evidence." He shrugged.

Gregor nodded. "Lead and I shall follow. I can keep up as long as you do not go above the trot. I will tell you commander what I may, but I fear my message is for your King."

The sergeant gave him a long measuring look. "May the Whispering Word have mercy on your soul."

Gregor shrugged. "Pray for me. I have long needed it.

Creaking wagons, and the musty smell of tents and mud and under it all the smell, almost more a taste, of the powder as they passed the powder wagon. All were only too familiar. It seemed that army camps were much the same no matter which side they were for.

His eyes swept the neat rows of undyed canvas, more gray than white from dust and wear. His guide stayed mounted and the Horse seemed to have become accustomed to him. Sounds of work parties and hammers on tent pegs rung in his ears. Many curious glances were directed his way, but no shouts. No calls... the army of Almarc was disciplined. He gave them that. Perhaps they hadn't called up the levees yet?

It was possible. Levees were always unchancy things and it was planting season. Taking hands away from the land at this time of the year was a good way to starve your people through the winter, then where would the war effort be?

He turned his thoughts to his guide. The man was of somewhat muddy shades, middle brown hair with just enough blond to look off, muddy eyes that were more or less brown but had their moments and flecks of blue. He only came up to Gregor's shoulder, but was broad and strong and most telling, didn't seem to be particularly worried about anything Gregor might attempt. Which meant he was either a fool or very, very good.

His guide navigated him through the rows of tents to a cluster of larger tents with a wide space next to them. One of the big tents would be the mess tent unless he missed his guess, and the delightful scent of something cooking tantalized his nose. He firmly instructed his stomach to mind its own business. He'd eat somewhere sooner or later. Probably later, which was his stomach's complaint. It was always 'later'.

They stopped before a single large tent with a piece of heraldry that Gregor did not recognize: a Winged sword on a scarlet field. His eyes narrowed as he saw the crown encircling the sword. Surely not!

"Your Highness, we encountered a stranger on the road. He did not hide from us, but said he had business with the king." The sergeant bowed formally. "He is called Master Bearskin."

"Well done, sergeant, if you are hungry, I'm certain the cooks will find you something to ease your hunger." The voice was a firm tenor, light seemingly young to Bearskin.

Gregor ducked under the tent flap (none of them were made for his height. Not one.) And the sergeant followed, quickly getting between Bearskin and the crown prince, for the king of Almarc had only one living child, much less son, as far as anyone knew, and letting an unknown of Bearskin's outward condition too near him was ill advised.

The prince simply watched them both and smiled with amusement. "Unnecessary, sergeant. I have heard of Master Bearskin and I see the ring."

Here the prince nodded his head with its honey brown hair at Bearskin, and smiled, though his blue eyes were speculative. He was tall for Almarc, lean and Bearskin could see muscle under the fine silk tunic he wore, an odd contrast. Maps were strewn about the table, and the familiar and comforting scent of inks and parchment and even paper wafted past him.

"Your Highness, surely you have heard the other tales of the man as well?" The sergeant glanced from the prince to Bearskin.

"I most certainly have," The prince snorted. "But somehow I don't think here, in the heart of the camp, we shall be set upon by bandits though assassins are more likely. He doesn't seem to change into the bear of the tales without proper provocation and I intend to offer him none. Now, go. You have done your duty and I am grateful, for that and for your concern."

The sergeant bowed stiffly and glared at Bearskin. Gregor decided that he would prefer to be set upon by Baron Hochritt's men again than discover what the sergeant would do to him if something happened to the prince. But the man left and the prince seemed to relax. "They think I am too young and brash for this."

Bearskin nodded in understanding and took a single step forward before going down on one knee. The prince's sword hand twitched as Gregor approached. Not so much the fancy he was pretending to be. The prince's smile broadened. "Perceptive man."

"I shall have to think more quietly about you, your Highness. There have been enough people lately who seem to be able to read my thoughts." It came out sourly, though Gregor had intended it as a jest. The prince eyed him speculatively.

"I have little time to spare for you, Master Bearskin, but I have heard much of the good you have done us, so you have some time to make your case. If you cannot. You will be fed, and allowed to stay the night before being sent on your way, provided you do not go towards Bayr." The Prince's tone was hard, and all the humor dropped from his voice. His blue eyes were cold and Bearskin stiffened.

"I have a message for your father, and something to give him. Something that may help in this war, though I did not know of it when I acquired these things." Gregor began slowly. "But I think it must be done in secret."

"I am listening," the prince said cautiously. "If you wish to lay the object or objects in question on the map table, please do so, but do not reach for a weapon."

"I have no weapon on me, your Majesty. I have never learned the sword and spear and staff even I cannot hide," Gregor pointed out. "But I must reach into my shirt, will you trust me enough not to assume there is a dagger there?"

The prince nodded once and Gregor pulled out the package the thief had given him and laid it on the map table. The Prince's brow furrowed as Gregor unwrapped it. Four objects lay there, shining with both jewels and gold as well as sheer raw power. The prince gasped.

"Where did you find these?" He leaned forward over the table, within easy reach of Bearskin's hands, caution obviously forgotten.

"I was given them by a man who simply said he was a superior thief. They were originally in the possession of one Baron Hochritt of Bayr and another man whose identity I could not discover," Gregor answered.

The prince nodded and leaned back, considering. "There is one missing, or one part missing of this one. Without it our evidence is incomplete, but still damning. Can you come to the court and make your case?"

Gregor paused then frowned. A piece missing? The little rhyme from the light sprite ran through his head. "That which you seek may still be found through bargain's end beneath the ground."

"What was that?" The prince leaned a little further forward, trying to catch the muttered words.

Gregor shook his head. "I think I may know where the final piece is. But I do not think you will be able to find it."

The Prince frowned. "Where?"

"Nevahs, which was once beholden to Baron Hochritt," Gregor said simply. "But I would not go there if I were you."

"Why?" The Prince asked simply.

"Because the Baron's men may be there looking for that piece. I have business there myself." Gregor trailed off, coming to his own decisions. It might be too late already, but this was worth doing even if the Devil got his due in the end. "Let me get it for you."

"What business have you there?" The Prince's eyes narrowed.

Gregor fingered his ring. "Let us simply say that seven years ago, a man named Gregor von Nevahs returned to his burned home, cast aside by the lord who no longer controlled his lands. That man must deal with the consequences of the folly of desperation. Should he see through I may be able to retrieve your artifact. Do you know what it looks like?"

The prince considered him for a moment then nodded slowly. "It is the simplest of them. A rod of iron in the shape of a nail. Only this nail is nearly a foot long. Along its length runes are carved in an unknown language."

Gregor blinked and then frowned. "I think I know what you speak of. If I am able I will return it to you."

"Bring it to my Father's court in one month's time. There has been a tribunal called to hear Bayr's case against us. These will help our cause there, but where was the Baron hiding them?" The prince turned the subject to the safer matters of the artifacts themselves, though Gregor saw the speculation in his eyes. Well. Let him speculate.

"What day is it? And month?" Bearskin asked, restraining the urgency.

The prince started. "The seventh of plowing."

Bearskin suppressed an urge to swear. Old Scratch *had* lied, if only by a few days.

The prince seemed to read or guess his dilemma for he waited with a strange patience.

"That question is best to be answered in the tribunal you mention. If I succeed, a man by the name of Gregor Bearskin will come to court with that object. You will know him because he will be wearing this." And Gregor pulled from his pouch the cloak of spun light.

The prince's eyes went wide. such a thing was heard of but the knowledge of such crafts was only held by the elves and the Sidhe. "I do not think there can be two such cloaks in even twelve kingdoms. Will the ring be the same?"

"It shall." Gregor acknowledged, "but if he is to come to court I must leave soon. It is far to Nevahs and my time is short."

"Can we give you no aid?" The Prince asked.

"No, I would endanger no one but myself in this. My enemy is not one who can be defeated with sword, spear, or lance. But if you are willing I would indeed accept the hospitality of a meal. I do not know when last I ate. I was long in the Dead Wood."

"The Dead Wood is tied up in this? No wonder it has been so difficult to unravel. Come Master Bearskin. I will have someone show you to the mess tent. Meanwhile I will see that none see these objects but myself. It is best if no one know of them until my father chooses his time."

Gregor bowed deeply and rose from where he knelt, folding the cloak while the prince secured the artifacts, and hiding it in his pouch once more.

Chapter 27
Trails of Trials

Bearskin threw himself flat in the dirt as the patrol thundered past. He could smell the horses and the men cursed as the horses veered wide around him. They could smell him as well. Dust filled his mouth and he spat it out once the patrol was clear. War indeed.

The deeper he pushed into the conquered lands, the more and more patrols he had encountered. None of them were levees. Where had Bayr gotten so many troops? They were all darkly complected, at least for the region. Ishani Mercenaries perhaps? Surely not Halvarsand? Surely Bayr would not be so mad.

But where they came from was of less consequence than the effect they had had on his pace. What should have taken him an easy week had stretched into nine days. He had heard the last patrol talking about how long they had been here. If he hadn't gone to the camp... But if he hadn't gone to the camp, Almarc wouldn't have had even the evidence it had. No. He would simply have to find a way.

He once more started edging through the woods, grateful that these seven years had given him skills he had never before needed to acquire. Now he must use all his skill not to be caught before he could get to Nevahs and deal with what he found there. He dared not touch the bear which had been growing more and more insistent as he approached Nevahs. Or was it as he approached his deadline?

Which ever was the truth he had little choice in this matter. No, that was not true. He left himself little choice in this matter. He could accept defeat, but after so long he would not give over simply because the road was difficult. He wormed his way through the brush freezing in place as another patrol thundered down the road, obviously not watching for those skulking in the shrubs and berry bushes. Where had they all come from? And where was von Neuen? He should have been in these lands, but there was no evidence of him or his patrol. Had they been pulled back while he was in the Dead Wood? It was possible.

Another few yards bought. Another cluster of shrubs. No more patrols. He glanced upwards and saw an owl blinking down at him in disgruntlement. Given the hour he didn't blame the beast. He would need to sleep himself soon. Too little sleep was had in enemy territory. Enemy. Many changes indeed for him to think of Bayr as the enemy.

A footfall sounded near to his outstretched hand and he froze in place.

"Captain, what makes you think there is a spy out here?" The voice was young and weary, but obviously of some influence or he wouldn't question a superior.

"I told your Lordship that this is where your witch said the trouble would come. If you would know more. Ask her not I. But I see nothing to raise her alarm," the second voice was gruffer, and more worn. It seemed older to Bearskin and he carefully listened not daring to so much as twitch.

A snort sounded from the direction of the first voice. "I sometimes wonder about that woman, but she is a perilous one to disregard, especially on things which have been put her rather than things she has simply Seen."

A pair of boots appeared in Bearskin's vision and slightly to his right, the direction the older voice came from. "All Powers are to be handled with care, your Lordship, whether wielded by mortal or immortal, or operating on their own. It doesn't make them always right."

"I know, but..." The speaker seemed to shake himself. "Perhaps we are off from the location this patch of woods isn't big let us try further back."

And the feet stamped off. Bearskin relaxed and held himself still for a few moments longer yet. That had been too close. A witch. Whose power was she stealing? Or was it simply an insult from someone afraid of magic? Mages held their own Power even though they could use outside sources. Witches and Warlocks did not hold their own power, and often couldn't see the Power lines which made them a bit mad to deal with as they often pulled from unchancy sources to fuel their abilities.

Or perhaps she simply had the Sight as Isela had, only with it focused on the future? It was possible. He wasn't quite willing to guess strongly based on such a small conversation. Better to assume she had greater power rather than lesser. It was less dangerous, and he had danger enough and to spare without adding more.

He gave the pair another five count and started carefully working his way towards the edge of the woods. He was so close. He could not afford to let them stop him so near to Nevahs. Was he the spy they spoke of? Or... He left the thought there and simply kept moving. Too little time remained.

Bearskin looked carefully down at the little clearing that was not half an hour's run from Nevahs. He eyed his options, this time the bark under his fingers was smooth and the underbrush had thinned. The moon was setting, and the greyness of false dawn had begun. False dawn before the fateful day. So close. He had to be careful. He had to be...

"We have the spy, M'Lord." The young voice from the patch of woods spoke clearly in the still night air. Gregor peered around the tree and almost growled. He knew those colors, and he knew the face of the man who was struggling furiously between two soldiers. His own Baron Hochritt, and the 'spy' was none other than Baron von Neuen. He didn't have time for this. He had to get to Nevahs. It was so close. And with the army here. With the army. He took a deep breath and held himself still. Maybe while they were discussing he could sneak past. Von Neuen was a valuable hostage. He would be safe. They'd ransom him as heir to a duke.

"Excellent. We've prepared the gallows already. After all what else does one do with spies and brigands?" Baron Hochritt smiled viciously and Gregor saw a jerk of movement from the younger lord.

Gregor closed his eyes and drew carefully on his bear. His eyes snapped open and suddenly the light of false dawn was bright and useful, and the scent of the woods were alive. And the scent of the men. Fear scent. Other scents as well. Odd. Fear scent from Hochritt. He glanced around the tree and could make out the expressions of the men holding von Neuen. Frowns and scowls. So the good Baron hadn't made himself any more popular since the last war.

The young lord shook himself and stepped one pace forward before bowing. "My Lord Baron, even in war, a trial must be had before a hanging. We caught him skulking in the woods not thieving nor threatening nor even near enough to our encampment to be listening in. He is of Almarc, certainly, but that is enough to imprison him until he can be ransomed after this war."

Bearskin wanted to laugh but smothered the thought. It was the most fundamental aspect of war in this part of the world, and the young officer's tone was a study as he tried to keep his tone polite. It was quite clear he thought the good Baron had taken leave of his senses. Honestly, the good Baron might very well have. He'd been in the Dead Wood after all, voluntarily!

"I have been given authority to deal with spies, traitors, and brigands in the disputed lands as I see fit," Baron Hochritt's eyes narrowed at the young lord. The youngster, commendably, stood his ground. "If you will not string him up, I will. Bring him."

The last was to the two burly men holding a struggling von Neuen. They glanced to the youngster, who seemed to be their own lord who shook his head. They stood their ground and did not move. Baron Hochritt scowled and called to two spearmen behind him. Two Gregor recognized as having survived capturing him. Von Neuen would have quite a bit of trouble with them.

As they went to seize von Neuen, and just as the others had loosened their grip to let the spearmen do so, von Neuen lunged sideways, digging his shoulder into the gut of one. Another reached for him only to get an elbow right below the sternum. He kicked. He fought like he'd grown up brawling, and turned it into an art. Alas, there were four of them and one of him and they eventually pinned him down and then the four of them hauled him to his feet. Only then did the young lord's men step back from the fray.

Gregor closed his eyes. He didn't have time for this. Seven years ended at dawn. Seven years. And yet, this man had fought with him. This man had trusted him when there was no cause for it. They had aided one another. He wasn't pleading for help, and Gregor knew he would not, even if he had known Gregor was here. Yet he would die if left alone. Die to the treachery of Gregor's own liege lord, another betrayal to the man's soul.

And yet, what if Gregor walked away? That, too, would be another betrayal. And it was not in him to betray a friend. He turned, eyes opening and as he did so he shifted.

It was the fastest he had ever transformed consciously and it hurt, but it was almost over before he could feel the pain of it. This time there was no rage. Only determination. Whatever the Devil did to him, he would not allow this one man to die simply to avoid his own folly.

As his front feet touched the edge of the clearing he let out a roar and picked up speed, there was nothing to hinder him here and many of the men had dropped their spears. He swatted them aside. He avoided the younger lord to go for Baron Hochritt's men, first those on von Neuen, then wheeling he charged the cluster diving for their weapons. Massive paws threw them about and then he turned on Hochritt.

Only to find the man fleeing afoot with his horse fleeing in the other direction.

A moment later he walked over to Rudigar von Neuen and helped him to his feet. The young lord was still there. He took a moment to salute them both.

"We found no spy, the good Baron's reason was disordered by this unusual attack by a bear." He called his men to him and they, too, left. How long the reprieve would last he did not know.

"It would seem I owe you my life, Master Bearskin, how may I repay you?" von Neuen rubbed his wrists and picked up his sword from where his captors had dropped it at some point in the scuffle.

Gregor shook his head. He didn't dare look at the sky. "That is not for me to say. Time is short and my doom is near, if you would not share it you must listen carefully."

"I am listening," von Neuen stood strangely calmly. Had he guessed it? It was possible.

"There is a town just northwest of here, burned out. The town of Nevahs. Go to the church. And whatever happens do not let yourself be seen. There are more perilous things about than enemy armies. If I win through you will know me by my ring, carefully test any stranger. Now *go*." Gregor gave him a shove in the right direction and von Neuen went. Running towards the steeple as fast his legs would carry him.

Gregor turned and pelted as hard as he could for his own burned out home, heedless of the roughness of the terrain. In the east, the sky began to turn golden.

Chapter 28
THE DEVIL'S DUE

Bearskin broke free of the trees and burst into the clearing just as the first rays of the rising sun broke over the trees. Everything stopped. There was no scent, the trees, the flowers, the mud and the sweat, all seemed to have been banished from the air. The light of the dawn seemed to freeze the specks of dust in the sky. The doves that usually called were strangely silent and Gregor walked to the center of the clearing to meet his fate.

"I see you are somewhat behind your time." A voice came from the direction of the house.

The tall, straight old man that he had first seen here seven years ago came from around the building, but there was no wall to conceal him. And he seemed somehow diminished from Gregor's Memory of their last encounter.

Gregor glanced at the sky. No, the sun had just peaked above the trees. He shook his head. "I am here, and I have fulfilled our bargain. You gave your oath. Seven years ago today we dealt with each other. It is sunrise and I am here to fulfill that dealing."

Old Scratch flung his head back and laughed. "Oh, you are a day late. Your time sense has been quite addled. You will be mine from here on here, Old Bear. and I will have all the knowledge out of that head of yours. You'll not interfere with my plans."

Once more Gregor shook his head, playing back through the days in his mind. Had he missed one? But he could find no flaw. "No. I have kept a careful track of days, old liar, I am here. I am within my time. I have completed my part of the bargain, it is time for you to complete yours."

"And your dealings with that interfering bard?" Scratch folded his arms. "I know she aided you in this."

It was Gregor's turn to laugh. "Is that the best you have, you old cheat? She sought me out. I sought no help from Powers after our bargain. Enough games."

"Very well, our bargain is concluded give me back my coat." The Devil held out his hand and Gregor gave him a bare-toothed smile. So the coat, not the bearskin, had been his connection.

"No, old liar. You still must fulfill your part. First take the bearskin." And Gregor heaved it off his shoulders flinging it towards the devil, who staggered back under the weight of it. Gregor stood straight for the first time in seven years and it seemed that his soul had shed even more weight as it came off. Even so, he dared not change his focus.

"Now, you will bathe me. You will cut my hair and my nails. Then you will give me new clothes, and the wealth you promised me, and it will be honest wealth, as you promised. Not poisoned. Not stolen. With neither trick nor string of any sort attached." Gregor stood there in the devil's greatcoat and towered over the man.

Old Scratch cast a hungry look at the coat, bowed most graciously and produced a bath, from where Gregor did not see, and motioned him towards it. His voice wheedled though his eyes never left Gregor. "To bathe you, you must take off your clothes."

Gregor nodded and took off first the great coat, holding it firmly in his hand. It was his only hold over the old liar and he wasn't about to give him the chance to back out. It was awkward getting out of his things one handed but he managed it.

As commanded he was bathed, and his hair cut, and his nails also. First one hand, then much to Scratch's frustration, he transferred the coat to his freshly clean and trimmed hand, and offered the other. Keeping the coat well out of reach.

When it was done he dressed one handed, stacking the items that could not be so adorned to one side and giving Scratch another toothy smile. "We are almost done you old thief, now. For the last of it and you shall have your great coat back."

The devil sighed, and once more waved a hand. A satchel appeared, and Gregor opened it. Many bags lay within it and as he opened them one by one, some contained jewels. Some contained gold, others silver. Boxes at the bottom contained precious oils. The fortune he had been promised. Nodding to himself he packed it all away and turned to the devil.

"Our bargain is concluded, my part and yours. I owe you nothing once I have returned your coat," Gregor said grimly.

"It would seem so," Old Scratch sighed and snatched at his coat and Gregor held it high out of his range.

"Say it," He commanded.

"Yes! Our bargain has concluded, you have won! Your soul is your own, now give me my coat!" Old Scratch hopped up trying to catch the tails, but he seemed to have shrunk even further.

"And you will lay no curse upon me nor will you otherwise interfere with me because of this," Gregor commanded.

"No more than any other mortal. Though I have no say over any curses you have taken upon yourself," The wheedling note was back.

Gregor simply nodded, "I had wondered if the bear was you or me. It would seem the bear was me then. Then here is your coat. And I have beaten you once, old liar. I recommend you stay clear."

"We shall see what we shall see. I have other souls to attend to."

Gregor tossed him the coat and he flung it about his shoulders vanishing with a maniacal laugh.

Gregor breathed deeply, smelling pine and earth and some early flowers. Savoring the sensation of the familiar air filling his lungs. The scent of ash was largely gone from the air, and he let himself treasure the moment. The silence of the woods slowly changed. First one bird broke into its usual song. Then a crow protested who knew what, probably a squirrel, all the little sounds of what he had once called home.

Home, a pang of sorrow touched. Even the future he had won would not bring his home back to him. Not in any way that counted. And yet, the grief had eased.

His eyes swept the landscape and carefully he picked his way to the graves behind his house. There he knelt in the grass and said a prayer. His first in seven years. He owed the Whispering Word much for this. But their souls were safe, and had never been hazarded. His wife and little boy were safe in the heavenly courts and it was his turn to move on. Move on at last. But there was one last thing to do here.

"What you seek may be found, through bargain's end beneath the ground," He murmured to himself. Then ran a hand over the simple stone that von Neuen had posted to mark the graves and stood. This time even his heart didn't look back.

Now where would it be? A simple spike of metal, carved with runes. Carved as a Delmin Bead would be.

He stepped into the mess of the house. Now the dirt floor was home to grass, and what was left of the wall was covered in rose vines, though while there were buds, there not yet blooms. Where? Where would it be? His hand fell to the pouch he had retained. The pouch that still contained what he had left of the Minstrel's gifts and the sprite's gift. It flared, then grew cold.

He nodded to himself. So this task was for himself. He carefully worked his way along the house itself. None of the spikes he had used to built it had been that big. None of the wooden pegs or jointing. He carefully worked his way down the crossbeam of the house, still scorched, but not rotten. It had been good timber, and thick and it would take many years for even the insects and time to weather it all the way away.

Yet, it also revealed nothing. He worked his way back down its length. Beneath the ground. Beneath the ground. He gripped the edge of the beam and rolled it. Once more carefully working his way down the length. Spiders scuttled off into the darkness. A little grass snake slithered away as fast as it could and worms buried once more into the ground, the faint hint of rotting wood reached his nose and mingled with the earth-scent. He ran his fingers down the muddy slime of the beam. Nothing.

He walked the length of the indention it had made, stooped near the earth as he could get, but still there was nothing, even with the sun's clear illumination.

Where? If not in the house then where? He stepped around the beam to the land he had once farmed, brushing his hands off on a scrap of his old rags that had been clean enough to bother keeping.

The fields had returned to wildflowers and meadows. A briar patch was forming in one corner of his fields. The stumps of the trees he'd cleared to warm them through the winter all showed signs of wear.

He turned back towards the graves and his eyes fell on the cellar door. The cellar where the center beam had required special strength to hold the dirt in the wet. Where had he found that central spike?

Under the stump of the tree that had provided the center beam.

With a little effort he pried the door loose. Had no one opened it these last seven years? It was possible, but how had Baron Hochritt's men missed it? Unless they hadn't returned to Nevahs yet for the search. If so that meant he had very little time indeed.

Propping the door open with a stone, he descended the steps: boards on the earthen ramp really. Now where? But there was only one upright and it was trivial to find the spike he had used: a spike that now gleamed faintly of its own light.

Now could he work it free without burying himself in the process? He circled the post. Placing both hands on the spike, h heaved. Nothing. The spike didn't budge.

Collecting a wedge-shaped bit of stone from above, he pried at the spike. Slowly, so slowly, it shifted. Now he could wrap both hands around it fully.

He glanced at the still open door. He might just have enough time. Bracing his feet against the hard packed floor, he gripped the gleaming spike with both hands. Once. Twice he pulled.

Let my strength be enough. He prayed.

A third time he pulled with all the strength and stubbornness he possessed. The metal slipped, but would not let go. Still he pulled, throwing all his considerable weight into it. Something gave. He stumbled back, the spike in his hand suddenly warm. So warm he almost dropped it.

A creaking shook him as the central support twisted. Gregor bolted for the door as the creak turned into a crack then a crash. He burst out into the light as the cellar collapsed behind him.

He rocked back on his heels and stood glancing up at the sun and then to where the church spire yet stood: the bell tower that was almost all that was left of the church. Dusting himself off, he picked up the satchel with his new won wealth and set his feet towards the town. He had kept von Neuen waiting long enough. It was time to begin again.

Chapter 29
One Last Task

R udigar paced back and forth across the scorched remnants of the cobbles of the church. Ghosts of smoke wreathed about him, though it was the climbing star vine that filled the air with perfume. Its shimmering white blossoms winking gently at him. Even in his agitation he was careful to keep his foot falls light, but it was not in him to hide, not even this deep in enemy territory.

The altar stood, intact, and he shivered slightly. He had never been the most religious and it seemed impious to stand here in the church that his own forces had burned. No bird sang. No mouse scuttled. All was unnaturally still beyond his own footfalls and heartbeat.

He took a deep breath and wiped, once more, the remnants of the blood away from his mouth trying to clear the iron tang of it away. He was no stranger to fear, but this was an unchancy business.

How had Bearskin found him? or was he truly here only on his own business? But that smacked too much of divine providence for his tastes. He was no one the Whispering Word or any other Power might be mindful of, unless they wanted something out of him.

"No, he doesn't wish anything out of you, Rudigar von Neuen son of a traitor." A woman's voice came from the door and Rudigar spun hand on sword hilt, but he dropped it at once when he saw who was standing there: garbed in olive green from her head to her feet with strange catlike ears protruding from the side of her hood and sweeping sideways rather than up. He'd heard too many descriptions of Fate's Minstrel to mistake her now.

He bowed cautiously. "This is an unexpected visit."

"I am usually unexpected," The woman said with a faint smile as she stepped further into the church, but held up a hand before he backed away. "Peace. I mean you no threat. I come simply to give warning as I am bidden."

"Isn't that how Master Bearskin came by his difficulty?" Rudigar asked as several things fell into place in his mind.

She laughed, a rich merry laugh that had him smiling along in spite of himself, that touched a joy he didn't understand and had too seldom felt. When she spoke her voice was more serious though a touch of that laughter echoed in it. "No, no. You might say I gave him the tools to win through, which he has done. You will recognize him, but not as 'Master Bearskin' when he comes. I have simply come to say, choose your own path wisely, and you need not fear to follow your father's fate. You may yet find your own joy, but that will depend on you."

Rudigar nodded slowly. "Then I thank you, my Lady, I have duties I would see to. I do not doubt your word, but..."

She nodded as he hesitated. "Think on it. The man you called Bearskin has another message for you. There is good work ahead of you if you choose."

"Are we not commanded by the Whispering Word?" Rudigar dared.

Her expression dimmed and she shook her head sadly. "Only if you choose to be. The other Powers seek you to compel your kind and they have no authority to do so. He does, but will not compel, only command as a lawful lord when loyalty is freely given. Yet mortals, and even some immortals refuse to believe that and so borrow more grief than they ought."

Footfalls came from outside the chapel. Once more Rudigar's hand went to his sword but this time the stranger stopped on their own. The man was huge, standing a good six inches taller than von Neuen himself and broad and well muscled, dark of hair and eye and darker of skin than most in this area, though not so dark as those from the southern sea. Delmin most likely then. His clothing was finely made, the traveling gear of a lower lord or very rich merchant, and the silver ring on his hand bore a bear. The face was, indeed familiar. He had seen it from the other side of a spear seven years back and its owner had spared his life. In battle no less.

The stranger bowed to Fate's Minstrel, and he spoke, and the voice was that of Master Bearskin, "My Lady, I had not thought I would see you again. Your gift has been of great use to me, and I have seen through. Unfortunately, there is little time for me to linger here on my gratitude."

"Gregor Bearskin, I have only this message for you: my gift should pass to another. The Lady must find her mother's past and will need it." Fate's Minstrel bowed slightly and smiled at Rudigar before turning to walk away, calling over her shoulder. "We shall meet again, Rudigar von Neuen. And you will see that I do not always bring doom in my wake."

Gregor Bearskin watched her go and Rudigar chuckled, a rusty noise. His humor stiff with disuse. The Delmin looked at him curiously. "She has given me much to think over... Master Bearskin? And also a soldier in Hochritt's levees?"

The man she had called Gregor Bearskin nodded and shifted his pack, which Rudigar now first noticed, on his back. "The same. Though it has been seven long years since he would have called me his vassal. I will never again call him my liege."

Rudigar nodded, "Such things cut both ways. What is your course Master Bearskin?"

"I must get to your court. And to your King. I am expected but I am not sure if I can gain entrance, even prosperous as I now look." Bearskin grimaced then chuckled ruefully. "My name is known in these parts, but I doubt it is known in the capitol."

"I wouldn't count on that," Rudigar retorted. "I was sending regular reports to the King. However, I can get you into court. There are advantages of being my father's son."

And it seemed disadvantages far beyond what even he had expected. 'son of a traitor'? What was his father up to? But that was a trouble for the future. For now the Delmin was watching him closely.

"I have something that may end this war before it grows again," The man said almost pleadingly.

"You need not convince me, Master Bearskin. I believe I have come to know you well enough to speak to the King on your behalf. And my reputation is enough that he should listen." Rudigar found himself relaxing in spite of the fact they were still in enemy territory. This man had fought beside and against him, and if they were to have to fight their way out of here he would prefer none other to fight beside. "Shall we go?"

The Delmin smiled and led him into the morning light towards the road, "And. My name is Gregor. It is good to be able to use it again."

Chapter 30
THE KING'S COURT

Candles blazed, filling the air with perfume yet very little smoke. The rustle of fabrics caught his ear with the soft murmur of voices. Which ones were the dangerous ones? Gregor Bearskin kept half an eye on Rudigar von Neuen. Taking his cue from the other man. He was not the tallest man in the room for once, but he stood head and shoulders over the crowed. He gave the northern... Heinrich? What was he doing here? He continued his polite bow and followed his guide. He could speak with Heinrich later.

Colors blazed from dresses and coats, tunics, and jewels. Bright silver, shining gold. And Gregor squared his shoulders under the cloak of spun sunlight. It did not glow much but it scattered light into the shadows left by the candles and more than one noble did not bother to conceal their speculation. Such fabrics were not typically for sale at any price.

Von Neuen's dress was more subdued. Black trimmed with silver and blue, and he seemed little interested in the spectacle his guest was causing. Gregor chose to take his cue from the actual noble. He certainly wasn't one. What he bore would gain him audience. Or at least a hearing.

Von Neuen spoke quietly with a Herald who glanced sharply at Gregor then nodded once. The man, in the ebony and gold of Almarc itself, stepped out into the center of the carpet leading to the throne.

"Ehdler Rudigar von Neuen, Junerzog of Neuensaltz, Freiherr of Narnoltz requests permission to present a stranger to the court. A stranger with significant bearing on today's tribunal, and craves the Crown's indulgence for the presumption of such a demand." The herald bowed and stepped back.

Gregor recognized the prince standing off to one side, dressed, one might say over dressed even for a prince, in bright scarlet and gold, trimmed with ebony. His sword was so gem encrusted Gregor wondered if he could use it. It was a far cry from the prince he had seen in the command tent.

The King was much more understated, wearing tunic and breeches of the Kingdom's colors. Yes, in fine fabrics, but his only affection seemed to be in the crown on his head and a pair of bracelets about his wrists, gold set with a single glimmering star stone, and matching the torc about his neck. A Delmin torc? rather than the necklaces all the 'civilized' kingdoms seemed to prefer? Well there was a story there he could not ask.

The king's intense blue eyes took in Von Neuen, and there was no liking there. Well he had no other ally to get him into court. And yet...

Gregor set the matter aside. His part in this was nearly done. The Powers had been clear on that. Best to finish this and pass his messages on to others. Out of the corner of his eye he saw his partner Johann von Algers and his daughters amongst the lower end of the nobility. Good.

Then the king turned those blue eyes on Gregor, and Gregor found himself holding very, very still. He met the king's eyes then lowered his own deliberately with a small bow. Not the bow of a vassal, nor yet the presumption of an equal. He owed no man fealty. But this man seemed to govern well so he would grant him respect. The King frowned slightly, but spoke clearly enough his eyes never leaving Gregor.

"Speak von Neuen. It is your right to introduce whom you will to court. It is my right to decide whether or not they may stay," The King motioned a hand to von Neuen and Gregor saw the flash of a signet ring.

Von Neuen stepped up to the King and Gregor watched as half the crowd tensed. He finally spotted the colors of Bayr on a reedy man near Heinrich who had suddenly begun to scowl. Von Neuen bowed deeply.

"Your majesties. Your Highness," the last was spoken more stiffly. And Gregor wondered if there was some bad blood between von Neuen and the prince. But Rudigar continued, seemingly oblivious to the undertones. "You have directed me to the northern border these past seven years, to quell bandits and to find evidence. That evidence has been found, though not due to my own efforts. I have written you often of a man called Master Bearskin who has done much in that region. I would now present to the courts, Master Gregor Bearskin. Who requests audience to give his own evidence. I have found him to be a man of deep honor and compassion. Whose virtues far exceed my own."

"That would not be difficult." Someone muttered nearby, but Gregor kept his focus on the king.

"I have heard of you from other sources as well, Master Bearskin." The King spoke carefully. "You may approach the throne. We will hear your business and see your evidence."

Gregor stepped forward himself and halted beside von Neuen, going down on one knee. "Your Majesties. Your Highness."

He stumbled over the plural for the Queen sat still as a statue. And between the silvery grey of her simple gown and the silver touching her black hair, she seemed almost to be a statue. It was hard to focus on her. Yet in his memory she was clear and sharp and vibrant. She caught his eye and nodded once smiling ever so slightly.

Gregor focused his attention completely on the king. "I have come as bidden by his Highness. There were certain objects I returned to him, but one piece was missing. I have that piece now and would return it to the proper owners. I dared not trust that duty to another."

The king leaned forward. "I may know something of this."

He cast a sidelong glance at his son, and there was resignation in his eyes. "You didn't tell me who had given you the artifacts."

The prince chuckled seemingly unconcerned. "It did not seem important at the time. Besides, would you have believed that the mythical Master Bearskin was taking a hand in all this?"

The king snorted, "bring the artifacts."

The prince bowed and stepped away from the throne and pulled from a satchel at his side each of the artifacts that Bearskin had given him, and laid them at a table nearby, then took up his place behind it almost like a sentry as his father continued to speak. "Master Bearskin what do you bear that is so important?"

"This," Bearskin drew from a pocket in that cloak the spike. The runes on it glowed and shifted. "It was found in Nevahs which once looked to

Baron Hochritt, in whose possession I found all the other artifacts as well."

"I protest!" The Ambassador from Bayr spoke up with a bluster that was ruined by his rather nasal voice. "For seven years we have demanded you provide proof of your accusations against us. Yet only now do you even try. This is far too convenient."

The king cut him off with a raised hand. With the other he motioned for the prince to retrieve the artifact. "Master Bearskin. Where did you find the other items? Where was Baron Hochritt holding them?"

"In the Dead Wood, your Majesty," Gregor said softly and dared meet the kings eyes as he handed the prince the spike. "Test me. Ask what you will. If you have a mage who can See truth, I will submit to them. My gift is Memory so ask what you will and I will answer."

"That is a dangerous thing to offer a king," The king murmured and glanced to his wife. "Your Majesty if you would?"

The Queen nodded once and frowned as her fingers traced a pattern in the air, then once more gestured to her husband. So the Truth finding didn't require it be the mage who asked the question? Interesting.

"Where did you find the artifacts you gave my son?"

"In a castle in the Dead Wood. I cannot tell you precisely where." Bearskin answered promptly, and something kept him from answering beyond the precise question. Whether the spell or something else he wasn't sure.

"In whose possession were they?"

"A man who called himself simply 'A Superior Thief' had just removed them from the Baron's office in that castle."

A murmur ran through the crowd at that, but Gregor didn't have the attention for it for the King had already moved on.

"How did you know it was the Baron?"

"He was my liege during the War, but the lands I had been bound to were no longer his. So he decreed me no longer his concern. When he captured me near the Dead Wood in the far north of what are technically the Neuenrittermark, I recognized his voice though did not immediately realize who he was. I had been tracking them from Eislathen.

"He wore an illusion and the colors of the von Neuen house. But the illusion was flawed or something else was at play for it did not disguise his voice and in moments of intense emotion it seemed to thin and show him for who he was. I do not know enough about magic to say how. Once in the castle in the Dead Wood the illusion was dropped and his ally called him by name: Ambrosius."

"Who is this ally?" The King leaned forward, and Gregor felt all the court leaning as well, and the first stirrings of the bear since leaving Nevahs. He squashed it firmly and focused on the king. The square face. Strong. The blue eyes. Intense.. The wide mouth that somehow seemed worried and... Gregor couldn't place what the lines about the King's mouth might mean.

"I do not know. He, too, wore an illusion. One of blandness. He was ordinary, remarkably ordinary. I saw only a glimpse past it. I would recognize the face if I saw it again, but it was none I knew. He also was a noble, though from where I cannot say." Gregor answered and this time the queen frowned.

"He speaks truth, and yet there is more," the Queen's voice was soft but he had no trouble hearing it. Odd. "What bothers you but was not in the purview of the question?"

"I... he was dark of hair, and had more of the look of the Delmin about him, though with sharper features and smaller. His boots were good, and those in the Dead Wood obeyed him without question. It seemed to me that whatever Baron Hochritt thought, this man was truly the enemy, the Master--or at least sought to be the Master of the Wood and perhaps more. But I cannot tell you more. There are simply too many fragments to explain in such a format and it is my suspicions only, not fact. Not truth. Merely belief. But this man was dangerous enough and ruthless enough that he was willing to use witch water and vice fungus and may be immune to them."

The queen let out a low hiss at that and a few others in the room winced, most simply shifted uneasily. No one lightly meddled with either. The water that flowed from the Witch Wood trees always, always had odd effects and in the Dead Wood...

The king slid a look to the ambassador from Bayr who stood silent and stunned. Gregor looked to the Ambassador. "I do not know, m'Lord if the Baron acted alone within Bayr or not. He desired greater place than he had, perhaps the crown. That I do know from his own mouth."

"I must take this matter to my master, the king. I see here the artifacts and I am enough of a student of magic to know that the casting was a true one," Here the man bowed with much more respect to the queen, and a small hint of apology.

"We have laid before you the evidence. Take word to your master. Perhaps he would do better to avoid risking all in another war on the behalf of a traitor," The king's tone was mild, but the Ambassador bowed deeply.

"Indeed and I think his Majesty will be having strong words with the good Baron very soon if the Dead Wood hasn't eaten him," The ambassador's tone was sour enough to rise a chuckle out of the courtiers.

"Sadly not," von Neuen said with a small smile of his own, which caused quite the stir. "He was in the Nevahs region, and has at least one mage or witch who was scouting out spies. One Master Bearskin prevented myself from being hung."

That led to a hiss and the ambassador stared at him in open astonishment, and even the nobles who had muttered disparagingly of von Neuen earlier looked affronted. That one noble would not offer another the chance at ransom. It was an alteration in the customs of war that boded poorly.

"Then this matter is settled. Let the court proceed to other matters," The King inclined his head to von Neuen and Gregor and both bowed and stepped back into the crowd.

Gregor settled himself with the merchant and his daughters, smiling at Isela who regarded him with more than a little startlement. He lowered his voice so as not to disturb the court. "M'Lady, I would speak with you perhaps when these proceedings are concluded?"

"I would be delighted, Master Bearskin. I look forward to getting to know my father's new business partner," She smiled brightly, going from quietly pretty to breathtaking, then turned her grey eyes back to the court proper.

Gregor himself watched, committing the proceedings to his excellent memory. He would likely not have another chance to witness such an assemblage, and he was content with that.

Petitioners came and went. Several cases were brought before the king to plead, mostly disputes between the nobility. Gregor found himself nodding along with the King as, as often as not, he steered the principles in these arguments into their own compromises without decreeing one for them. Clever. More likely to stick as well.

Then the court seemed to break up into more social activities at a signal that Gregor had not seen. He looked first at Johann von Algers, who seemed to have had a weight lifted off his shoulders. Gregor smiled, "Would you still consider Gregor Bearskin for a junior partnership now that he stands before you?"

"Master Bearskin, I will gladly take you into my business, and my home if certain others are amenable. If not, or if you are not so inclined, I can help you find lodgings you will find suitable," Johann clapped the man on his shoulder and gave Isela a wink.

The girl blushed mightily, and Gregor smiled. It might be presumptuous, but after this long and all the letters, he was willing to hope. He reached into a pouch and pulled out a string of brightly carved beads mostly in amber. A stone of power and significance for the Delmin. With the second of Anna's carved beads in the center, the match to the one he had given her so long ago. "To that, I will have to speak with the lady."

He bowed his head, and stepped up to Isela who looked up at him, blush fading only a little but grey eyes bright. "You know little of me outside of the letters we have exchanged these last three years. I have grown fond of the woman in those letters, and would like to become fonder still. My dead are buried, and no ghosts haunt me any longer. I told you once, you would know me by the mate of this bead. Isela von Argers, would you consent to marrying a man, newly made?"

"Master Bearskin, nothing would give me greater pleasure. I, too, have grown to care deeply for the man in the letters. He is one I would be honored to spend my days with. And nothing I have seen today has changed that opinion of him." She curtsied deeply and accepted the necklace of beads. Some of the courtiers about them who saw chuckled and he saw approval in most of their faces. After all it wasn't as if anyone important was actually getting married, and...

"There is one other matter," The voice came from the direction of the throne, as the king spoke loudly enough to cut through the overwhelming murmur of voices. "We have the truth of the War as much as is likely ever to be known. And in that case, there are decisions that must be rendered at last. First, A formal acknowledgment that Johann von Argers bears no responsibility for the loss of these artifacts. Not with the Powers that were invoked against him. But the larger issue is the assignment of the lands from Bayr. These seven years I have hesitated to assign them to any. "

His blue eyes landed on von Neuen and they were hard and cold, but Rudigar seemed to meet his gaze without challenge. Which drew a frown from the prince. Why the prince? Gregor wondered then turned his attention back to the king wondering where the man was going with these decrees.

The king's eyes sought, and found several other nobles whose heraldry Gregor knew, but beyond that knew nothing of. "Many have petitioned for control of these lands. Some invoking right of conquest. Some invoking redress of wrongs. And on and on the arguments went. Yet, an iron hand would likely bring these already restive lands to open rebellion and that is as undesirable as a renewed war. So an alternative ought to be found."

Gregor frowned as the king's eyes fell on him and he straightened first, then bowed in acknowledgment. The king smiled, "Gregor Bearskin approach the Throne."

For the second time that day Gregor did, kneeling though he kept his back straight. He was not this man's vassal. He was a free merchant. The king inspected him carefully then nodded as if to himself. "Gregor Bearskin, you have spent seven years routing bandits, feeding the poor, and rescuing my subjects in the conquered lands. You have aided those I sent down there to keep the peace."

Here his eyes flickered to von Neuen who started to frown then just sighed and gave a resigned nod to the king. He knew where this was going.

The king returned his attention to the puzzled Gregor. "Such subjects are difficult to find, and Freiherr Rudigar von Neuen speaks highly of you. Of your nobility of character and your strength of spirit. I know you are a vassal of no man, but that may change. Your fealty is yours to give and owed to no other. Would you give your oath to a king who was once your enemy?"

Gregor stared for a moment in stunned shock at the king and von Neuen chuckled, almost in sympathy, though there was some resigned resentment there as well, but Gregor could not spare the time to track that down. The king was regarding him and this close he could see the twitch at the corner of the man's mouth. Gregor closed his eyes and then nodded. The decision had made itself long ago.

"Your Majesty. I have seen the care you have had for your lands, even those newly conquered. You did not try to break them, rather brought them into your kingdom as vassals in truth not merely in name, to be still enemies in fact. It is wiser than I had thought to find. I have learned something of your lords and nobles in my wandering, and I would be honored to count among the ones I have met." Gregor's voice was firm.

Rashness came in many ways, he knew, but he would not back down from this either, and responded in the Delmin fashion of offering allegiance to a tribal or clan chieftain. "I offer your Majesty no sword, for I have none. Instead I offer my strength in all its forms, and my honor which I have ever held close. Will you take a strength which has never yielded, neither to Powers nor to Magics nor to the Dead Wood not even to the Devil himself? Will you take an honor that will not let a wrong pass by?"

The king nodded, "Such a strength is a greater treasure than a thousand swords, for swords can be laid down and abandoned, but such strength is all you are. I would be honored to call such a strength my own."

He stood and drew his sword holding it before the kneeling Gregor. "Place your hand on this sword hilt and repeat after me."

Gregor reached out and laid his hand on the hilt of the sword, but his eyes locked with the king's as he repeated the words of the oath. "I, Gregor Bearskin, swear on my honor to use all my strength to uphold the crown of Almarc, to give obedience and advice to those appointed above me, and justice and care for those beneath me. Whether called to peace or war, prosperity or ruin. And to hold her good over all others."

The king placed his other hand on Gregor's preventing him from pulling back, silently reminding him that such oaths had two parties. "I hear your oath, and accept it, and this I swear in return: To give back what is given and more. Strength for strength. Justice for Justice. A listening ear to hear the wisdom of those who have walked other paths than mine. As I may call you to war, or to peace. You may call on my strength in your need. And as you uphold these oaths in that measure will I reward you. Loyalty with trust, Courage with honor, and betrayal with vengeance. Rise, Count Gregor Bearskin, Lord of the Northern Marches."

Astonished, Gregor stood and even Rudigar von Neuen cheered.

Also By

Poetry

Lift High the Candle

Novels

Spiral of Worlds Universe
Whirlwind of Stars
Persistent Powers Universe
Bearskin

About the Author

I am old enough to worry about growing old gracefully, but not old enough to be graceful about it yet. After a stint in the Army and a longer stint as a geophysicist, with some bouts of IT work and other odds and ends thrown in the work, I've finally settled down on 10 acres with my family.

All along the way there have been stories, some big and some small. Some that are forever lost on 5.25 inch floppies (the ones that actually flopped!) and are probably the better for it. Now, these stories are starting to come out of trunks, and the depth of my mind and get themselves finished and find their way into the world, along with a fair few new ones. After all, stories never come alone. They always bring worlds with them, and sometimes those worlds bring friends of their own. And poetry and songs. Those that I had always thought would be just for me, but life is sometimes strange in delightful ways.

I hope you have enjoyed this book and that it has brought you a glimmer of the joy tales and poetry have brought me throughout my own life. Feel free to reach out to me either on my websites or by e-mail, I can't guarantee I'll respond to everything but I will try.

Publisher: www.wyrdbardtales.com
Personal: www.dreaminginplot.com
E-mail: heather@dreaminginplot.com
Ko-fi: https://ko-fi.com/wyrdbardtales